MW01133010

THE GHOST
AND THE MUSE

The Ghost of Marlow House

The Ghost Who Loved Diamonds

The Ghost Who Wasn't

The Ghost Who Wanted Revenge

The Ghost of Halloween Past

The Ghost Who Came for Christmas

The Ghost of Valentine Past

The Ghost from the Sea

The Ghost and the Mystery Writer

The Ghost and the Muse

The Ghost Who Stayed Home

The Ghost and the Leprechaun

The Ghost Who Lied

The Ghost and the Bride

The Ghost and Little Marie

The Ghost and the Doppelganger

The Ghost of Second Chances

The Ghost Who Dream Hopped

The Ghost of Christmas Secrets

HAUNTING DANIELLE - BOOK 10

BOBBI HOLMES

The Ghost and the Muse
(Haunting Danielle, Book 10)
A Novel
By Bobbi Holmes
Cover Design: Elizabeth Mackey

This novel is a work of fiction.
Any resemblance to places or actual persons,
living or dead, is entirely coincidental.

ISBN-13: 978-1539029847
ISBN-10: 1539029840

To my family.
Because that's what's really important in life.

ONE

Steve Klein went fishing every Thursday evening. At least, that was what he led his wife, Beverly, to believe. On Thursdays, she played bridge with her girlfriends. She had missed the last two bridge nights because she had been out of town. What Steve had failed to tell his wife was that he hadn't been fishing for over six weeks.

But here he was—after almost two months of skipping his weekly fishing night—sitting alone on the Frederickport Pier, fishing pole in hand and cursing himself for leaving his thermos of decaf coffee sitting on the kitchen counter back at home.

Had he remembered his coffee, he wouldn't have run into Carla at Pier Café. If he had just realized his oversight before pulling into the parking lot, he could have stopped somewhere else and picked up some coffee. He certainly wouldn't return home to grab his thermos. What would Beverly say? She'd wonder why he bothered returning home when it would be easier to buy take-out coffee on the pier.

The bridge ladies had started showing up at his house before he had stepped onto his front porch. Beverly had practically pushed him out the door, which was one reason he had forgotten his thermos and had left it sitting on the kitchen counter. She had shoved the sack with the tamales Baron had given him into his hand and kissed his cheek, telling him to have fun.

Steve had to admit, Beverly was a good wife and mother. Having the affair with Carla was nothing personal. It had nothing to do with his feelings for Beverly. In fact, it wasn't even about his feelings for Carla. He had no feelings for Carla. But a man had certain needs, Steve told himself. As long as he didn't neglect his wife or get some foolish notion to leave her for his mistress, then what was the harm? Steve congratulated himself for doing the right thing and breaking it off with Carla before things got awkward. *The next time it won't be someone in Frederickport,* Steve told himself. *Too close to home. I won't make that mistake again.*

He glanced over to the unopened sack and cup of coffee sitting on the pier next to his chair. His stomach began to grumble.

ANTOINE PAUL HAD RECOGNIZED Steve Klein the moment he had walked onto the pier, clumsily carrying an armful of items, which included a fishing pole, tackle box, folding chair, and paper sack. Antoine had seen him on the pier before—on the night Jolene Carmichael had been murdered.

At the time, Antoine thought there was something vaguely familiar about the man, yet considering he was average looking, Antoine initially assumed the middle-aged man simply resembled someone he once knew. The morning after Jolene's murder, learning the man's name was Steve Klein prickled his memory, but it wasn't until he learned Steve was the manager of a local bank did it all fall into place.

Naturally curious, considering he now knew who Steve was, Antoine discreetly shadowed the banker, watching as he entered Pier Café and set what he had been carrying onto a bench in the front entry of the diner before he went up to the counter and ordered coffee.

A waitress with rainbow-streaked hair took his order and didn't seem particularly friendly. In fact, she was downright hostile, and Antoine imagined she wouldn't be getting a tip. After placing the order and paying for it, Klein turned his back to her, waiting for his order.

Antoine watched as the waitress went to pour coffee into a large Styrofoam cup. He found it curious when her eyes darted to Steve, whose back still faced her, and then she hastily slipped something into his drink before securing the lid.

That alone would not have piqued Antoine's curiosity, but when Steve placed his coffee on the bench with his other items and then went to use the men's room, Antoine watched as the waitress quickly scurried from behind the counter and began going through Steve's belongings. From Antoine's vantage point, he could tell she removed something—but what exactly, he wasn't sure.

By the time Steve returned from the restroom, the waitress had disappeared into the kitchen. Steve collected his belongings, never knowing they had been tampered with.

STEVE SAT on the folding chair under the moonlight, his feet propped up on the railing. Eyeing the Styrofoam cup, he set his fishing pole by his side, its line still out in the water, and reached for the coffee.

Antoine leaned back against the railing, the line of Steve's fishing reel just a few inches from his left elbow. With his arms folded across his chest, he looked down at Steve. "I wouldn't drink that coffee. She put something in it."

Steve removed the lid from the Styrofoam cup, but instead of taking a sip, he tossed the lid aside and set the cup back on the pier. He then picked up the sack and opened it, removing a foil package.

Antoine reserved comment, yet continued to watch as Steve quickly ate the contents of the first foil packet and then the second. When he was done, he scrunched the foil into tight balls and shoved them back into the sack before picking up the coffee.

Antoine began shaking his head. "I wouldn't do it. Really. You don't want to drink that."

Steve quickly downed his first swig of coffee. Antoine surmised it must be lukewarm. Steve was about to take another drink when he suddenly froze, his hand gripping the cup so tightly it began to crumple.

Antoine watched in fascination as Steve released hold of the now smashed cup, paying little notice to the fact it had just fallen onto his lap, the remainder of its contents spilling onto his pants and soaking his crotch. Steve began to cough, and then he gasped for air. He reached frantically for his tackle box and flipped open its lid. In a panic, he rummaged through the box, and when he could not find whatever he was looking for, he hastily dumped it upside down and began tossing the contents in all directions, desperately looking for something that was not there. Stumbling to his feet, he tried to catch his breath.

"I warned you. But they never listen." Antoine shook his head in disgust. "Never."

Unstable on his feet, Steve weaved from side to side, his hands grasping the railing in an attempt to keep upright. Making a gasping sound, his eyes rolled back into their sockets and he swung around, his back now to the railing. Steve's hands clutched his throat as silent screams tore from his gaping mouth. In the next instant, his body stiffened. As if in slow motion, he fell backwards, toppling over the pier's railing, plunging headfirst to the ocean below.

Casually, Antoine looked over the railing. He heard the splash as Steve's body hit the seawater. Shaking his head in disgust, Antoine continued to gaze down, the moonlight casting a golden glow on the rippling water. He couldn't see Steve. Antoine assumed he had simply sunk to the bottom, or he had already been washed out to sea.

Turning from the rail, Antoine's gaze moved over the now empty folding chair and the scattered tackle. With a shrug, he stepped over the debris and made his way down the dock. As he walked, he reached up to his red bow tie and gave it a gentle tug, straightening it.

DANIELLE HAD GROWN ACCUSTOMED to seeing Walt wearing the fashions from his era—typically a gray or blue pinstriped three-piece suit, circa 1920s. What she didn't know, he rarely gave much thought to his clothing, unless it was a dream hop, and then he would make it a point to dress for the occasion. But in his day-to-day life—or more accurately death—his manner of clothing was simply a habit, wearing what he had normally worn when he had still been alive.

Yet this evening, he was dressed more casually than what was typically his norm, wearing dark slacks and a white dress shirt, its unbuttoned cuffs casually pushed up toward his elbows. He lounged lazily on the parlor sofa, his stockinged feet propped up on the sofa's armrest, crossed at the ankles.

"I can't say I'll miss the sound of that damn typewriter." Absently, he watched the smoke curl upward from his thin cigar.

Danielle glanced up from the book she was reading and looked over at Walt. Watching him a moment, a random thought flashed through her head. Sitting there fidgeting with his cigar, dressed casually for his era yet overdressed for her generation—considering the setting—he suddenly reminded her of a character from one of those old movies—his role being that of the handsome yet elusive bachelor.

Pushing the silly thought from her head, she shrugged. "I can barely hear it in my room."

Walt flicked the cigar from his hand. It vanished. "Then maybe you need to get your hearing checked."

Danielle shrugged and closed her book, setting it on her lap. "Hillary's visit has taught me one thing."

"Typewriters will no longer be allowed on the premises?"

Danielle laughed. "Walt, no one uses typewriters anymore. I don't think that'll be an issue."

Meeting her gaze, Walt arched his brows. "What have we been listening to the last month?"

"Okay…I mean, aside from Hillary. Most people really don't use typewriters these days. Even writers…well, at least I don't think so."

"If not outlawing typewriters, then what exactly has her visit taught you?"

"Well…I prefer the short-term guests. Those who stay for the weekend or the week at most. The fact is, even if it's someone I really like, after a few weeks under the same roof, they kinda get on my nerves."

Walt didn't respond immediately. Instead, he stared expressionlessly at Danielle for a few moments before asking, "Do I get on your nerves?"

Surprised by the question, Danielle stared back at Walt. After a moment considering it, she smiled. "No. Actually…you don't."

Walt cocked his brow. "Why do you sound so surprised?"

"I don't know." Danielle shrugged. "I never really thought about it before. But no…you don't."

Walt smiled. "How about Lily?"

"You know I love Lily."

Walt laughed. "That wasn't the question. Does she get on your nerves? After all, you two have been under the same roof for months now."

Danielle fidgeted with the book on her lap. "That's different."

"How so?" Walt sat up on the sofa—placing his feet on the floor—his eyes still on Danielle.

"She's like family. And with family, even if they sometimes get on your nerves…well, it's okay. What about me?"

Walt frowned. "What do you mean what about you?"

"Do I get on your nerves?"

Walt smiled. "All the time."

"Oh you!" Wrinkling her nose, Danielle hurled the book at Walt. It disappeared through his body and fell onto the sofa.

Walt's laugh was interrupted by Hillary's voice at the open parlor door.

"Danielle…oh, I'm sorry, I didn't know you had company. I didn't mean to interrupt, but I just wanted you to know, I'm taking a little walk on the beach, since this is my last night, and it's a full moon out."

Danielle stared dumbly at the now empty doorway. She looked from it to Walt.

"Did she just say she could see you?" Danielle stood up, rushed to the doorway, and looked into the hallway. Hillary was no longer there. Danielle stood there a moment, staring at the front door, before walking back into the parlor.

Walt stood up. "Is she still out there?"

Danielle shook her head. "No, she already left."

"I didn't hear the door."

"Walt, she saw you!"

He chuckled. "No, she didn't. She heard you talking to me and assumed you were in here with someone."

With a frown, Danielle sat back down. "It just seemed like she saw you."

"Don't be ridiculous. She barely looked in here, and considering the only light on is the reading lamp by your side, it's not really surprising she made that assumption. And if I was you, I'd let her continue believing someone was in here with you tonight."

Danielle stood back up. "Why do you say that?"

"When she leaves here tomorrow, do you really want her telling people you regularly talk to yourself and occasionally fling objects around the room?" Walt picked up the book from the sofa and handed it to Danielle. "By the way, that is no way to treat a book."

Reluctantly Danielle accepted the book and set it on the desk. "True. It's not the book's fault you're a brat."

Walt laughed again. Max, who had been napping on the back of the sofa, lifted his head and opened his eyes. Yawning, he looked at Walt and meowed.

Danielle turned off the reading lamp. "I think I'm going to bed now. Come on, Max."

"You aren't going to wait up for Hillary?"

Danielle walked to the doorway. "No. She has a key. And I'm exhausted."

Together, Walt and Danielle made their way up the staircase, with Max reluctantly trailing behind them.

Midway to the second floor, Walt asked, "Did Chris get on your nerves?"

Danielle paused and looked at Walt. "Chris? What are you talking about?"

"When Chris stayed here for so long, did he get on your nerves?"

Danielle continued up the stairs. "He didn't stay that long."

"Longer than Hillary."

Danielle shrugged. "I'm still processing the fact I get on your nerves."

Walt chuckled. "You know I was teasing you."

"My dad used to say behind every jest there is a truth."

"You aren't going to pout now, are you?" Walt teased.

"I would if I had the energy. But I really am tired." Danielle yawned.

Just as they reached the second-floor landing, Lily stepped out of the bathroom, a towel wrapped around her recently shampooed hair. Wearing plaid pajama bottoms and a gray T-shirt, Lily paused in the hallway a moment and faced Danielle.

"You going to bed?" Lily removed the towel from her head and briskly rubbed it over her damp rusty curls.

"Yeah, I'm exhausted. It's been a long day." Danielle nodded to Walt. "Walt's with me."

"Hi, Walt." Lily glanced from where she imagined Walt stood to the closed door leading to Hillary's room. In a whisper she said, "I guess Hillary will be leaving in the morning?"

"You don't have to whisper," Danielle told her. "Hillary went out for a walk. But yeah, she told me earlier she wants to get on the road right after breakfast."

Lily frowned and glanced back to Hillary's door.

"Night, Lily…Walt…" Danielle yawned and walked to her bedroom. Flashing a weary smile in Lily's direction, Danielle opened her bedroom door. Once inside, she waited for her cat, Max, to join her before shutting the door again.

Still standing in the hallway, Lily was just about to say something to Walt when she heard the door open and close in the attic. Glancing to the ceiling, Lily let out a sigh. She knew Walt didn't need to open doors to enter a room. It was simply his way of telling Lily he had left the second floor.

Letting out a sigh, she walked toward her bedroom, yet paused by Hillary's doorway. Impulsively, Lily opened the bedroom door and looked in. Frowning, she gently shut the door.

Glancing back to Danielle's room, she shook her head and muttered, "I don't know what you've been smoking."

TWO

Hillary had forgotten to bring along a jacket for her late night stroll. Spring evenings in Frederickport tended to be chilly and damp. She didn't miss the jacket, nor would she have noticed the oversight, had she not run into Heather Donovan.

Pausing in front of Heather's house, Hillary watched as the young woman, clad in a flannel bathrobe, struggled to drag her trash bin to the curb. Instead of the pigtails she normally wore, Heather's jet black hair fell straight past her shoulders, gently swaying from side to side as she made her way to the street.

"I forgot it's trash day tomorrow," Heather explained when she reached the curb and found Hillary standing there watching.

"Looks like you remembered."

"Yeah. After I was already in bed." Heather looked Hillary up and down. "What are you doing out in the dark. Aren't you cold?"

"I'm checking out in the morning. Thought I'd get in one more moonlight walk along the beach. And why would I be cold?"

Heather frowned. "You aren't wearing a jacket." She shivered. "It's freaking freezing out here."

Hillary shrugged. "Maybe I'm not over those hot flashes."

Hugging her robe tightly around her, Heather shivered again. "I don't know about hot flashes, but I'm freezing. Have a nice walk." Heather turned toward her house and started back up the driveway.

"You will one day!" Hillary called out with a laugh. Chuckling, she continued down the block several doors before crossing the street and cutting between two houses, making her way to the ocean.

Hillary found herself alone on the beach under the moonlight, its glow casting a golden shadow over the water. Breathing in the salt air, she stood at the water's edge, looking out to sea.

She wasn't sure how long she had been standing there before motion in the water, some distance from shore, caught her attention. Leaning forward and narrowing her eyes, she studied the stretch of rippling water illuminated by the moonlight. The shimmering path glimmered and sparkled, reminding Hillary of buoyant diamonds—a fanciful notion, but one that popped into her head. In the midst of those diamonds was what appeared to be the arms of a man swimming toward her, his feet kicking furiously behind him.

With a steady stroke, he persistently made his way toward her. The moment he reached the shore, he stumbled from the water and stood upright. By his expression, it was obvious he was surprised to find someone standing on the beach, watching him.

Hillary's eyes widened. She recognized the man. "Steve Klein? What in the world are you doing out swimming at this time of night? And do you always go swimming in your clothes?"

Steve stared at Hillary. At first, he hadn't recognized her. But it was Hillary Hemingway, the mystery writer staying at Marlow House. He had initially met her after she had first arrived in town, when she had come into the bank and needed some assistance in transferring funds. He'd seen her around town a few times, the most recently less than two weeks earlier, when he'd seen her at Pier Café the night Jolene Carmichael had been murdered.

"I fell off the damn pier. Isn't that obvious?" Steve took a step toward Hillary.

"Well…not really." Hillary glanced up the beach in the direction of the pier. "Are you saying you swam all the way down here? Why didn't you just swim up to shore by the pier?"

Hands now on hips, he looked at Hillary. "Aren't you even curious how I managed to fall off the pier?"

"Umm…yes…of course. Are you alright?"

Steve scratched his forehead. "I think so. But I knocked my head on the pier when I fell." He turned slightly so she could see his injury.

Hillary leaned closer and looked. "That's nasty looking."

"It doesn't hurt anymore. It all happened so fast."

"You didn't break anything, did you? That's quite a fall."

"You're telling me! But no, nothing seems to be broken. One minute I'm fishing quietly on the pier, and the next minute I get a severe allergic reaction, and I can't find my damn EpiPen. I always keep one in my tackle box. Especially when I'm fishing."

Hillary frowned. "Why especially when you're fishing?"

"I'm allergic to shellfish—it's a pretty bad allergy. Sometimes just handling shellfish can cause me a problem."

Hillary arched her brow. "You've a severe allergy to shellfish, and you were fishing…on the pier…in the ocean?"

He shrugged. "Well, it's only shellfish. And while I've had a couple mishaps before, I always had the EpiPen. It's not like I'm fishing with shrimp."

"So what happened?"

Hands still on his hips, he turned to face the pier, shaking his head. "I just finished eating my tamales, drank some of my coffee, and then, well, it just hit. I couldn't breathe, and the next thing I know, I'm falling off the damn pier, hit my head. Could have killed myself."

"Was it something you ate—drank?"

He shook his head. "No. I mean, not what I ate exactly. But what probably happened, there must have been some raw shellfish on the dock, maybe on the railing. I might have touched something down there and then transferred it to my food—and into my mouth."

Hillary frowned. "Are you saying something like that could actually send you into anaphylactic shock, one severe enough to make you fall off the pier?"

Steve shrugged. "It must have."

"If that's the case, do you think it's wise to go fishing—especially ocean fishing?"

Steve let out a sigh. "I may have to rethink that. Well, I guess I better go get my car, it's still at the pier, along with my fishing equipment, providing no one took off with it." With a farewell salute, Steve turned from Hillary and started down the beach toward the pier.

Hillary continued to stand in the same spot under the moonlight, watching Steve until he was no more than a dark silhouette. It was then she noticed a second person, walking in her direction from the pier. Whoever it was, he or she stopped, as did Steve. She surmised the two were talking. After a few moments, Steve started back on his way, and the second shadowy figure started walking again—in her direction.

Looking back to sea, Hillary took a deep breath and smiled. The night before she had finished her newest book. She had already tucked the manuscript into her briefcase. After she returned to Vancouver, Washington, she would have it typed up—using a word processor—so she could do the rewrites on the computer. While it was true she used a manual typewriter when writing her first draft, she'd never consider making tedious rewrites using the typewriter. She often led people to believe she never used a computer, which she felt better fit her image—that of a serious, old-school writer.

Her thoughts shifted from the tools of her craft to the source of her inspiration—her muse. If she wanted to get technical, the term muse was somewhat misleading. A muse was typically a female. Her muse was definitely not a female. She wondered, was Danielle right? Was she really a clairvoyant and the regular appearance of her muse was nothing more than her clairvoyant gift showing her real events in her dreams—giving her clues that might help her solve over a dozen cold cases?

Letting out a sigh, Hillary felt overwhelmed. She had promised Danielle she would try remembering her past dreams and pay closer attention to the faces of the killers, and perhaps use that information to help local authorities solve the old crimes. Yet the truth was Hillary didn't really want to get involved. After all, how would she explain her information to the police? The more she thought about it, the more she didn't want to have anything to do with playing real-life detective.

She could recall what it had been like when the police had once brought her in for questioning—suspecting she might have been involved with the past murders, because why else did she know what she did? No, she did not want to go through that again.

Turning from the ocean, she glanced back toward the pier. She could no longer see Steve in the darkness, but the second person—the shadowy form who had minutes earlier been talking with Steve, stepped into view.

Hilary's eyes widened when she saw his face. Without thought, she asked with a gasp, "What are you doing here?"

"Hillary? Seriously?" He groaned. "What are you doing here? Oh—never mind. I know the answer to that question."

"You know who I am?" she asked in surprise.

"Well, of course. Haven't we known each other, what—ten, eleven years now?"

Confused, she shook her head in denial. "This doesn't make any sense."

"Oh, it will."

Abruptly, Hillary stepped back, taking a defensive stance. "If you try to kill me, someone will hear me. I can scream very loud, and we're not that far from a house. I imagine I could scream loud enough for someone at the pier to hear me!"

He laughed sardonically. "Seriously? That's what you're thinking?" Turning from her, he continued his walk down the beach—away from her—away from the pier.

Perplexed, she watched him for a few moments and then called out, "Wait!"

He paused a moment and turned and faced her. "What?"

"You mean you aren't going to kill me?"

Wearily, he shook his head. "Now I understand why it never worked. You were never the right one to help me."

"What are you talking about?"

"It really doesn't matter now."

"You don't care that I recognized you?" she asked.

He shrugged and turned away again.

"You don't care that I saw you kill her?" she called out, unable to resist asking the question.

Pausing a moment, he turned back to face her again and smiled. "Not particularly."

She stared at him for a moment before asking, "Who are you? What's your name?"

He smiled again. "Do you know, that's the first time you've ever asked me that question. In all these years, you never asked. Antoine Paul. I'm Antoine Paul."

"Antoine Paul?" The name meant nothing to Hillary.

Shoving his hands into the pockets of his black dress slacks, he turned from Hillary again and proceeded to walk down the beach, leaving Hillary Hemingway staring at his departing form with a look of confusion on her face.

THREE

Danielle overslept on Friday morning. When she finally managed to pry open her sleep-laden eyes and look at the clock radio sitting on her nightstand, it took her a few moments for reality to sink in, and when it did, she bolted from the bed and hastily dressed. It was almost 9 am. She never slept in that late when guests were in the house, and Hillary had announced she would be leaving right after breakfast—right after an 8:00 a.m. breakfast.

Dashing into the hallway, she looked over to Hillary's room. The door was shut. If Hillary was preparing to check out, she would expect the door to be open. Danielle hoped to find her guest downstairs at the breakfast table. She prayed she hadn't left already. Danielle would feel horrible if she had missed saying goodbye to Hillary.

Once she reached the first floor, Danielle went to the dining room and looked in. The table was set, but by its appearance, breakfast hadn't yet been served. She headed for the kitchen.

"Good morning, sleepyhead," Lily greeted Danielle when she burst into the room. Lily sat with Joanne at the kitchen table as the two drank coffee.

Danielle headed for the coffee pot to pour herself a cup. "Why didn't you wake me up?"

Lily shrugged and sipped her coffee. "Why would we? I figured you needed your sleep. And since Hillary hasn't come down yet, I didn't see what the big deal was."

"I thought Hillary wanted to get an early start back to Vancouver?" Joanne asked. "I expected her to be downstairs an hour ago."

Danielle joined Lily and her housekeeper at the table, a fresh cup of coffee in hand. "That's what she told me. You mean you haven't seen her this morning?"

"Her door was still shut when I came downstairs," Lily said.

"Maybe she got in late last night." Danielle sipped her coffee and then paused. She looked at Lily. "She did come back, didn't she?"

Lily frowned and set her cup down on the table. "About that. I don't know what the heck you were talking about last night. But Hillary was sleeping soundly in her room when you went to bed last night."

Danielle shook her head and frowned. "No, she wasn't. I was in the parlor when she stopped by to tell me she was going for a walk."

"Did you see her leave the house?" Lily asked.

"No, but I just assumed she did. When I walked out into the hall, she was already gone."

"She must have changed her mind and came back upstairs and went to bed. Who knows, maybe Hillary's a sleepwalker. All I know, when I looked in her room after you went to bed, she was sleeping."

"I don't know anything about Hillary going out last night," Joanne said. "But don't you think one of you should wake her up? She did say she wanted to get on the road early. From what she told me yesterday, she intended to leave by now."

Danielle stood up. "You're probably right."

"I'll get the bacon on." Joanne stood.

"YOU DON'T HAVE to come upstairs with me," Danielle told Lily as the two headed to the second floor.

"I just wanted to tell you I thought you were losing it last night," Lily said in a low whisper before giving way to a mischievous giggle.

"Why didn't you tell me she was in her room last night?"

"I didn't know until after you went to bed." Lily shrugged.

"Why did you look in on her, anyway?" Danielle stepped onto the second-floor landing.

"I don't know. Being nosey, I guess. You know, she never locks her door." Lily followed Danielle to Hillary's room.

"I noticed that. I always lock my bedroom door, at least when there are guests in the house," Danielle confessed.

"Me too."

Together the two women stood outside Hillary's bedroom door. Danielle knocked.

No response.

Danielle glanced to the bathroom across the hall from Hillary's room. Its door was open and the light was off. Hillary was obviously not in the bathroom. Danielle knocked again, this time louder.

No response.

"Wow. I didn't realize Hillary was such a sound sleeper," Lily said.

Danielle knocked again even louder. When there was still no response, she gingerly turned the doorknob and pushed the door open. She peeked inside. The morning sunlight streamed through the window; the curtain had not been closed the night before. Danielle could see Hillary sleeping in the bed, her back turned to them.

"Hillary! Oh, Hillary!" Danielle called out in a loud whisper. Still no response.

Hesitantly, she walked to the bed and reached out, gently touching the older woman's shoulder, giving it a gentle nudge. "Hillary, wake up…" Danielle froze.

The next moment, Danielle snatched back her hand. "Oh my god!"

Not waiting for Danielle to explain, Lily rushed to the other side of the bed and looked at Hillary's face. Hillary stared at her through open, unblinking eyes.

"LOOKS like she's been dead for hours," Officer Brian Henderson told Danielle as the responders took Hillary's body out to the waiting van.

Notepad in hand, Brian stood in the middle of the living room, the door leading to the hallway wide open, making it possible for the living room occupants to witness Hillary's departure.

Ian, who had arrived at Marlow House just minutes after

Danielle had called for the police, sat on the living room sofa, Lily by his side, her hand in his. Across from the pair, Joanne sat on the edge of a chair, her hands nervously twisting in her lap. Danielle stood by the fireplace with Walt—who only Danielle could see.

"Do you have any idea what happened?" Lily asked.

"Looks like a heart attack. She had heart medication in her purse." Brian looked up from his notepad. "We'll know more later. Did she give a name of someone to call in case of an emergency?"

"Heart medication?" Danielle asked. "I didn't realize she even had a heart problem."

"Maybe a family member?" Brian rephrased the question.

Danielle shook her head. "I really don't know. She never talked about family. I don't think she had any kids. If she did, she never said anything to me. She did mention she'd been married twice. But I have no idea if she was divorced from her husbands or widowed."

"Widowed twice." Ian spoke up. "She didn't have any children."

"You knew her well?" Brian asked.

Ian shook his head. "No, I'd never met her before—not until she checked in here. But I was a fan. I've read every Hillary Hemingway mystery. I've seen a few of her interviews, read some articles about her. But other than knowing she has no children and lost two husbands, I've no idea who her closest relative might be."

"What about Melony?" Lily suggested.

"Melony?" Danielle looked at Lily. "That's right."

"Melony?" Brian asked.

"You know, Melony Jacobs. Jolene Carmichael's daughter. She was Hillary's attorney—well, she represented her once. I imagine she'd know who we need to contact," Danielle explained.

"If she doesn't, I'm sure I can find out who her agent is," Ian offered.

"Didn't Melony go back to New York?" Brian asked.

"Yeah, but she's friends with the chief. I'm sure he could call her."

Brian nodded and jotted something down in his notepad. He then looked up. "Joanne mentioned something about you thinking Hillary had gone out last night?"

"Oh, that was just a misunderstanding," Danielle said quickly. "I thought she had gone out, but she must have gone back to bed."

"And died…" Brian mumbled, again jotting something down on the paper.

"Hillary did see me last night," Walt said suddenly.

Danielle looked over at Walt, her expression questioning.

"Last night, when she came into the parlor, she saw me. That was Hillary's spirit we saw last night. She was already dead when Lily looked into her room," Walt explained before vanishing. He went to the attic to look outside to watch the activity on the street in front of Marlow House.

"When was the last time anyone saw Hillary last night?" Brian asked.

"I imagine that would be me, when I peeked into her room last night before going to bed. She was sleeping. Or…well, I assumed she was sleeping." Lily squeezed Ian's hand. Silently, he looked into her green eyes and returned the squeeze.

"What time was that?" Brian asked.

"It was 10:15. I looked at the time when I went to bed a few minutes later," Lily explained.

"Hillary's dead?" a new voice called out from the doorway.

They all turned to face the new arrival. It was Danielle's neighbor Heather Donovan. The fact Heather looked more girlish—than the young woman she was—was partly attributed to her habit of wearing her hair pulled back into two regular, three-strand braids, with her severe bangs cut straight across her forehead.

"I saw the police cars—the ambulance. I just saw them put Hillary into the ambulance, and she's dead?"

"I'm afraid so," Danielle said sadly. "We think it might have been a heart attack. I found her this morning. But we'll know more after the autopsy."

Heather walked into the room. "I can't believe it. I just saw her last night. Damn…I was kind of short with her. I was tired, cold, just wanted to get back in the house." Dejected, Heather took a seat on an empty chair.

"When did you see her?" Brian asked.

"Last night. I was taking out my trash. It was late, I'd already gone to bed when I remembered today's trash day. So I got up, took the can out to the sidewalk and ran into Hillary. She told me she was heading down to the beach to take a final moonlight walk. She said she was checking out this morning."

"Do you have any idea what time that was?" Brian asked.

"Sure. I looked at the clock when I got out of bed to take the trash out. It was 10:15."

FOUR

Beverly Klein had just started to make herself a sandwich when the landline began to ring. Abandoning the opened loaf of bread on the cutting board, she walked to the far end of the kitchen and answered the phone.

"Beverly, hi. This is Susan Mitchell. Is Steve there, by chance?"

"Steve? Why would he be here? Isn't he at work?"

"He hasn't come in today. I tried calling his cellphone. But he doesn't answer. He has an 11:00 meeting."

Holding the phone's receiver to her ear, Beverly glanced at the wall clock. "It's almost 11:30."

"I know. That's why I'm calling. Do you know where he is?"

Moving the receiver from her right hand to her left, Beverly leaned against the wall. "He should be at work."

"Do you know what time he left this morning?"

"Not really. When I got up, he was already gone. I assumed he was at the bank."

"This isn't like him. He never misses meetings."

Beverly stood up straight and glanced to the door leading from the kitchen to the garage. "No, this isn't like him. Let me see what I can find out, and I'll call you back. Do you have my cellphone number?"

"Yes. I have both yours and your husband's."

"Good. If he shows up, please call me immediately. If I'm not at the house, you can reach me on my cellphone."

When Beverly got off the phone, she went directly to the garage. Steve's car wasn't parked in its normal spot. She glanced around. His tackle box, which he kept on the workbench, was absent, as was his fishing pole.

Going back into the house, she grabbed her purse and car keys.

Fifteen minutes later Beverly pulled into the Frederickport Pier parking lot, where she found her husband's car. After parking next to it, she got out and peeked in the windows. Nothing looked out of place. Turning from the vehicle, she made her way to the pier.

No one seemed to be around save for one man who was fishing along the same side of the pier as the café and the row of shops. Yet on the other side of the pier, she spied a folding chair she recognized. Instead of approaching the chair, she surveyed the area from afar, noting what appeared to be Steve's tackle box, open and upside down, with tackle scattered around the chair's perimeter. Steve was nowhere in sight. She went immediately to the lone fisherman.

"Excuse me!" Beverly greeted the man when she approached.

Preparing to bait his hook, the man paused and looked to Beverly. "Yes?"

"Did you notice where the man who was fishing over there went?"

He shrugged. "I haven't seen him. No one's been over there since I got here. Figured whoever it was is probably at the café, getting something to eat."

"How long have you been here?"

Again the man shrugged. "Couple hours, I guess."

"A couple of hours? And in all that time, no one's been over there?"

"Nope. But now that I think about it, not a good idea to just leave your gear lying around on the pier. Anyone could walk off with it."

"Umm, yes, you're right. Okay, thank you." Beverly smiled and turned away from the man, making her way to Steve's fishing spot.

When she got to the other side of the pier, she surveyed the area. It was Steve's folding chair and tackle box, but the sack he had taken with him was nowhere in sight. She remembered he had forgotten to take his thermos the previous night, and if he had picked up coffee on the pier, there was no evidence of that. She didn't notice the fishing pole immediately. What she noticed first was a section of broken railing directly in front of the chair. Her gaze moved down, and then she saw it, Steve's fishing pole lying on the pier, its line still dangling out in the water.

Beverly turned and made her hasty way to the Pier Café. The moment she entered the door, she practically ran head-on into a waitress with rainbow-colored hair.

"Mrs. Klein," Carla squeaked, coming to an abrupt halt before slamming into the banker's wife and spilling the pot of coffee she carried.

"Hello, Carla, is my husband here?"

"Your husband? Why would he be in here?"

Beverly cocked her brow. "I would assume to get something to eat."

"Umm…oh yeah…" Carla laughed nervously. "No…no, he isn't."

"Has he been in at all this morning?"

Carla shook her head. "Not since I got here. But I don't know about before that."

"How long have you been here?" Beverly asked.

Carla glanced to the wall clock. "I've been here for about an hour."

"Did you happen to see him last night?"

"He came in to buy some coffee. Is there some problem?"

"I don't know." Beverly glanced to the window. "He came down here to go fishing last night. And he never came home. His fishing equipment is still on the pier."

"Why would he leave his fishing equipment on the pier?"

"And his car in the parking lot," Beverly added.

SERGEANT JOE MORELLI guessed Beverly Klein was a good ten years younger than her husband, somewhere in the early forties range, which would make her a few years older than himself. Yet unlike Joe, who was still single and unmarried, Beverly was not only married, she had two grown, college-aged children, a boy and a girl.

When Joe had learned about Steve's affair with Carla, his first reaction was—why? Why would a man like Steve Klein risk it all for a flighty waitress not much older than his own daughter while he had a wife that looked like Beverly at home? Rumor had it that in Beverly's younger years she had been Miss Colorado, or was it Miss Connecticut? He couldn't recall exactly. Whichever state it was, he suspected the story of Beverly Klein once being a beauty queen was true, considering how she now looked. Beverly Klein—with her trim yet curvy figure, startling green eyes, and perfectly coifed strawberry blonde hair—was an attractive woman. Far more appealing than the younger Carla, Joe thought.

He stood with Beverly at her husband's fishing site. Together they looked over the area.

"And you didn't realize he hadn't come home last night?"

"No. But that's not so unusual. Thursday night is bridge and fishing night. I spend the evening with my girlfriends and he goes fishing. There's lots of times he doesn't get home until after I've fallen asleep and then he's already gone to work before I wake up in the morning. I just figured he was at work. I didn't realize anything might be wrong until Susan from the bank called me, looking for Steve after he missed a meeting. When I went into the garage, his car wasn't there and neither was his tackle box. He never leaves that in his car when he comes back from fishing. He always keeps it on the workbench in the garage. When I didn't see that tackle box this morning, I just knew he never came home last night."

Hands on hips, Joe looked at the upside-down tackle box, its lid askew and its contents scattered along the wooden pier under and around the folding chair. When Beverly leaned down, preparing to right the box, Joe reached out and grabbed her wrist, stopping her.

"No. I don't want you to touch anything."

Beverly paused and looked up at Joe, her eyes wide. "What are you saying?"

"WHAT'S THIS about Steve Klein going missing? That he might have drowned?" Danielle asked the chief as she walked into his office late Friday afternoon.

Looking up from his desk, MacDonald tossed his pen aside and leaned back in his chair. "It has been one hell of a day, that's for sure."

Danielle took a seat in front of the desk and tossed her purse on the floor by her feet. "I heard something on the radio coming over here about him going missing while fishing last night."

"He was fishing on the pier last night—his chair, pole and tackle box are still there, but he hasn't been seen since last night, when he went into Pier Café to buy some coffee. What's disturbing, the railing along the pier is broken. And from what we've learned, it wasn't like that yesterday morning."

"Are you saying he fell off the pier?"

"His tackle box was upside down, and everything was scattered all over the place. I don't know if there was some sort of altercation down there—did he get in an argument with someone—it escalates —someone kicks over the tackle box and then—"

"Someone shoves Steve over the rail," Danielle finished for him.

The chief gave Danielle a nod. "One thing that I don't imagine was mentioned on the radio, we found blood and hair on one of the pillars of the dock. As if someone fell over and hit his head. It's being tested now."

Danielle winced then said, "According to the radio report, they didn't notice he was missing until this afternoon. I know Beverly's back in town, I saw her at the grocery store the other day. If he went fishing last night, how is it no one noticed he was missing until today?"

"I guess when she woke up this morning, she assumed he'd gotten in after she went to sleep, and left for work before she got up this morning."

Danielle considered his words for a moment and then with a gasp said, "Carla!"

"Carla? What do you mean?"

"Carla works at Pier Café. If she was there last night, maybe she and Steve had words. I can't see her doing anything like that intentionally, but if she did get in a fight with him and it got out of hand, I imagine by now she is freaked out and would probably tell you whatever you wanted to know."

"As a matter of fact, Carla did work last night. Joe spoke to her. Steve stopped into the café to buy some coffee, and she swears she didn't see him again last night."

"Not even when she locked up to go home?"

The chief shook his head. "No. According to Carla, she locked up and went out the back door last night, so she wouldn't have seen him fishing, even if he had still been there. Joe thought she acted a little uncomfortable during the interview, but not like someone who'd recently shoved an ex-lover off the pier."

Danielle slumped back in her chair, folding her arms across her chest. "I just think it's a little weird that Steve chose to go fishing right outside the door where his ex-girlfriend works."

"Maybe. But right now, I have another problem and it involves you."

"Me? How?"

"I spoke to the coroner, and while he's fairly certain it was a heart attack, he may not be able to give me anything official until Tuesday."

Danielle frowned. "Why is that a problem?"

"Brian is asking questions—questions I can't answer, yet I have a feeling you can."

"Questions about what?"

"Like why both Lily and Heather claimed to have seen Hillary at exactly the same time—the exact same time, 10:15 p.m."

Danielle slumped farther down in her chair and groaned. "I knew that was going to be a problem."

"Heather didn't actually see Hillary last night, did she? I mean, not the living Hillary."

With a sigh, Danielle stood up and started pacing the room. "Technically speaking, I don't think Lily saw the living Hillary either. I'm certain she was already dead when Lily peeked in the room."

Danielle went on to tell the chief about her and Walt's encounter with Hillary the previous night and how Lily had looked into Hillary's room before going to bed.

She stopped pacing and turned to face the chief. "You know, Heather seems to be getting more and more sensitive to spirits. She saw Jolene and now Hillary. What makes me nervous, one of these days she's going to catch more than a glimpse of Walt. Not so sure how that will turn out."

FIVE

Sitting alone on the beach, the cup of hot coffee warming her hands, Heather played over in her head last night's phone conversation with Danielle Boatman.

"The next time you talk to Brian Henderson—and I have a feeling he's going to be calling you or stopping by your house—you may not want to stick to that 10:15 time frame for seeing Hillary. Maybe suggest it was earlier than that —that it was 10:15 when you got back in bed after taking the trash out," Danielle had suggested.

Heather couldn't believe what Danielle was asking of her. *"You want me to lie to the police?"*

"Heather, haven't you figured it out yet? You saw Hillary's spirit last night. It wasn't the flesh and blood Hillary. She was already dead—and her body was in the bed at Marlow House. Lily saw it, just like she said this morning."

Glancing down at the hot cup of coffee, Heather blew softly and then took a sip.

"If there was some way to prove *I was* talking with Hillary's spirit last night, the last thing I'd want to do is lie about when I saw her." She took another sip.

Settling back in the sand, telling herself she should be jogging instead of sitting and drinking coffee, she set her cup next to her on the beach, wiggling it slightly, burrowing it in the sand so it would stay put. She then removed her jogging shoes and socks. Burying her feet in the cool sand, she wiggled her toes.

"This would feel much nicer in the summer." Heather picked up her cup, its lower half now coated with sand, and took a sip. Looking out to the incoming waves, she watched as what appeared to be a massive heap of seaweed washed up onto shore not thirty feet from her.

Her gaze still on the pile of seaweed, she watched as wave after wave gently nudged the heap farther and farther onto shore, and closer to her. She was just about to take another sip of coffee when she noticed movement on the beach to her right. She glanced over and looked. There was a man walking in her direction. A man wearing a black suit and red bow tie.

"Another weirdo," Heather muttered as she stumbled to her feet, deciding to cut her coffee break short and get on with her jog before having to talk to the oddly dressed man—oddly dressed for a stroll on the beach.

Just as she stood and started to toss out what remained of her coffee, she glanced back to the heap of seaweed and noticed something sticking out of it.

"Oh crap!" Heather cried out. She looked to the man walking in her direction and shouted, "Quick, it looks like a body!" Dashing to the seaweed, Heather looked down and discovered she had been correct. There, tangled in the mass of sea foliage, was the bloated body of Steve Klein, and by the way the back of his head looked, it appeared as if he had been hit in the head.

When she looked back to the approaching man, she discovered he was no longer there.

"What the…?" Heather looked around and then promptly dug her cellphone from her pocket.

"I'M GIVING UP JOGGING," Heather told Brian later that morning. She sat on a bench along the boardwalk and watched Steve's body being loaded into the waiting van.

"If that would cut down on the number of bodies we've been finding on the beach lately, then I'm all for that," Brian mumbled as he jotted something down on his notepad.

"No, I'm serious." She sounded serious. "This is just getting ridiculous. Dead bodies, ghost ships. What the hell? I thought living on the beach along the Oregon coast was going to be calming—relaxing. DO I LOOK LIKE I'M RELAXED?"

Surprised by Heather's outburst, Brian inadvertently slammed his notebook shut. Startled, he said, "I know this must have been traumatic for you—"

"You don't know anything!" Abruptly, Heather stood. "And I did see Hillary Thursday night."

"I never said you didn't. But the time—"

"Well, I was right on the time. 10:15. Yes, 10:15! The same time Lily saw her. You know why that is, Officer Henderson?"

"Umm…no…but I think you're going to tell me."

"Because I saw Hillary's ghost! She was already dead. Hillary wasn't alive when Lily saw her in that bed."

Not expecting that answer, Brian blinked, somewhat confused.

"Yes, her ghost! There, I said it! I see ghosts! I saw Harvey Crump's ghost. I bet you don't even know who that is. He was the teenager haunting Presley House, the poor kid my great-grandfather murdered."

Heather leaned over and roughly brushed the sand from her jogging pants. "And I saw Jolene's ghost. Did you know that? I didn't just find her body; I saw her ghost. Ask your boss. I told him. He believed me. Oh, he didn't say he did. But I know he believed me. And I bet if I stick around here long enough, I'll see Steve Klein's ghost. But you know what? I don't want to see any ghosts today! I don't want to see any more dead bodies either. I'm going home!" With that, Heather turned and started to stomp away.

"Heather!" Brian called out. "I'm not done with you."

"Well, I'm done with you!"

"SHE SAID ALL THAT?" Joe asked Brian later Saturday afternoon when they were back at the station. Joe and Brian sat with the chief in his office.

"I told you she was an odd one." Brian looked over at the chief. "Did she really tell you she saw Jolene's ghost?"

Absently tapping the end of his pen against his desktop, MacDonald looked over at Joe. "The day she found Jolene's body, she claimed she saw Jolene running to the pier. But then a few minutes later she found the body, so she figured the woman she saw running to the pier was Jolene's spirit."

Suppressing a laugh, Brian said, "Not to be disrespectful, but I can't imagine Jolene running anywhere—alive or dead. It was probably some woman who resembled Jolene, and when Heather found the body, she got this crazy idea that the first woman was a ghost. And considering what a nut she is, I'm probably spot on."

Joe frowned at the chief. "You didn't actually believe she saw Jolene's ghost, did you?"

"I'm just telling you what she told me. As for Jolene's ghost—since her murder has been solved, I think we need to focus on the murder at hand."

"You think it was murder?" Joe asked. "You don't think it's possible he stumbled and fell off the pier on his own?"

"According to the coroner, the only abrasion was on his head—consistent with hitting the side of the pier during the fall," the chief explained.

Joe frowned. He looked from Brian to the chief. "If that was the only abrasion they found, that would mean no defensive wounds, which would indicate Steve possibly fell off that pier on his own—which is hardly murder."

"Call it a gut feeling," the chief said. "I think there is something more to this."

"I have to admit, seeing that tackle box upside down and everything scattered around, it did look like something went on," Joe said.

Brian thoughtfully considered the possible scenarios. "I'll be curious to see what the autopsy comes back with. It's possible he was drinking a little more than coffee, got wasted, and stumbled off the pier on his own. Might just be a stupid accident."

"How did Beverly Klein take the news?" Joe asked.

"I suspect she had a gut feeling this would be the outcome," the chief told him. "But she looked a little dazed, in shock. Said she had to call their kids. Their daughter lives in Portland and their son recently joined the military. I think he's stationed in Texas, not sure. I called Susan over at the bank, figured there would be someone she should get in contact with at work."

"Does Carla know?" Joe asked.

"I haven't talked to her yet. But I don't think my duties include informing someone their ex-lover is dead. But speaking of Carla, I think we need to tread lightly during this investigation. For the moment, I'd rather Beverly not learn about her husband's infidelity," the chief said.

"I know Danielle found out about her husband's infidelity when he was killed. I imagine that made his death even worse," Joe said.

"Why?" Brian scoffed. "If my wife died and then I found out she'd been screwing around, it would be easier for me to get on with life and not moan over something that was obviously a lie."

The chief shook his head. "Damn, Brian, you're cold. If you really were in love with your wife and she died—and then you found out she was cheating on you—trust me, it would not lessen the pain. It would make it worse."

Brian shrugged. "Maybe you're right. But when my wife cheated on me, seeing her dead didn't sound like such a bad thing at the time."

Ignoring Brian's comment, the chief said, "Depending on what the coroner says, it's possible this will be ruled an accident, and if that's the case, there's no reason for Beverly and her kids to learn about Steve's wandering eye."

"More than his eye wandered," Brian sneered.

"And if the coroner suspects foul play?" Joe asked.

"Then I guess it won't be kept a secret." The chief shrugged.

SATURDAY EVENING CHRIS JOHNSON sat with Danielle, Lily, and Walt in the living room of Marlow House, waiting for Ian to arrive so they could all go out to dinner. All except for Walt, who'd be staying home with Sadie and Max.

"I'm glad we don't have any guests right now," Danielle said with a sigh. "There are a lot of people who wouldn't be thrilled to know someone had recently died in their room. As it is, some guest aren't going to want to stay in a room where someone has died."

"Then I guess that makes Hillary's room, the parlor, and the attic off-limits for guests," Lily said.

Danielle cringed. "Umm…that doesn't sound very good, does it?"

"You guys haven't seen her at all?" Lily asked.

Danielle shook her head. "Nope. Only that one time, when she was leaving the house. My guess, she was in that unaware state. Sort of like when you showed up here from California after the accident."

"I wouldn't say being intentionally hit over the head was an accident," Lily argued. "And I wasn't dead. But I know what you're saying."

"Maybe she's moved on," Chris suggested. "Between Danielle, myself, Walt, and Heather, I'd think if she were lingering nearby, one of us would have seen her."

"About Heather, does this mean she can see me?" Walt asked.

Danielle shrugged. "I know from what she's told me, she's seen glimpses of you. I've alluded to the fact you may be around—but I've also made it clear I do not want to go public about my abilities. I'm hoping she'll continue to respect that."

"I'm not sure I'd want someone like Heather to be fully aware of my presence. Something about her is a little unsettling."

"I guess I'm all the unsettling you can handle at one time, right?" Chris winked at Walt.

"Oh brother…" Walt muttered and then waved his hand for a cigar.

"You haven't seen Hillary, but what about Steve Klein? Do you think his spirit is still lingering?" Lily asked.

"I haven't seen it. But maybe I will when we go over there tomorrow," Danielle said.

Chris looked curiously to Danielle. "Why are you going over there?"

"Lily and I are going to take a casserole over to Beverly and give her our condolences."

SIX

Beverly Klein sat alone in her living room, staring blankly at the television. It wasn't turned on. There was a funeral to plan. She had just gotten off the phone with her daughter after successfully talking her into delaying her trip to Frederickport until the funeral. It wasn't as if it was an especially long drive from Portland to Frederickport, but Beverly wasn't ready yet to deal with her daughter's grief over the sudden and unexpected loss of a father. Beverly had her own emotions to wrestle with.

As for the funeral, the date hadn't yet been set. Steve's body had only been found twenty-four hours earlier, and it would be a few days before it could be released—after the autopsy was complete. Beverly wondered, *What will the autopsy show? Why did Steve fall off that pier?*

Beverly's solitude was interrupted a few minutes later when the doorbell rang. She stood up and went to answer the door.

"Baron!" Beverly greeted Baron Huxley, a longtime friend of her husband, when she found him standing on the front porch.

Opening his arms, he gathered Beverly up for a comforting hug. "I'm so sorry. I read about Steve in this morning's paper. I can't believe it."

Beverly accepted the hug. When it ended, she silently ushered Baron into the house and to the living room.

"Can I get you some coffee?" she offered when she showed him to a chair.

He gently nudged her to a nearby seat. "Don't be silly. The last thing I want is for you to be waiting on me. But I'll be happy to get *you* some coffee. I want you to know, if you need anything, I'm here for you."

Now sitting, Beverly smiled sadly and patted Baron's hand, which lingered on her knee. "Thank you, Baron. I appreciate that."

Baron withdrew his hand from her knee, yet not before giving it a final pat.

Beverly tilted her head slightly and studied him for a moment. "I suppose you understand what I'm going through—having lost Melissa like you did."

He shook his head. "Tragic, senseless circumstances. I suppose losing a spouse is always devastating, but when it's from pointless violence—or in Steve's case, a senseless accident—it's almost impossible to make sense of it all. From what I read, he fell from the pier while fishing?"

Beverly nodded. "You know how he went fishing every Thursday night. I never really considered fishing alone, especially on the Frederickport Pier, to be especially dangerous. He's been doing it for years."

"Do you know when the service will be?" Baron leaned back in the chair and studied the widow.

"I don't know yet. The autopsy might take a few days. And until that's complete, I don't really want to set a date."

"When are Roxane and Steven arriving?"

"After I called Roxane yesterday to tell her, she wanted to leave right then and come home. But I didn't want her driving when she was all emotional. I asked her to wait and come closer to the funeral date. Steven will come for the funeral, naturally."

"I still can't believe it. I saw Steve Wednesday morning when I dropped off the tamales."

Beverly smiled. "Steve loved the tamales you'd bring him."

"Carlos's wife makes the best ones…You never liked them, did you?"

She laughed. "You know I don't. Something about masa that just makes me gag. I think it's the texture. Lucky for Steve you kept him in tamales. I sure would never buy them. In fact, he took the tamales with him that night."

"I never could understand how he could eat them cold." Baron shook his head and chuckled.

"Hot or cold, tamales aren't for me. But to be honest, Steve and I always had very different eating habits. I tried to get him to cut down on red meat, eat more salads, but I swear, the moment I leave town, he's eating burgers every day."

"I think it's a man thing." Baron flashed her a smile.

"I suppose. And now, considering everything, I should have let Steve eat all the burgers he wanted." Beverly's eyes filled with unshed tears.

"Unfortunately, when it's our time, I really don't think there's much we can do about it."

"Do you think it was truly Melissa's time to go?" she asked.

He didn't answer immediately. Finally, he said, "I think Melissa was simply in the wrong place at the wrong time."

"How many years has it been now? Ten?"

"It was eleven years this past February," he told her.

"Are the police still looking for her killer?"

"It's not just a cold case—it's an ice block. I don't know if you remember, but several witnesses at the time claimed they saw her leaving the bar with a man wearing a dark suit and red bow tie. According to witnesses, they were arguing. But this mystery man, he vanished. No one has ever been able to identify who he may have been."

"I remember Steve telling me that." Beverly dropped her gaze briefly to her lap, regretting for a moment broaching the sensitive subject.

"I've never believed there was anything—between her and that man—like some of the police implied at the time. Sure, we were having a rough spot, but Melissa wasn't the type to go picking up strange men. He must have done something to convince her to go with him. Melissa was always naïve."

Before Beverly could respond, the doorbell rang.

DANIELLE HUGGED to her chest a warm, covered casserole dish —wrapped in a clean towel—filled with a batch of macaroni and cheese she had baked that morning. *Comfort food,* she thought. Beverly Klein needed comfort food. Next to her stood Lily, who carried a sack filled with homemade chocolate brownies. *Chocolate always helps*. Together they stood on Beverly's front porch, waiting for someone to answer the door.

They didn't plan to stay long. Just long enough to give their condolences and drop off the food. Initially they had considered calling first, but then decided to just stop by. Danielle wasn't especially close to Beverly. She and Lily had first met the woman at Marlow House's open house in July—the disastrous open house where Cheryl had taken off with the Missing Thorndike and had tragically gotten herself murdered.

But Beverly had always been friendly when Danielle had run into her around town—like at the grocery store or at some function at the museum. Danielle hated knowing about Steve's infidelity, and she hoped his wife would never have to discover the truth. What was the point? Danielle knew firsthand what it felt like to discover your husband's betrayal while trying to come to terms with his death.

"Danielle! Lily!" Beverley greeted them after she opened the front door.

"We understand if you don't feel like seeing anyone," Danielle began. "But we wanted to drop this off—it's some homemade macaroni and cheese and some brownies. I know that when going through something like this, the last thing you want to think about is cooking—or eating. But you really need to eat."

"We're so sorry to hear about Steve," Lily added.

"Oh, this is so sweet of you!" Beverly looked as if she was about to cry. She ushered the women into the house, taking the casserole dish and sack of brownies from them.

Following Beverly down the entry hall, they paused a moment while she quickly darted into the kitchen to deposit the food. When she returned, she led them to the living room. Baron stood the moment the three women walked into the room.

"Oh, I'm sorry, I didn't know you had company," Danielle said.

"No, it's fine. This is a good friend of Steve's, Baron Huxley." She turned to face Baron. "Baron, this is Danielle Boatman, she owns Marlow House, and this is her friend Lily Miller."

After a brief round of hellos and nice to meet yous, Lily and

Danielle took a seat on the sofa while Beverly sat back down in the chair next to Baron.

"If there's anything you need, please let us know," Danielle said. "If you need a place for any of your family to stay, I'll be happy to let them use a room at Marlow House. No charge of course."

"That's so sweet, Danielle, I really appreciate the offer. But to be honest I'm not really sure when the funeral will be. I don't want to plan anything until after the autopsy—and they release Steve's body."

Danielle glanced toward the doorway leading to the hallway and asked, "Are your kids here?"

"No. But they'll be here for the funeral. Roxane wanted to come right away, but I didn't want her driving right now, she was so upset."

Danielle frowned. "I thought you had small children."

Beverly smiled. "No. Not so little anymore. Although they'll always be my babies. Roxane is twenty-one and lives in Portland. Steven is in the army, stationed in Texas."

"Oh my! I had no idea your kids were that old! I just assumed they were in grade school." Danielle told her.

"You look way too young to have college-aged kids," Lily added.

Beverly smiled. "Why, thank you. But at the moment, I feel every year of my age."

"Times like this, people often say they know what you're going through," Danielle began. "They're just trying to be helpful, I suppose. In some ways, I guess I know a little of what you're going through, because I lost my husband in a car accident over a year ago. But even then, I have no idea what you're going through. We all grieve in our own way. And I imagine right now, you're probably feeling something akin to shock, trying to process it all. But if you ever need someone to talk to, you can call me."

Beverly smiled sadly at Danielle. "Thank you, I appreciate that. I remember Steve telling me you had lost your husband." She turned briefly to Baron and said, "Baron here is a widower. I suppose in some ways it helps to know that there is life after such a loss…you both have done it."

There was a moment of awkward silence.

"Do you live in Frederickport?" Lily asked Baron.

"I have a vacation home here," he explained. "But I live in Vancouver."

"I assume you mean Vancouver, Washington?" Danielle asked with a smile.

"Yes."

"Baron and Steve used to work together before we moved to Frederickport," Beverly explained.

"Are you in banking too?" Danielle asked.

"In a manner of speaking."

"Baron owns his own finance and consultant company," Beverly explained.

"Are you Steve's old boss?" Lily asked.

"No, but we used to work together. But then Steve decided it was time to get a real job and work for a company that had benefits and vacation pay."

"Steve just preferred a little more security." The moment the words left Beverly's mouth, she started to cry.

SEVEN

"Do you think it was the irony of her words that made her cry?" Lily asked. She sat in the passenger seat of Danielle's Flex as they drove back to Marlow House.

Danielle glanced briefly to Lily. "How so?"

"You know, the thing about Steve wanting security, which implies playing it safe, planning his future. And here he goes and gets himself killed, falling off the pier while fishing."

"Either that or it just hit her that she's a widow. That friend of Steve's was sure good looking for an older guy."

"How old do you think he is?" Lily asked.

"I don't know. Late fifties, I guess. He has great hair. Why don't all men let themselves go gray like that? What was it that my mother used to call it? Oh yeah…a silver fox. He was that."

"I was sort of surprised he was in financing." Lily reached up and adjusted the sun visor.

"Why did his line of work surprise you?"

"He's built pretty good for a man of his age—solid, nice shoulders, arms. Like he's in construction."

"I think he's a little old for construction," Danielle said.

"I know. I just meant his build. And from what I could see, he had a nice tan. He's solid like he's used to manual labor. Although, I imagine if I inspected his hands, they're probably all soft like a baby's bottom, considering those slacks he was wearing and that designer golf shirt."

Danielle laughed. "He had nice gray eyes too."

"Yes, he did. Sexy."

"And did you notice how they were always on Beverly?" Danielle asked.

"What are you saying?"

"I don't think he was there just to offer his condolences; I got the impression he was staking an early claim, getting there before anyone else."

"Danielle! Why would you say that? Beverly said he was a good friend of Steve's and had just learned about Steve's death this morning. I certainly don't think the first thing he'd think about is jumping the widow."

Danielle laughed. "Oh, Lily, so naïve."

Lily frowned over at Danielle. "Why do you say that?"

"I remember once my mother telling me that after her father died, a number of grandpa's friends hit on grandma—and I'm talking about *married* friends. Mom said that often happens to a woman when a husband dies. I didn't really take it seriously, not until Lucas died."

Turning in her seat, Lily faced Danielle. "Are you telling me some of your married friends hit on you after Lucas died?"

"Yep. I would have been totally shocked had I not remembered what my mother had told me. Beverly is an attractive woman, and I imagine she'll encounter more than one of her married friends making a pass. At least with this Baron guy, he's not married. At least, I don't think he is. She mentioned he'd lost his wife, and she didn't say anything about a current wife, and I didn't see a ring. So at least it won't be quite as sleazy."

"Still sleazy if you hit on a vulnerable widow before her husband is laid to rest. Even if a guy is single."

Danielle shrugged, her eyes still on the road and her hands steering the wheel.

"So who were they?" Lily asked.

"Who was what?"

"The married guys who hit on you."

Danielle tossed out two names and Lily gasped. "Why didn't you ever tell me? Is that why you dropped out of that book club?"

"Well, I didn't have time to read for any book clubs back then, with Lucas suddenly gone and me trying to deal with the business. But I certainly didn't feel comfortable sitting around discussing books with a couple of women whose husbands dropped by my house uninvited to offer their condolences—in what they hoped would be the most intimate way."

"I hope they didn't stop by at the same time!" Lily teased.

Danielle laughed. "No, thank goodness I only had to deal with one obnoxious guy at a time."

"I don't understand, why would they do something like that and risk the friendship? You and Lucas used to do a lot with those couples. I imagine it made it extremely awkward for you when you ran into their wives—who were your friends."

"I've given it a lot of thought. I have a theory. They see a new widow as someone who is vulnerable—ripe—someone who they can manipulate by giving her what she needs—comfort and human contact. I wanted someone to hold me after Lucas died. I just didn't want it to be another woman's husband. I don't believe for a moment they were offering real comfort—even in a misguided way. They were nothing but predators, in my opinion."

"I'd be tempted to tell their wives," Lily said angrily.

"I thought about it. For about two seconds. But then I remembered how Cheryl had hit on Lucas before our wedding and how she had tried to blame him. But I didn't blame Lucas, I blamed Cheryl, and it caused a bigger rift in our relationship."

"I thought she really was the one at fault."

"She was. *That* time, Lucas really was innocent. But my point is, chances are those women would not have believed me—their husbands would've probably made up some story about how I hit on them. And then I wouldn't just lose them as friends; they would hate me. No, it was better to just pull away."

"That really sucks."

Just as Danielle turned onto Beach Drive, she spotted a man walking on the sidewalk. Something about him looked familiar. She slowed down and glanced up in the rearview mirror.

"Did you see him?" Danielle asked.

Lily looked out the back window. "See who?"

"There was a man walking on the sidewalk. I swear he looked like Hillary's muse."

Lily rolled down the window and looked up the street where they had just come from.

"I don't see anyone. If he really is a ghost like you suspect, maybe you really did see something. You suppose he's haunting the neighborhood, looking for Hillary's spirit?"

Danielle parked the car along the street in front of Marlow House. She quickly got out of the vehicle and looked back up the street. She didn't see anyone.

"There's no one there now. But I swear I saw something. Someone."

HEATHER DONOVAN STOOD at the bathroom mirror, staring at her reflection. She had just removed the rubber bands from her hair and combed out the tangles, leaving her jet black hair smooth and straight, falling past her shoulders.

"Why can't anything go right for me?" Heather asked herself. "I've tried to be a good person. I've tried to make amends for past sins."

Turning from the mirror, she walked from the bathroom, flipping off the light on her way out. In the hall her calico Bella greeted her, weaving in and out around Heather's feet. Stopping for a moment, Heather reached down and scooped up the cat, taking her in her arms as she headed to the living room.

Sitting on the coffee table was the laptop computer. It mocked her. The book she had promised to write was never going to get written. At first she wanted to blame her failure on Danielle. After all, Danielle refused to collaborate on the story of Harvey's haunting—yet the truth was, she simply didn't have it in her.

Writing a book, Heather decided, was excruciatingly boring. Being an author sounded much cooler than actually doing the work to become one.

Flopping down on the sofa with the cat still in her arms, Heather lifted one foot and used it to slam shut the laptop computer. She slid it to the far end of the coffee table before propping her feet on the edge of said table.

"I don't know what we're going to do, Bella. I'm going to have to get a damn job." Heather stroked the now purring cat.

"In another month, my savings will be gone. If mom would have paid those damn taxes on Presley House, I could've sold the property and got something. I suppose I could try selling this house—but what's this place really worth now, once a buyer finds out about the mold? I'd be better to burn it down, like Presley house."

Suddenly bored with the attention, Bella stood up and then jumped to the floor, abandoning Heather.

"Fine, leave me. Everyone else does."

By the time Bella was down the hallway and out of sight, Heather was leaning back on the sofa, staring up at the ceiling.

"What is the point in all this? Why couldn't it have been me that died in my sleep instead of Hillary Hemingway? Maybe she was an old woman, but at least she had something to live for. What do I have?"

Letting out a dejected sigh, she lifted her head from the back of the sofa and proceeded to stand up. Just as she did, she glanced to the living room window, its blind wide open. To her surprise, there was a man looking through the glass pane. He stood in her flower planter just outside the window—staring in.

Heather let out a scream.

"HE WAS RIGHT THERE!" Standing in her front yard, Heather pointed to the flower planter under her living room window.

Sergeant Joe Morelli stood next to her and looked down into the planter.

"I don't see any footprints, and none of the flowers are smashed. Are you sure that's where he was standing?"

"Are you calling me a liar?" she shrieked.

"No. But maybe he wasn't standing in the planter—"

"He was standing in the planter, I saw him! He was the same man who was down on the beach when I found Steve Klein's body. Of course, then he couldn't be bothered to help. Now he turns into some freaking peeping tom and starts looking into windows!"

With a sigh, Joe took out his notepad and pen. "Okay, can you give me a description of what he looked like—how old do you think he was, how tall, any distinguishing marks you might have noticed, anything that might be used to identify him."

"I guess he was about your age. Not really sure how tall he was, average, I suppose. Not short but not tall. He had dark hair—oh, and dark eyes. I noticed that. Kind of an olive complexion. Nice looking, or at least he would have been had he not been looking in my window. What kind of sicko does that?"

"And you say you saw him on the beach yesterday?"

"Yes. And he was wearing the same thing he was wearing yesterday. I can understand wearing the same thing two days in a row—but a suit and red bow tie, to the beach?"

"What kind of suit?"

Heather shrugged. "Black suit with a white shirt and this goofy red bow tie. Such a nerdy thing to wear."

"You sure this was the same guy you saw yesterday?" Joe asked.

Heather looked at Joe as if he had just said the most stupid thing in the world. She rolled her eyes, exaggerating the gesture. "You honestly believe there are two guys walking around the neighborhood wearing a black suit and red bow tie? Seriously?"

Joe shrugged and jotted down a note and then closed the notepad.

"What are you going to do?"

"We'll keep an eye out for this guy. I'll see if there's anything out on someone who meets that description. While technically it is illegal for someone to be going onto private property and looking into people's windows, it's not really that uncommon here. Tourists are always checking out potential rental houses and often assume something is empty when they look in. I doubt this guy is dangerous, but we'll see what we can find out."

Heather expelled a frustrated growl and turned abruptly from Joe, making her way to her front door. "You people are useless. Utterly useless!"

EIGHT

The room had been closed up like a tomb since they had found her body. Other than Hillary's purse, which had been rummaged through on Friday morning in search of emergency contact information, nothing else had been disturbed. The only information the purse had offered up was proof Hillary had a heart condition, if the medication she was taking was any indication.

Joanne wasn't coming back to work until Friday. On Friday, she would clean the room and change the sheets. But Danielle couldn't leave the room untouched until then. She needed to pack up Hillary's belongings and send them—send them where she wasn't sure yet.

And so, Danielle found herself on Monday morning standing at Hillary's now open doorway, looking into the room and dreading the task at hand.

Why am I always left to sort through a person's belongings after they've moved on? Danielle asked herself, thinking of how that task had fallen to her after her parents' death and Cheryl's. Of course this time it was only one room, yet still, it was not something she wanted to do.

Telling herself to stop being a wimp, Danielle marched into the empty room and went straight to the window. *What this room needs is some fresh air.* She attempted to open the window, yet its rusted latch refused to budge. Prying and pushing had little influence over what now appeared to be a stubbornly stationary object. Danielle let out a curse and then heard Walt's voice.

"You need a little help?"

The latch suddenly unlocked and the window flew open. Danielle leapt back in surprise. With a laugh, she turned from the now open window and faced Walt.

"Thanks," she said with a smile.

"No problem." Walt glanced around the room. "Are you packing up Hillary's belongings?"

"Yeah. You haven't seen her, have you?"

Walt shook his head. "Not since she left the house on Thursday night."

Danielle walked to the bed and proceeded to pull off the sheets, dropping them in a heap on the floor. "I sort of expected her to return. She obviously had no clue she was dead when we saw her. I wonder, is she just wandering around, or has she moved on?"

"Each of our journeys is different, Danielle. Hillary is traveling her own path; she'll get to where she needs to go."

"You sound like a philosopher now." Danielle tugged the pillows from their cases.

"Would you like me to help? I could pack Hillary's things. I'm quick."

Danielle laughed at Walt's offer. "No, thanks. I remember how you packed Cheryl's suitcase."

Walt shrugged and took a seat at the desk chair; he glanced down at the typewriter. "I won't miss that."

"I'm sort of sad I have to send that back. I'm tempted to ask her estate if I can buy it from them." Danielle picked up the linens and blankets now on the floor and tossed them on the center of the bed while neatly piling the pillows next to them.

"Why in heaven's name would you want that annoying machine and its clacking keys? Your laptop is much quieter."

"Oh, I don't want to use it. I thought it would look good in the library, sort of a tribute to Hillary—after all, she wrote her last book here, on that typewriter."

"A nice promotional gimmick."

Danielle paused and looked at Walt. She scrunched her nose. "True, but that's not why I want it. Poor Hillary is dead."

Walt shrugged. "We're all going to be dead someday. I already am. Actually, I think it's a good idea. You should ask to buy it. It's not like you're asking them to give it to you. And trust me, there are plenty of people who would conveniently forget to ship the typewriter and then declare they don't know anything about it."

"*That* would be just wrong."

Before Walt could respond, Danielle's cellphone beeped. She had an incoming text message. Removing her cellphone from her pocket, she read the message and then looked up to Walt.

"That was from the chief. He got the addresses from Melony where to send Hillary's belongings. I'm going to go ahead and box them up and then take them to the post office. The sooner I get this done, the better."

"Even the typewriter?"

"Yeah, even the typewriter. I think I have some boxes in the attic."

"Let me get those for you." In the next moment, Walt vanished.

Flashing a smile to the space Walt had occupied just a moment before, Danielle walked to the dresser. Before she had a chance to open the first drawer, her cellphone rang. It was Chris.

"What're you doing?" he asked.

Holding the cellphone to her ear, Danielle glanced around the bedroom. She sat down on the edge of the unmade bed.

"Getting ready to pack up Hillary's things. Walt went to get me some boxes from the attic."

"Handy to have a ghost around the house."

"It can be." Danielle smiled.

"I was wondering if you wanted to go out to lunch with me. We could stop at the post office first and send Hillary's boxes."

"Sure. Lunch sounds good, and I could use some help wrestling with the boxes."

"What are you doing about Hillary's car?"

"I guess her estate is having someone pick it up. I'm not mailing that."

DANIELLE AND CHRIS sat together at Pier Café. Carla had just brought them their order. She wasn't her normal talkative self.

"I think Carla's taking Steve's death hard," Danielle whispered after the waitress left their table.

"She looks like she's on the verge of tears." Chris picked up his French dip.

"It's hard enough to deal with losing someone you care about, but to have to hide your grief, well, I feel sorry for her, even though I don't approve of what she and Steve did."

Chris shrugged. "We never know what goes on behind closed doors."

"You mean like what Steve's marriage was like?"

"That and all of it. We don't know what brought Carla and Steve together or why Steve didn't just leave his wife. People are complicated. Relationships are complicated. Who am I to judge?"

Danielle paused and looked up from her plate. "You think I'm judging?"

Chris shrugged again. "A little. But that's okay. We all do it to some extent. And I know where you're coming from, considering what you went through with your husband."

"True." Danielle took a bite of her chicken salad.

In the next moment Heather Donovan walked through the diner's doorway. Danielle stopped eating a moment and looked Heather's way. The young woman, her hair pulled up on top of her head and haphazardly secured with a clip, glanced around the diner, looking for someplace to sit.

"Heather's here. Can we invite her to sit with us?" Danielle asked in a whisper.

"Sure." Chris took a bite of his French dip.

Danielle called out to Heather. She looked their way. Danielle waved her to the table. Reluctantly, Heather approached.

"I don't want to interrupt anything," Heather said when she reached the table.

"Don't be silly. Join us," Danielle said as she scooted over to make room.

When Heather sat down, Chris said, "And I'm treating."

"You don't have to do that." Heather sounded out of sorts. She dropped her purse on the floor by her feet.

"Are you okay, Heather? Is something wrong?" Danielle asked.

"Do you have all day?"

Before they could respond, Carla showed up at the table and took Heather's order.

"What's wrong?" Danielle asked after Carla left the table.

Heather shook her head. "You don't need to hear my

troubles."

"What are friends for?" Chris asked.

Heather looked up into Chris's eyes and asked in a somber voice, "Are we friends?"

"Well, certainly," Danielle said quickly.

"Not just friends, but neighbors and onetime roomies. Well, we were practically roomies." Chris grinned at Heather.

"I'm sorry if I sound like a drama queen. But first I find Steve's body and then the peeping tom…"

Danielle reached over to Heather's hand and gave it a brief squeeze. "That's right, you found Steve's body. It's totally understandable that you'd be upset."

"It wasn't just Steve. I also found Jolene. Damn, it's like I don't even want to go on the beach anymore!"

"What's this about a peeping tom?" Chris interrupted.

Heather picked up the glass of water Carla had filled when taking the order. She took a sip and then said, "I saw a man on the beach when I found Steve, but he took off, didn't help. But then last night, the jerk was looking in my window!"

"What window?" Danielle asked.

"My living room window. He was standing in the planter, looking in. Of course, that idiot Joe Morelli points out there are no footprints in the planter, so I guess that makes me delusional or something. He is such a jerk."

"What did the guy look like?" Chris asked.

"Looked like he was in his early thirties. Nice looking, if he wasn't a freaking peeper. Weirdo was wearing the same thing yesterday that he had on the day before, a black suit and a red bow tie. I mean who wears a red bow tie, much less a suit, when walking on the beach? The jerk."

Danielle's eyes darted to Chris; their gazes locked. She knew they were thinking the same thing. Hillary's muse. Heather had seen Hillary's muse—or more accurately, the ghost who had been hopping into Hillary's dreams for over a decade, showing her real murder scenes, which she then had used as inspiration for her books.

"I'm just so tired of it all." Heather looked as if she was about to cry. "I wish it was me instead of Hillary."

"Heather!" Danielle gasped. "You don't mean that!"

Chris set his beef dip on the plate and studied Heather.

"I don't? Look at me, Danielle, what do I really have in my life? What better way to go than in my sleep? I wouldn't want to go like Steve. I keep trying to set things right, but crappy things keep happening to me. Karma can be such a bitch."

Danielle took Heather's hand in hers. "Heather, you aren't responsible for what your great-grandfather did. And yeah, some crappy things have happened lately, but you'll get through it. If you ever need a shoulder, I want you to know I'm here for you."

NINE

"This muse thing concerns me, especially considering Heather's mental state," Chris said after they had finished lunch, and Heather had said her goodbyes. He sat alone with Danielle in the booth, waiting for Carla to bring the bill.

"What do you mean?"

"Heather seems unstable—more unstable than normal. I think she's suffering with real depression. She looks horrible."

"It doesn't look like she's slept for days. But what does that have to do with the muse?" Danielle asked.

"Remember when I suggested that maybe the muse was an opportunist? An evil one. According to Hillary, in her first dream the killer was the muse. We wondered how the muse happened to show up at all those murder scenes; after all, we know ghosts aren't clairvoyant, they can't tell the future."

"At least we don't think they are," Danielle reminded him.

"True. But from our experiences, we've never heard of a ghost who can see into the future."

"I'm still not sure what you're getting at."

"I wonder if maybe the muse just wanders around, looking for confrontation, and when he finds it, eggs it along. Like in Jolene's case, maybe he used his powers to help Pete find that wine bottle. If he hadn't, maybe Pete wouldn't have killed Jolene in a fit of anger."

"So what does that have to do with Heather?"

"What if the ghost senses Heather is facing an emotional crisis. She's vulnerable, plus she is susceptible to paranormal influences. What if he nudges her toward…suicide?"

Danielle cringed. "I don't even want to think about that. But I see what you mean. Maybe we need to talk to the chief."

Absently stroking his chin, Chris asked, "Exactly how is that going to help? Is he going to put an all-points bulletin out on a ghost?"

"Of course not. But maybe if we can figure out who the muse is —or was—then maybe we'll have a better idea on how to handle him."

"I don't want to handle him. Walt's about the only ghost I want to put up with these days. And that's only because I have no other choice," Chris grumbled.

"When have we ever had a choice in all this? You certainly didn't with Trudy," Danielle reminded him.

"Exactly. Which is why I'm reluctant to seek out any restless spirits."

"Don't you want to help Heather?"

Chris sat quietly for a moment and then reluctantly agreed. "I suppose we don't have a choice. I don't want Heather to do anything stupid, and I certainly don't want you to deal with this muse fellow alone."

"I think I saw him yesterday."

Chris frowned. "Where?"

"On our street. It was a few doors down from Heather's, so maybe it was about the time he looked in her window."

"If she saw him at the beach, then maybe he figured out she could see him, and that intrigued him. Maybe that's why he was looking in her window," Chris suggested.

Before Danielle could respond, Carla came to the table.

"I think I changed my mind," Chris said when Carla handed him the bill.

"What, you want me to pick up the tab?" Danielle teased.

Chris grinned. "No, I'm paying." Chris handed the bill back to Carla. "But I've decided I want dessert. Apple pie. Warm it up and add a scoop of vanilla ice cream, please."

Carla, who seemed to be only half present mentally, took back the ticket and then looked at Danielle. "You want something?"

Danielle sighed. She considered the question for a minute. "I probably shouldn't."

"Give her a hot fudge sundae. Extra fudge. No nuts," Chris instructed.

After Carla left the table, Danielle chuckled. "I think you know me too well. But I really shouldn't."

"Aww, screw it, life's short. And you can afford a few extra calories."

"Not really." Danielle sighed again.

"You look great to me."

Just as Carla returned to the table with the desserts, the diner door opened. It was Adam Nichols. The minute Adam walked into the diner, he spotted Danielle and Chris and headed to their table.

"That looks good. I think I'd like some pie too," Adam said. "But first bring me a cheeseburger." Without invitation, Adam sat down on the booth's bench next to Danielle, forcing her to hastily scoot over toward the wall.

"Hello to you too," Danielle halfheartedly grumbled as she dragged her dessert to her end of the table, yet not before Adam grabbed the spoon and helped himself to the first bite of the ice cream. When he started to take a second bite, Danielle snatched the spoon from Adam.

"No double-dipping!" Danielle looked at the spoon and then realized she didn't have a clean one.

Adam laughed. "Sorry. That was bad of me." Adam stood up and snatched a clean spoon from the next booth. He handed it to Danielle.

"You aren't sorry." Danielle took the spoon.

Across the table Chris chuckled and scooped up a bite of pie.

"True. But are my germs really that scary?" Adam asked with a faux pout.

Danielle scrunched her nose at Adam. "Seriously? I don't even want to imagine what kind of stuff you've picked up."

Adam frowned and then slumped back in his seat. "I wish you were right. Sad to say my life is boring."

"Have you heard from Melony?" Chris asked.

"Nahh. But I didn't really expect to."

"How come? I thought you two had something going on. I like Melony. I think she's good for you."

"Lord, Danielle, now you're starting to sound like Grandma." Adam groaned.

Danielle shrugged and took a bite of her sundae. "At least I figured you'd be talking to her about her mother's house. I thought she was going to list it."

"She isn't ready to sell yet. I don't think she knows what she wants to do with it."

"I sort of got the idea she wanted to move back to Frederickport," Danielle said.

Adam shrugged. "She talked about it, but I don't think she was serious. She has a pretty good practice back in New York. Plus, her divorce isn't final. I wouldn't be surprised if she holds onto the house for a while and then calls me one day out of the blue to have me sell it. But move back to town? I don't see that seriously happening."

"I like Melony. Hope she at least visits," Chris said.

Adam sat up in the booth and leaned forward, turning to Danielle. "So what is this about Hillary Hemingway dropping dead at Marlow House?"

Danielle frowned. "She didn't exactly drop dead. The poor woman died in her sleep."

Adam shrugged again. "Same thing."

"We're pretty sure she had a heart attack." Danielle scooped up a spoonful of fudge.

"And what's this about Steve Klein? Holy crap. They're dropping like flies around here!" Adam shook his head.

"They say he fell off the pier when he was fishing," Chris said.

"Yeah, I read that. You think he was drinking?" Adam asked.

Just then Carla came to the table to refill the water glasses. "Your order is almost up."

"Hey, Carla, were you working the night Steve fell off the pier?"

Carla flinched at the question. She stared at Adam, frozen to the spot as if unable to move, oblivious to the fact the pitcher of water she was pouring was about to overfill the glass. Adam reached out and grabbed the pitcher, tipping it upright just as the water began to spill onto the table.

Danielle and Chris quickly grabbed napkins to soak up the water while Carla stood mute, frozen to the spot.

Gently tugging the water pitcher from her grasp, Adam studied Carla. "Hey, are you okay?"

Without a word, Carla turned and fled from the booth, disappearing into the kitchen.

"What in the hell was that about?" Adam asked.

"I guess she's upset over Steve's death," Danielle suggested.

THE NEXT STOP for Danielle and Chris was the police station to see Police Chief MacDonald.

"I just heard from the coroner," the chief told them after they each took a seat in the office.

"Was it a heart attack?" Danielle asked.

"Yes." Edward MacDonald leaned back in his office chair.

"Thanks for getting that address for me," Danielle told him. "I boxed up everything this morning. Chris helped me take it to the post office. I found her new book, by the way."

"She finished it?" the chief asked.

"She told me she intended to finish the first draft, but that she'd have to go through it again. I'm pretty sure that's what this was. I imagine her publisher will hire someone to go through it before it goes to the final editor."

"Did you read it?" MacDonald asked.

Danielle shook her head. "No. I didn't really have time. Walt's read it, though. He used to stand behind her shoulder and read while she was writing."

"So annoying," Chris muttered.

"That would drive me insane!" MacDonald said with a laugh.

"Well, Hillary didn't know he was standing there," Danielle reminded them.

MacDonald smiled. "I guess not."

"Now I just have to wait for them to pick up her car," Danielle said. "But I didn't stop by just to talk about Hillary."

"What do you need?"

Danielle then proceeded to tell the chief what she knew about the recent sightings of Hillary's muse, and of her and Chris's concerns regarding Heather.

"So Heather really did see someone looking in her window?" MacDonald asked.

"I'm certain of it. I can't imagine she would just happen to come up with a description of a man who perfectly matched Hillary's muse."

"How is it Heather has never seen Walt? She stayed at Marlow

House for a while. She saw the ghost of Presley House, Jolene, Hillary, and now this muse character. Why not Walt?"

"I think she did get glimpses of him. But I have a feeling her paranormal abilities are getting stronger. The last few times she's been by the house, Walt's made himself scarce. Now that he knows she could possibly see him, it's easier for him to avoid being seen," Danielle explained.

"So what now?" the chief asked.

"Danielle suggested that if we could identify this ghost, figure out who he was, then maybe we'd have a better idea on how to handle him. Perhaps even encourage him to move on."

"You honestly think he played some role in Jolene's murder? In all those other murders?" the chief asked.

Danielle considered the question a moment before responding. "I still believe a spirit is very limited in his or her capacity for physical violence. Yet that doesn't mean it's not possible they might be able to harness enough power to do harm. Look at Darlene. Maybe she didn't drive Chuck's car off the side of the road, but she frightened him enough to cause the accident."

"If we want to identify this spirit, I suppose we could start with a police artist. You've seen him, right?"

"Yes, but I only got a good look at him in the dream. Maybe you could ask Heather. It would probably make her feel better to think you are really looking for this guy."

"Unfortunately, he's out of my jurisdiction."

Danielle smiled. "You know what I mean."

The chief considered it for a moment and then nodded. "Okay. I'll have her come in, see if we can get a good likeness of this guy."

"I sort of wish Hillary hadn't left so abruptly," Danielle said with a sigh.

"It often happens that way," Chris reminded her.

Danielle nodded.

"How do you know she moved on?" the chief asked. "Heather saw her in front of her house, and according to her, she was going down to the beach. Maybe she's still there. Have you tried looking?"

"I haven't gone looking, but my house does face the ocean. I haven't seen any sign of her," Chris said.

"What about Steve?" the chief asked.

Chris and Danielle shook their heads no.

"How is that investigation going?" Danielle asked. "I saw his wife yesterday. Lily and I went over there to take her some food and give her our condolences. She said she hadn't planned the funeral yet, that she didn't know when they're releasing his body."

"And they probably won't for a few days," the chief said.

"Why is that? From what I read in the paper, it looked like he simply stumbled and fell off the pier. There was some mention of him hitting his head as he fell, but that there were no other marks on his body to indicate foul play," Chris said.

"I can't go into it right now. But the blow to the head didn't kill him. And it wasn't exactly a simple drowning."

"Do you suspect foul play?" Danielle asked.

"It's possible." MacDonald glanced from Danielle to Chris. "And I expect whatever we talk about not to leave this room."

"Fair enough," Chris agreed. "I suppose I should tell you about Carla's odd behavior at the diner this afternoon." Chris then went on to tell the chief what had happened after Adam had asked Carla about seeing Steve the night of the accident.

"That really doesn't surprise me, considering everything, and the fact she was the last one to see him alive."

"She was on the pier with him?" Chris asked.

"No, in Pier Café. He went in to buy some coffee, and she waited on him. As far as I know, no one else saw him after that."

"Maybe she's with her body," Danielle blurted out.

Both Chris and the chief looked to Danielle.

"Carla's with Steve's body?" Chris frowned.

"No, silly. *Hillary*. Maybe Hillary's with her body. You know spirits are often attracted to their own bodies. Before they move on, they always seem to want one final look—not sure why, to make sure they're really dead, maybe? I don't know. But they do. And they often don't move on until after their service. So if Hillary isn't wandering on the beach, maybe she's at the morgue. Her body's still here, isn't it?"

"It's at the funeral home. They're having her cremated here and then sending her ashes to Vancouver for the memorial service."

"I suppose that makes sense," Danielle said. "Any word on when the service is?"

The chief shook his head. "No."

"So what about it, guys? Should we go see if we can talk to Hillary before she moves on? It would probably be my last chance to ask her any more questions about her muse."

TEN

Before leaving for the funeral home, Danielle called Lily, telling her where she and Chris were heading. She asked Lily to pass on the information to Walt. Both Danielle and Chris were a little reluctant about going to the funeral home. Neither one was especially anxious to bump into any lost spirits. As it turned out, there were no spirits lingering at the funeral home, not even Hillary's.

"How can they call themselves a funeral home; not one stinking ghost," Danielle said as she got out of Chris's car. She slammed the door shut and looked into the open window. Chris sat in the driver's seat, the engine running. They were parked in front of Marlow House.

"It's not really necessary to talk to Hillary. If you and Heather can help the artist draw a good likeness, it's possible we can figure out his true identity."

"You're right. Hillary didn't even know her muse was really a dead guy."

Chris flashed Danielle a grin. "I wouldn't let Walt catch you referring to a ghost as a dead guy."

"True, but Walt isn't too thrilled with the term ghost either."

"Speaking of Walt, he's standing at the parlor window, watching us." Chris pointed to the house.

Danielle glanced behind her. Sure enough, Walt was standing at the window, and he didn't look happy. She waved at him. Instead of a wave in return, Walt gestured for her to come into the house.

"I guess he needs something." Danielle frowned. Instead of hurrying to see what Walt needed, she turned back to Chris and said, "Thanks for going with me to the post office and for lunch."

"No problem. I enjoyed it."

"Oh, and I like your new car too." Danielle stepped back on the sidewalk. She gave Chris a little wave and watched him drive down the street to his house.

By the time Danielle got to her front door, Walt was pacing in the entry hall, waiting for her.

"What's up?" Danielle asked as she walked inside, closing the door behind her.

"Where have you been?"

"Didn't Lily tell you? We went to see if we could find Hillary. I thought maybe she was with her body; she wasn't."

"I know that," he said impatiently.

Danielle set her purse on the entry table. "If you know that, why did you ask where I've been?"

"I meant I already knew Hillary isn't with her body."

"How did you know that?" Danielle frowned.

Walt gestured up to the ceiling. "Because she's here, in her room."

"Hillary is here?" Danielle glanced up to the ceiling. "When did she get back?"

"Not long after you talked to Lily. Who is over at Ian's, by the way. I've been dreading her coming back and having to explain to Hillary why Lily's ignoring her."

"You're saying Hillary doesn't know she's dead?"

Walt nodded. "That seems to be where she's at. She's been looking for you and for her things. She's especially panicked because she can't find her manuscript."

"I hate having to tell someone they're dead." Danielle started for the stairs.

"I know what you mean. Nothing like ruining someone's day by informing them they're dead."

"I assume she saw you?" Danielle asked as she started up the stairs.

"Of course, she's dead. Spirits on this plane see other spirits. We aren't invisible, you know."

"Who does she think you are?"

"A new guest. Although, she kept looking at me as if there was something vaguely familiar."

"The portrait?"

"Probably."

Danielle found Hillary in her room, sitting on the edge of the bed, the pile of soiled linens still heaped in the center of the mattress. The moment Hillary noticed Danielle, she jumped up.

"Where are my things? My typewriter, my manuscript?"

"They're safe, don't worry. But we need to talk."

Hillary's gaze darted about the room. "Why aren't they here?"

"Don't you remember? You were checking out on Friday. Everything has been packed up and safely stored."

"Who packed for me?" Hillary frowned. "I don't remember packing."

"I had to do it for you. You weren't here. I waited, but it's Monday—three days after checkout. I did it this morning."

"It's Monday?" Hillary looked confused.

"Hillary, do you remember going to bed on Thursday night? You told me you wanted to check out the next day, after breakfast."

"Yes. I guess so."

"Do you remember getting up and seeing me that night?"

Hillary sat back down on the edge of the mattress and considered the question. "Why, yes. I remember now. I wanted to take a walk on the beach—a final walk. You were in the parlor with that handsome young man—your new guest. He was here when I got back."

"What else do you remember about that night?"

"I remember heading for the beach—oh, and I ran into your neighbor Heather. She can be rather abrupt, by the way. Oh, I saw Steve Klein! I almost forgot. How could I forget?"

Danielle turned the desk chair to face Hillary and sat down. "What do you mean you saw Steve Klein?"

"You know, the bank manager."

"I know who that is. But what do you mean you saw him?"

"That silly man fell off the pier!" Hillary laughed. "Can you imagine that? I was standing on the beach, enjoying the evening, and all of a sudden I notice something in the water—it was Steve Klein, fully clothed, swimming to shore. When he got out of the water, he had a nasty gash on his head. He told me he hit his head on the side of the pier during the fall."

"Did he say how he fell?" Danielle asked.

"He said something about having an allergic reaction. He has a severe shellfish allergy and went into anaphylactic shock after eating something, and then his EpiPen wasn't where he kept it in his tackle box. The next thing he knows he's falling off the pier."

"Did he say what he ate?"

"He just assumed there was raw shellfish on the pier, which he happened to touch, and somehow ingested when he was eating. I told him it's awful foolish to be ocean fishing if he's that allergic."

"Did he say anything else?"

"Not that I can recall. He headed back to the pier to get his car and fishing gear."

"Do you remember what happened after that?"

"Well…I remember him walking down the beach toward the pier and then…" Hillary let out a gasp and stood up abruptly. "I saw him. The man from my dreams!"

"Your muse?"

"Well, who I thought was my muse all these years." Hillary started pacing the room. "We need to call the police!"

Danielle studied Hillary. "Why do we need to call the police?"

Hillary stopped pacing and stared at Danielle. "Isn't it obvious? That man, that killer, he's here in Frederickport." Hillary gasped again, remembering another detail. "And he knows who I am!"

"Hillary, why don't we go downstairs? We can talk in the library."

"Why should we go to the library? We need to call the police! That man is dangerous! And he knows I know he's a killer!"

Danielle stood up. "How does he know that?"

Hillary frowned. "Umm…I suppose I sort of told him."

"And he didn't get angry with you? He didn't try to hurt you?"

"No. I wonder why?"

"Come on, Hillary, let's go downstairs."

"I don't see why we need to go downstairs," Hillary said as she followed Danielle out of the room.

Because the portrait of Walt's in the library.

As Danielle headed downstairs, she pulled her phone from her back pocket and dialed Lily.

"Are you back? Did you find her?" Lily asked when she answered the phone.

"I'm just calling to tell you to stay over there. I don't want Ian over here until I give you the okay."

"What's up?" Lily asked.

Glancing over her shoulder, Danielle looked at Hillary, who continued to follow her. "Hillary and I are having a little discussion, and I'd rather avoid any interruption."

"Hillary? She's there?"

"Yep."

ELEVEN

Once they were in the library, Danielle asked Hillary to take a seat on the sofa.

"I really think we should be calling the police," Hillary told her.

"We will…but I have a few things I need to tell you first."

Hillary let out a sigh and leaned back against a cushion. "Okay, what is it?"

"Some people believe that after a person dies, their spirit can visit you in your dreams."

"Oh, I believe that," Hillary said with a nod.

"You do?" Danielle asked in surprise.

"Why certainly. After my first husband died, I used to dream about him all the time. I think he really came to me. I don't believe it was just a dream."

"I call it a dream hop."

"A dream hop?" Hillary asked.

"Yes, when a spirit enters your dream. Do you believe in…ghosts?"

"Ghosts?" Hillary frowned.

"Ghosts. You know, a spirit of someone who has died."

Hillary shrugged. "I suppose I believe in the possibility. I know when my second husband died, I could swear I saw him in our kitchen on the day of his funeral."

"I believe all people have a little bit of psychic ability—where you're sensitive to paranormal activity. You probably did see your husband."

Hillary smiled. "I like to think so."

"The thing is—I am very sensitive. The first spirit I ever saw was my grandmother when I was a little girl."

Hillary didn't say anything.

"You know who else is sensitive to paranormal activity?"

Hillary shook her head.

"My neighbor Heather. She swears she saw Jolene Carmichael's ghost not long after she was murdered."

Hillary leaned forward and whispered, "I think Heather is a little odd."

"You know who else can see ghosts?"

"Who?"

"Other ghosts. Take Lily, for example, she can't normally see ghosts. Oh, like you, she has had a rare occasion of seeing one—but generally speaking, she can't. However, when Lily dies, if she were to run into another spirit, she could see him."

"I suppose it's nice to know when I'm a ghost someday I'll be able to see other ghosts."

Danielle pointed to Walt Marlow's portrait. "Hillary, I want you to look at Walt Marlow's portrait and tell me if you notice anything."

Growing impatient, Hillary shook her head and said, "I don't know what you expect me to see." She stared at the painting.

Several moments later, Walt appeared in the room. "Danielle, can't you just get to the point? Must you drag this thing on so?"

Hillary slowly stood up, her gaze moving from Walt to his portrait and back to him. "You're Walt Marlow!"

"It's nice to meet you, Hillary Hemingway. I like your new book."

"It's not even published yet, how do you know you like it?"

Walt smiled and leaned against the edge of the library desk. With a wave of his hand a thin lit cigar appeared. He took a puff and then said, "I confess, I've been reading over your shoulder for the last month. I especially appreciated that twist at the end. I never saw that one coming."

Hillary plopped back down on the sofa and looked at Danielle. "What does this mean?"

"Remember the night you first saw Walt in the parlor with me, before you went for your walk and ran into Heather?"

Hillary nodded, her eyes wide.

"Do you remember first going to bed?"

Hillary considered the question a moment and then nodded.

"Can you remember anything about what happened between the time you went to bed and then got up again to go for a walk?" Danielle asked.

Furrowing her brow, Hillary carefully considered the question. "I had a sharp pain in my chest. It was excruciating—I thought I was going to die. But then the pain, it just stopped. It went away."

"It's because you did," Walt said.

Hillary turned to Walt. "I did what?"

"You died." Walt took a puff off the cigar.

"No…that's impossible…" Hillary muttered as she shook her head and gazed across the room, lost in her thoughts. Finally, she looked to Danielle. "I suppose that explains what I'm wearing."

Not sure what she meant, Danielle noted Hillary was wearing the same blue sweat suit she'd been wearing the night she had left the house after dying.

"What do you mean?" Danielle asked.

"I just remembered…" Hillary sounded surprisingly calm. "The pain stopped, and then there I was, standing in my room, and I just knew I wanted to go down to the beach—one last time. But then I looked at myself—I was in bed sleeping, wearing my nightgown. Then I looked down and realized I was also standing next to the bed, wearing the same nightgown. I thought that would not do. I could not go traipsing around on the beach in my nighty, and the next thing I knew, I was wearing this outfit."

"And you didn't find that a little odd…there being basically two of you?" Danielle asked. "Or that your clothes magically changed?"

Hillary shrugged. "I'm not really sure what I thought about there being two of me, but I must say being able to change clothes that fast was rather handy." Hillary smiled.

"Then you understand…you have died?"

Hillary sighed and leaned back on the sofa. "I suppose that makes sense. I knew it was going to happen one day. But never imagined that when it did I could still communicate with living people." Hillary paused a moment and looked at Danielle. "You are alive, aren't you?"

Danielle smiled. "Yes. Like I said, I have a gift…I can communicate with spirits."

"Like my gift when I was alive? Being clairvoyant?"

Danielle shook her head. "No, Hillary. You weren't clairvoyant. I just said that to help you make sense of everything."

Hillary sat up straighter. "What are you talking about? Of course I was clairvoyant! Oh my, I saw who I thought was my muse—and he saw me—which means he's like you, he can see spirits too!"

Again Danielle shook her head. "No, Hillary. The man you call your muse, he's a spirit like you and Walt. He visited you in your dreams—remember, we talked about dream hops? Whoever he is, he's been dead for over a decade."

"He's Antoine Paul," Hillary announced.

Danielle frowned. "Excuse me?"

"His name. It's Antoine Paul."

"You never told me you knew his name."

"I didn't. But when I ran into him on the beach, I asked him his name and he told me."

"Did he tell you anything else?"

Hillary shook her head. "No, not really." She began to laugh.

"What's funny?" Danielle asked.

"Now what he said makes perfect sense. When I asked him if he was going to kill me…foolish me, I was already dead."

"You seem to be adjusting to the news of your recent demise," Walt noted.

Hillary shrugged. "I suppose there really isn't much I can do about it now, is there? And like I said, I knew it was eventually going to happen. I'm just glad I finished my book…" She paused and looked at Danielle. "So what did you do with my things?"

"Melony got us in touch with your attorney in Vancouver. He gave us instructions where to send everything. I sent your manuscript to your agent."

Hillary let out a sigh. "I just hope she doesn't mess up on the rewrites. I would have liked to have done that myself, but I suppose it is what it is. What did you do with my body?"

"It's at the funeral home right now…preparing to be cremated."

"Cremated!" Hillary shrieked.

Surprised at the outburst, Danielle asked, "Didn't you want to be cremated?"

Hillary considered her question for a moment and then shivered. "It's not that I *wanted* to be cremated per se—I did make arrangements for cremation for when that time came—but now that that time has come, it doesn't sound so terrific. I am quite terrified of fire, you know."

Walt chuckled. "Hillary, stay away from the funeral home, and you won't feel a thing."

Hillary shivered again. After a moment of silence, she suddenly remembered something. "Does this mean Steve Klein is like you and Heather and can communicate with spirits?"

"No, it means Steve's dead," Walt said.

"He is?"

"Yes. He fell off the pier. His body washed up on Saturday. Heather found it," Danielle explained.

Hillary frowned. "That Heather certainly gets around. So did she see his spirit too, talk to him?"

Danielle shrugged. "Not that I know of."

"Interesting, everything makes sense now," Hillary noted. "I didn't realize how jumbled things have seemed since I took off for that walk. But now it's crystal clear. What now? I assume Walt here is haunting this house."

Danielle glanced over to Walt and smiled. "Something like that."

"Was Antoine Paul haunting me?"

"I suppose he was, in a sense," Danielle said.

"And Steve Klein, is he haunting the pier? The beach?"

Danielle smiled. "I haven't seen him down there. But when someone dies, their spirit doesn't generally stick around and haunt. They move on."

"Move on?" Hillary frowned.

"I like to think of it as the next leg in our journey."

"Are you talking about Heaven? Is there a Heaven?"

Danielle shrugged. "I'm not sure if it's Heaven exactly. But from what I understand, when you get there, you'll be reunited with your loved ones. Those who died before you."

Hillary cringed. "You mean like my husbands?"

Danielle nodded.

"Both of them?"

"I suppose."

Hillary shook her head, folded her arms across her chest, and stubbornly declared, "Then I'm not going."

"What? You don't want to see them?" Danielle asked in surprise.

"If you had two dead husbands, would you want to see them? Both of them?"

"Umm…well, I don't know. I never really thought about it."

Hillary shook her head again. "I can't even imagine what those two have been doing all these years. Comparing notes? And when I get there, who will I be married to? Will I be a bigamist?"

"I don't really think it works that way." Danielle smiled.

"I certainly am not going to chance it. I'm staying here."

"Here? You can't stay here!" Danielle insisted.

"Why not? He is?" Hillary pointed to Walt.

"In my defense, this was my house."

"So I'll find somewhere else to haunt."

"Hillary, you really don't want to do that. Our spirits aren't meant to stay here and haunt indefinitely. You have a journey; you need to take it."

"Oh poo, what do you know? I don't see you asking pretty boy here to leave."

Walt arched his brows. "Pretty boy?"

"Hillary, if you don't want to leave, perhaps it's a sign that you need to first solve the murders," Danielle suggested.

"What murders?"

"The murders your muse told you about, of course."

"Those aren't my concern anymore. I'm dead myself."

The next moment Danielle's cellphone buzzed, indicating an incoming text message. After reading it, she said, "That's Lily, she wants to know if she and Ian can come over now."

"Why is she asking?" Hillary asked.

"Ian doesn't know about Danielle's gift, yet Lily does," Walt explained. "So when they come over here, they won't be able to see or hear you."

"But I can see and hear them?"

Walt nodded. "Yes."

"This sounds interesting." Hillary smiled and leaned back in her seat. "Have them come over."

Danielle groaned and then called Lily. When Lily answered, she said, "There's really no reason to stay away. Hillary understands she's dead, but she's not ready to move on."

BY THE TIME LILY, Ian, and Sadie arrived at Marlow House, Danielle, Walt, and Hillary had moved to the living room. Danielle sat on the sofa while Walt sat next to her, perched on the sofa's arm. Hillary stood by the fireplace, giddy at the prospect of playing the invisible woman while eavesdropping on the unsuspecting mortals. She forgot for a moment that while Lily could not see or hear her, she was still aware of her existence. It was only Ian who would be totally unaware of her presence.

Sadie galloped into the living room, Lily and Ian trailing behind her. The moment Sadie spied Walt, she ran to the sofa to greet him. Danielle reached down to Sadie, patting her back while giving her a gentle nudge. Sadie sat down, leaning against Danielle's legs while looking up at Walt.

"We were wondering if you wanted to go to Pearl Cove with us for dinner tonight," Ian asked when he entered the room with Lily. "Maybe Chris would like to go too."

Before Danielle had a chance to answer the question, Sadie noticed Hillary standing by the fireplace. With a bark, she leapt up and dashed to Hillary, planting herself before her. With her butt in the air, tail wagging, front paws firmly planted wide apart and her head lowered, she persistently barked.

Hillary's eyes widened as she looked down at the large golden retriever, who appeared to be ready to pounce at any moment. Jumping back, Hillary let out a scream.

"I thought they couldn't see me!"

"Sadie, stop that!" Ian ordered, to no avail. Sadie continued to bark, her pouncing stance more determined as she focused her attention on Hillary.

"Get her off me!" Hillary shouted.

"She's not on you…yet." Walt chuckled.

Danielle and Lily exchanged glances.

"Sadie!" Ian shouted again.

"I think she sees something," Lily whispered.

"Whose voice is that? I can hear someone talking to me!" Hillary shouted. "Someone do something!"

Walt laughed again. "It's Sadie. She's not going to hurt you. You're dead, remember? Sadie is just saying hello."

The dog lunged at Hillary. Shrieking, Hillary ran from the room, Sadie trailing behind her.

TWELVE

Monday's moon, more than half full, cast a golden trail across the ocean's surface while the stars above hid from view. Picture windows flanked the west wall of Pearl Cove, providing a scenic backdrop for its diners.

The server led the four friends to a half-circle booth under one of the windows. Lily and Danielle sat down first, each entering from an opposite end of the booth. Once scooted in, they were sitting next to each other. Ian entered the booth seat on Lily's side while Chris sat next to Danielle. After ordering cocktails, they each picked up a menu and proceeded to glance through it.

When making plans for dinner, Danielle had informed Chris of Hillary's appearance. Hillary, who had managed to escape Sadie's pursuit by running into the downstairs bedroom—through its closed door—refused to leave the bedroom. Danielle had no idea if she was still there, she was just glad the newly departed mystery writer hadn't followed her to the restaurant.

"Have you heard anything about Hillary?" Ian asked just as Danielle took a sip of water. His question—considering she had heard from Hillary—prompted her to choke. Chris gently patted her back.

Frowning, Ian studied Danielle. "Are you okay?"

"Umm…yeah…" Danielle coughed. "It just went down wrong."

"We stopped by the police station this afternoon," Chris told him. "It looks like it was a heart attack, just like we suspected. Her body is being cremated and then sent to Vancouver for the memorial service."

"Lily said you boxed up all her belongings and mailed them to her attorney?"

"Not her attorney exactly, but the address he gave Melony," Danielle explained. "We mailed her manuscript to her agent."

"Really? That sort of surprises me."

Before Danielle could ask Ian what he meant, the server arrived with their cocktails. After she left the table, Danielle asked, "Why does that surprise you?"

Ian shrugged. "I would think it would go into probate. I imagine that manuscript is worth a fortune, considering everything."

Danielle picked up her cocktail. "From what I understand, it had something to do with the terms of the contract Hillary had with her publisher and agent."

Ian raised his glass in toast. "Here's to Hillary Hemingway, may your books remain on the bestseller list for decades to come."

Joining Ian in the toast, they all raised their glasses briefly and then took a sip.

After a few moments, Danielle asked, "Ian, do you know which of Hillary's books was her first murder mystery? I remember her telling me she used to write romance, but switched genres about ten years ago."

Pondering the question, Ian sipped his cocktail. "*Beautiful Rage*."

"*Beautiful Rage*? Do you know anything about the real murder—the one some believed Hillary based her murder scene on?" Danielle asked.

"I want to know why it was called *Beautiful Rage*," Lily asked.

Ian glanced to Lily. "That's easy. The killer in the book was very handsome, some even described him as beautiful."

"Ahh…so Mr. Beautiful went into a rage and killed the victim?" Lily asked.

Ian nodded. "Pretty much."

"Do you know anything about the real murder?" Danielle asked again.

"Actually, I do." Ian sat back in the booth seat, his left arm casually draped over Lily's shoulders. "In the book the victim is a young woman—mid-twenties—and she's coming out of a restaurant with—" he paused a moment and smiled at Lily "—*Mr. Beau-*

tiful. They're arguing. It appears they're walking to a car parked in the parking lot, but then Mr. Beautiful grabs hold of her arm and drags her off to a nearby alley. They're arguing, and the next thing we know he begins shaking her, and she falls to the ground. The scene ends with him kneeling by her body as he strangles her."

"So what happened in the real story?" Danielle asked.

"The woman who was really killed—if Hillary did pattern the scene after her murder—was also in her mid-twenties. Very attractive and married to a wealthy businessman. She was last seen leaving a restaurant with an unidentified man, who, according to witnesses, was good looking. They appeared to be arguing and walking toward the parking lot. She was found the next morning in the alley. She had been strangled."

"Do you know where this happened?" Danielle asked.

"I'm pretty sure it was Portland."

"You wouldn't happen to remember what the killer was wearing?"

"I do. It was one of the reasons some insisted Hillary patterned the scene after that particular murder. Like the man the witnesses described leaving the restaurant with the victim, Hillary's killer also wore a black suit and red bow tie."

WHEN DANIELLE and Lily returned home Monday evening, Hillary was not there. According to Walt, she had left shortly after they had, saying she was looking for someplace interesting to haunt.

Danielle had showered and shampooed, slipped on clean pajama bottoms and a T-shirt, and sat on her bed, the laptop computer open on her lap. Her damp hair, still wrapped in a towel, was piled atop her head.

"I thought you were going to sleep?" Walt asked when he appeared in her room, taking a seat on the edge of her mattress.

Danielle looked up from her computer. "I'd like to find out a little more about Hillary's muse since the guy seems to be hanging around."

"Do you honestly believe he's dangerous?" Walt asked, remembering what Danielle had told him earlier.

"Like Stoddard, I'd rather he not hang around. If I just knew something about him, maybe I can figure out some way to nudge him onto the next level."

"Considering he murdered that woman, I don't imagine he's anxious to move on."

"Perhaps. Do you think Hillary's going to come back here?"

Walt shrugged. "If she can't find anyone to talk to, I wouldn't be surprised. I imagine she'll get a little bored wandering around, being strictly an observer, unable to make any comment someone can actually hear. After all, she is a writer. Writers tend to want to express themselves. And if she continues to wander about, she won't have enough energy to do anything more than make an occasional light flicker."

"Of course, if she decides to land somewhere, she could manage to harness her energy."

"True. But let's not tell her that. Okay? I would prefer she not attach herself to Marlow House."

"I agree." Danielle turned her attention back to the computer.

"I'll leave you to play detective." Walt disappeared.

It took Danielle just a few keystrokes to find Hillary's *Beautiful Rage*. Clicking on its thumbnail, Danielle watched as *Beautiful Rage*'s book cover filled the screen. Dark and shadowy, the image was of a man dressed in a dark suit and red bow tie, his arms folded across his chest as he leaned casually against a wall facing a dark back alley. Sprawled lifeless at his feet was the murder victim, her blonde hair fanning around her, framing her crumpled body. The man on the cover looked nothing like the muse who'd invaded Danielle's dream, yet that did not surprise her. After all, how would the cover artist know what the real killer looked like?

Leaning back against the headboard and settling into the bed, she adjusted her laptop. Leaving the website featuring Hillary's first book, she began searching for information regarding the first murder.

Pausing mid-keystroke, she looked up and said aloud, "Antoine Paul. That's what Hillary said his name was."

Quickly typing *Antoine Paul*, she was disappointed when nothing useful came up in the search. She added a second word to the search: *Portland*. Still nothing.

After fifteen minutes of futile search, Danielle abandoned her efforts and focused her attention back on the real murder that had inspired *Beautiful Rage*.

"Bingo!" Danielle cried out when she found what she was looking for.

IT WAS past midnight when Danielle slipped out of her bedroom. A towel was no longer wrapped around her head, and she drew a brush through her tangled hair as she headed to the attic.

Just as she stepped onto the stairwell leading to the upper floor, Lily walked out of the hall bathroom. Like Danielle, Lily wore sleepwear.

"Where are you sneaking off to?" Lily teased.

Danielle paused and turned to Lily. "Good, you're awake. Why don't you come with me to see Walt."

"Gee, are you sure you want me to come?" Lily smirked.

Danielle tossed her head dramatically. "I did a little research on the muse's victim. I thought you'd like to hear too, but if you aren't interested…" Danielle turned back to the stairs, resuming her brushing as she continued on her way.

"Hey, you aren't getting rid of me that quick." Lily hurried to the stairwell, following Danielle to the attic.

When they entered the attic, Danielle found Walt standing by the spotting scope while Max napped on the nearby sofa bed.

Danielle glanced around quickly. "Any sign of Hillary?"

"None." Walt strolled to the sofa and sat down.

Looking toward the spotting scope, Lily smiled. "Hi, Walt."

"He's no longer standing there, Lily. He's sitting on the sofa next to Max now."

Lily glared at Danielle. "I think you do that just to mess with me."

Danielle frowned. "Do what?"

"Look where Walt's not standing when talking to him."

"He was standing by the window when we came in. I can't force him to stay in one spot!"

Walt leaned back on the sofa and casually summoned a cigar. "You two didn't come up here just to argue, did you? There was a purpose for this midnight visit?"

Danielle let out a sigh and walked to the sofa, taking a seat next to Walt. "Of course. I wanted to tell you—" Danielle paused a moment and looked at Lily, who now stood by the spotting scope

"—and Lily, what I found out tonight. I did a little online sleuthing."

"Ahh, playing Nancy Drew again, are we?" Lily grabbed a nearby folding chair and dragged it to the sofa. She sat down and faced Danielle.

"Yep. I first did a search on the name Hillary gave me for the muse. But nothing came up. Oh, I found a few people named Antoine Paul, but none looked remotely like the spirit who barged into our dream hop."

"Maybe that's not his real name," Lily suggested.

"Perhaps. But the murder took place over a decade ago. If that was his name, he didn't leave any sort of online presence."

Walt fiddled with his cigar, absently watching the smoke curl as he asked, "Did you find anything interesting about the real murder?"

"Not really. I saw a picture of the woman who was killed. So sad. Just like Ian told us, she was young, mid-twenties. I guess she was married to an older guy; he had a lot of money. They didn't have any kids. It's still a cold case. What they do know about her last hours pretty much matches what Hillary wrote in her book. She left the restaurant with this good-looking guy. He was wearing a dark suit and a red bow tie, and she was strangled."

"What about the husband?" Walt asked.

"What do you mean?" Danielle asked.

"It's been my personal experience a spouse is often the killer."

"Yeah, well, this spouse was in California when his wife was murdered. I don't think he was considered a suspect for more than two seconds."

Walt shrugged. "My wife was in Portland when I was murdered. And we know how that turned out."

"I suspect Melissa Huxley's murder had more to do with a bored young wife looking in the wrong place for a little excitement and finding more than she bargained for," Danielle suggested.

"Melissa Huxley? Was that the name of the woman who was murdered?" Lily asked.

"Yes."

Lily frowned. "Why does that name sound familiar?"

"You know a Melissa Huxley?"

Lily shook her head. "No, the name Huxley. I swear I just met someone with that name."

THIRTEEN

When Danielle went to bed that night, she kept thinking about what Lily had said. *When had she heard that name?* In the morning her thoughts were still on the murder, yet instead of trying to figure out why Huxley sounded oddly familiar—as if she had just met someone by that name—she decided to search on *Newspaper Archives*, looking for any old newspaper articles on Antoine Paul and if possible, any connection between him and the murdered woman.

The first article she pulled up did not mention Paul, but it did give a brief biography of the murdered woman. Settling back on the bed with her laptop, Danielle began to read about the tragic death of the lovely Melissa Huxley, who had been brutally murdered at such a young age, and of her husband, the wealthy and successful Baron Huxley…

Danielle bolted up straight in the bed. "Baron Huxley?" She read a few more lines and then frantically searched for a photograph showing the widower. After a few more minutes of searching and skimming articles, she shoved the laptop onto the mattress and leapt from the bed. Danielle dashed into the hallway and to Lily's room, knocking frantically on the door. She was about to open the door when it flew open.

Lily stood in the doorway, her sleepy eyes glaring at Danielle. "What?" she asked sharply. "Please tell me the house is on fire or I *will* have to kill you."

"I know why the name sounded familiar!" Danielle said excitedly.

"What in the world are you talking about? And what time is it anyway?" Lily turned from Danielle and stumbled back into her room, looking for the cellphone she had left on the nightstand. She picked it up and looked at the time.

Following Lily into the room, Danielle said, "It was Beverly's friend. The guy at her house on Sunday."

"Do you know it isn't even six yet? I may miss teaching, but I don't miss getting up this early…wait, what did you just say?"

"Huxley. That's the last name of the man we met at Beverly's house. Not only that, he has the same first name as Melissa's husband."

Rubbing sleep from her eyes, Lily sat down on the edge of the mattress. "I don't get it."

"The first murder—the one that inspired Hillary's first book—the victim in the real crime was named Melissa Huxley."

Waving her hand dismissively, Lily shook her head and said, "Yeah, yeah, yeah. I get that. But what's all this about a husband?"

"Melissa Huxley, the one who was murdered, her husband's name was Baron Huxley."

Lily frowned. "Baron Huxley?"

Danielle pulled the chair out from the dressing table and sat down, facing Lily. "Yes. And that's the name of Steve Klein's good friend, the one who was visiting Beverly when we stopped over there on Sunday. Plus, Beverly mentioned he was a widower."

"Are you saying this guy, the one we met on Sunday, it was his wife Hillary's muse murdered?"

Danielle shrugged. "If his wife was Melissa, then yeah. I tried to find a photo of him online but couldn't."

"No photo at all? Seems like everyone has a business website these days."

"I was only searching the newspaper site, looking for articles about the murder. The articles only had her picture, none of her husband."

Lily sighed. "I suppose you might be able to find Baron Huxley—the one who was at Beverly's—but that won't prove it's the same man unless the article mentions his late wife. You think it really is the same person? What a bizarre coincidence if it is."

"It's just that the name isn't that common."

Lily shook her head. "Weird."

JOE MORELLI STOOD with Brian Henderson at the break room doorway, watching Police Chief MacDonald lead Heather Donovan and Elizabeth Sparks to the interrogation room. Elizabeth, a tall slender woman in her mid-thirties, with long dark hair, carried a sketchpad in one hand and a purse in the other.

"I don't understand why the chief had Elizabeth come down here," Joe said after the three walked into the interrogation room, closing the door behind them.

"Elizabeth is the closest thing Frederickport has to a criminal sketch artist," Brian reminded him.

"I understand that. I just don't get why he's going to all this trouble, trying to get a likeness of a man Heather imagined seeing."

The two officers walked back into the break room, each carrying a cup of coffee.

"You still don't think she really saw anyone?" Brian sat down.

"She insists the guy was standing in her planter. There wasn't a footprint or so much as a flattened flower petal. No one had been standing in that planter."

Brian shrugged. "Maybe she thought he was standing in the planter, but he was standing in the yard."

"The lawn around the planter is pretty sparse and the dirt was a little muddy. I didn't see any footprints."

"I DIDN'T KNOW the police department had a sketch artist," Heather said as she sat down across the table from Elizabeth and the chief.

Elizabeth opened her pad of drawing paper. "I'm not exactly a police sketch artist." She dug into her purse and took out a drawing pencil.

Heather frowned. "Then why am I here?"

"Technically speaking, Elizabeth is not a police sketch artist—but she could be if she wanted to. Fact is, many large police departments don't even have one. But Elizabeth is one of the most talented artists I know—she also teaches art locally. Trust her."

The chief stood. "I'm going to leave you two ladies alone, so I don't get in your way. When you're done, I'll be in my office."

"Okay, Chief," Elizabeth called out as she focused her attention on her drawing pad.

Heather let out a sigh and leaned forward, taking a closer look at the blank sheet of drawing paper. "Okay, what do you want to know?"

"Let's start with the shape of his face. Was it round, oval—"

"Oval. Definitely oval."

DANIELLE WAS WALKING up the front entry of the Frederickport Police Station as Heather exited the building. Danielle paused on the sidewalk as her neighbor walked in her direction.

"Hey, Heather, what are you doing here?"

"Hi, Danielle," Heather greeted her, sounding happier than she had been the last time Danielle had seen her. "The chief asked me to come in and help the artist make a drawing of the man who'd been looking in my window. I think it turned out pretty good. Looks just like the guy."

"Terrific. Any clue on who he might be?"

"No. But he promised me he'd have the newspaper run the picture, saying he was a person of interest."

Danielle smiled. "You seem a lot happier than you did the other day."

"I'm just glad my complaint is being taken seriously. I don't think Joe Morelli believed someone was looking in my window. I didn't appreciate his snotty sanctimonious attitude."

Danielle chuckled. "Tell me about it. I've been on the receiving end of his misguided beliefs."

Heather smiled. "Oh, that's right. He arrested you for murder, didn't he?"

"Yep." Danielle glanced over to the door leading into the police station and back to Heather. "Joe isn't a bad guy, he's just not very good at seeing outside the box. And he has actually saved my butt a few times. So don't go too hard on him; he does mean well."

"What do they say? The road to hell is paved with good intentions."

"If that's true, then I'd say the road to hell is paved with all intentions—good and bad."

Heather shrugged. "So why are you here?"

"I have some questions about Hillary," Danielle lied.

"Oh, right, do you know when her service is?"

"I don't know, but I imagine it will be in Vancouver."

"Are you going?"

Danielle shrugged. "I'm not sure. I probably should. I suppose it will depend on when they have it."

Heather glanced at her watch. "I better get going, I wanted to stop at the store on the way home."

"Okay, see you later." Danielle watched as Heather practically skipped to the parking lot.

"I HAVE TO SAY, you made Heather happy," Danielle told the chief when she walked into his office a few minutes later.

MacDonald looked up from the sheet of paper he was holding. "How's that?" Sitting behind his desk, he waved to one of the empty chairs for her to sit down.

"I ran into her outside. I haven't seen her that cheerful since… well, not sure if I ever have. She was thrilled you got a sketch artist. I didn't know you really had one."

"We discussed getting one. Don't you remember?"

"Sure. But I didn't think the Frederickport Police Department actually had one."

"We don't." He stood up and leaned across the desk, handing Danielle the piece of paper he had been looking at. It was the drawing Elizabeth Sparks had done. "Does it look like him?"

Danielle stood up briefly and accepted the drawing. She sat back down, staring at the face in the picture.

"Wow, this is good. It looks just like him." She glanced up at MacDonald. "Who drew it?"

"Elizabeth Sparks, she's a local art teacher. At one time she was going to become a police sketch artist, but decided it wasn't for her."

Danielle studied the picture for a few more moments and then let out a sigh before tossing the drawing onto MacDonald's desk. "I feel bad I didn't call you sooner."

"What do you mean?" He frowned.

"Hillary dropped in for a visit yesterday."

MacDonald leaned back in his chair and studied Danielle. "So her spirit is still here?"

"Well, it was yesterday. When Chris dropped me off after visiting the funeral home, she was waiting for me. She was a little upset her things were missing—and she didn't quite understand she was dead. But Walt and I walked her through it, and during our conversation, she told me the name of her muse."

"I thought she didn't know who he was?"

"She didn't. But while her spirit was wandering around, she ran into his spirit on the beach. I guess it freaked her out. She still thought she was alive and assumed he was too."

"I suppose it would be a little frightening to run into a man you had been dreaming about for years—one who you believed was a killer."

"He is a killer, if there is any truth to her dreams."

"But still, no reason for her to be frightened now," the chief reminded her.

"Yes, but she didn't know that at the time. Anyway, she asked him his name, and he told her. Antoine Paul."

"Did you get any hits when you looked him up online?"

Danielle frowned. "How did you know I tried looking him up?"

MacDonald laughed. "I know you. I can't imagine you not going into Jessica Fletcher mode the moment you have something to look up."

"Well, unfortunately my amateur detective skills are slipping. I didn't find anything on Antoine Paul. Oh, I found a few Antoine Pauls online, but none that looked like him." Danielle pointed briefly to the drawing.

MacDonald picked up the drawing and studied it a moment. "I suppose had I known his name before I called Elizabeth in, we could have skipped this—and not gone through the farce of placing his picture in the newspaper. The guy is obviously dead, so all this is going to do is make locals a little nervous about peeping toms."

"It did make Heather's day. That girl needed some cheering up. And really, what harm will it do running that drawing in the local paper?"

FOURTEEN

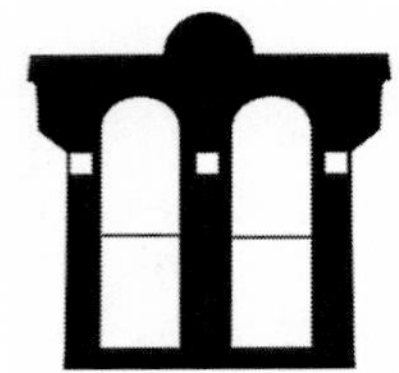

"You're right." MacDonald tossed the paper aside and turned his attention back to Danielle. "I'll see if I have better luck than you in tracking down Antoine Paul. We know he's been dead for eleven years, so I'll start there."

"I did try some obit sites. But I came up empty."

"Don't worry, *Jessica*, I've got some better sources than Google."

Danielle wrinkled her nose. "Oh hush! At least I got the name."

"You mean Hillary told you his name. You cheated." He chuckled.

"Since you're obviously unimpressed with my detective skills, I won't bother telling you about the bizarre coincidence I stumbled on."

"What bizarre coincidence?"

"I thought you said you weren't interested?"

"I didn't say that."

Danielle flashed him a grin. "Okay, I suppose you didn't." She leaned forward, propping her elbows along the edge of his desk. "Hillary's first book was called *Beautiful Rage*."

"And?"

Danielle leaned forward again and rested her elbows back on the desk. "The murder scene in *Beautiful Rage* was based on the murder of a woman named Melissa Huxley. I'm sure it really was, considering the man Melissa Huxley was seen leaving with before she was murdered was wearing a black suit and red bow tie."

"Like your muse ghost."

"Well, in all fairness, I don't think he was ever really a muse. But I suppose some might argue he was. Anyway, the description of Hillary's villain from that book, as well as its book cover, featured a handsome man dressed in a black suit and red bow tie."

"I suppose we need to figure out how Antoine Paul was connected to the victim."

"The interesting thing, Chief, I think I may have met Melissa Huxley's husband the other day at Beverly Klein's house."

"Why do you think that?"

"Beverly's friend was named Baron Huxley. According to one of the articles I read, that's the same name as Melissa Huxley's husband. Actually, he was more Steve's friend. He'd stopped by to pay his condolences. I guess he and Steve used to work together."

"I've never heard of the guy. Does he live in Frederickport? Seems like I would have heard of him if his wife had been murdered."

"He has a vacation home here, but he doesn't live here full time."

"That's interesting." The chief picked up the drawing again and looked at it.

"You know, I wanted to learn more about Antoine Paul and why he murdered Melissa Huxley, because I'd hoped it would give me something to use to convince him to move on. It makes me nervous, him hanging around, especially if he attaches himself to someone who's vulnerable and sensitive to spirits like Heather. I don't think she's in a very good place. But now I realize, if we could solve this murder, look what it will mean for Melissa's family. For her husband. Finally, they can have some closure."

The chief tossed the paper aside. "Let's not get ahead of ourselves, *Jessica*. One thing at a time. Let's first see if we can find your dead guy."

"Would you please stop calling me *Jessica*! I'm much too young to be Jessica Fletcher," Danielle said as she snatched her purse up off the floor.

The chief laughed.

Danielle stood up, purse in hand. "By the way, I got a call from someone who's handling Hillary's estate. They're sending someone over in the morning to pick up her car."

"Good. Glad they're handling everything. I'm glad her autopsy is finished. Now if they would get Steve's autopsy back to me."

"Oh…" Danielle sat back down. "I forgot to tell you something." She smiled sheepishly.

"What?"

"Umm…Hillary ran into Steve as he was swimming in from the ocean."

"I'm assuming you're talking about Steve's spirit."

Danielle nodded. "Of course, Hillary thought she was alive at the time—thought Steve was too."

"He didn't happen to tell her how he fell off the pier, did he? Was he pushed? Did he get into a fight with someone? Carla maybe?"

"Carla?"

"You suggested it yourself. Steve's fishing on the pier, not far from the entrance to her place of employment. He comes in, buys coffee from her. Maybe she decided to go talk to him, they argued, and one little push—over the pier he goes. He did hit his head, might have knocked him out."

"According to Steve, no one pushed him. He went into anaphylactic shock, didn't have his EpiPen, and fell into the ocean. It doesn't sound like murder to me. Just a tragic turn of events."

"Did he say what caused it?"

"I guess he was highly allergic to shellfish. He figures he might have inadvertently touched some raw shellfish left on the pier, transferred it to the food he was eating, and ingested it."

The chief cringed. "Hard to believe someone with that severe of an allergy wouldn't make sure he had his EpiPen with him if he was going to be fishing on the pier and putting his hands anywhere near his mouth."

Danielle stood back up. "According to Hillary, Steve said he normally kept an EpiPen in his tackle box, but it wasn't there when he went to get it."

WHEN DANIELLE GOT BACK to Marlow House, she found Beverly Klein standing on the front porch, holding her now empty and clean casserole dish. It was the dish Danielle had used to hold the macaroni and cheese she had taken to Beverly on Sunday.

"You didn't need to bring it back," Danielle said, taking the dish from Beverly.

"I think I just needed an excuse to get out. It's driving me crazy hanging around the house. I'm not sure what to do with myself."

Danielle unlocked her front door. "Have you had lunch yet?"

"No, but…I really should go. You're probably busy."

Danielle opened the door and motioned Beverly inside. "Don't be silly. I'd love to have some company. We don't have anyone staying here right now. And if you like chicken salad…"

Beverly stepped into the house as Danielle continued to hold the door open. "If it's half as good as your macaroni and cheese, I don't think I can pass it up."

"Who do we have here?" Walt asked as he appeared in the entry hall. He looked the attractive woman up and down.

Beverly stood in the entry hall and glanced around as Danielle closed the door. "The last time I was here was at your grand opening. We spent most of our time out back, playing croquet. That was a lot of fun." Beverly closed her eyes for a moment and then let out a sigh. "I can't believe he's really gone."

"Who is this woman?" Walt asked.

Danielle set the dish on the entry hall table and dropped her purse to the floor. She rushed back to Beverly and placed an arm around her shoulder, giving her a reassuring half hug. "Why don't we go into the living room; I can bring us our lunch there."

Beverly shook her head wearily. "I'm not really hungry. I should probably go. This was a bad idea."

"Come, Beverly," Danielle urged, nudging her toward the living room. "I'll bring us some tea, and in a while, if you feel like eating, I'll make some sandwiches. It's not good to be alone at this time. I know. I went through this when my husband was killed."

"Is this Steve Klein's wife?" Walt asked, following them into the living room. "Now that I look at her, she does look familiar. I seem to recall her from the open house."

Fifteen minutes later Danielle and Walt sat together on the sofa while Beverly took her place in a chair across from them, balancing a saucer with a cup of hot tea on her knee. The moment Beverly had entered the room she had been greeted by Max, who weaved in and out between her ankles, yet took his place on Danielle's lap after she returned with the tea.

"I think it's starting to set in," Beverly said as she took a sip. "That he's really gone."

"You still don't know when Steve's service will be?"

Beverly shook her head. "They haven't released his body yet."

"When will your kids be coming in?"

"Steven is waiting until we schedule the service. Our daughter wants to come now, but frankly, I'm not quite ready to deal with her grief. I imagine that sounds horrible. A mother should be there to comfort her children."

Danielle smiled softly at Beverly. "Maybe it will be better for her if you get a handle on your own emotions before you have to deal with hers."

"At least she has a good support system where she is. I like her boyfriend. He seems to adore her. I think that's important in a relationship."

"What was her husband thinking?" Walt asked. "Why don't people realize what they have before they risk losing it all?"

"Family keeps calling, asking when the service will be. To be honest, I don't even want to answer the phone or deal with it."

"Like I told you before, there's no one staying here right now, so we have plenty of rooms. The fact is, we're going to be closed until May."

"Why? You'll be missing spring break…oh, is it because of Hillary Hemingway? I was so wrapped up in myself I forgot, she died here, didn't she? The same night as Steve's accident?"

"Yes. It was a heart attack. She went peacefully in her sleep, so I suppose that's to be considered a blessing. But no, her death isn't the reason. We'd already planned to close down for about a month."

"Why, are you taking a vacation?"

"We've been having issues with the furnace; it has to be replaced. I want to do it before next winter, but I don't want to do it in the middle of the summer season, so we had already decided to close down after Hillary left. I'm not really sure how long it's going to take. This house is old, and it's going to involve a little more than just replacing a unit. I didn't want to risk being in the middle of repairs and having clients checking in."

FIFTEEN

A while later, after the conversation had shifted directions, Danielle asked, "Umm, Beverley, you know that friend of Steve's who was at your house on Sunday?"

Beverly looked up at Danielle. "Baron? What about him?"

"His name sounded familiar. I remember reading about a murder case in Portland, and the woman who was killed had the same last name."

Beverly moved her saucer and tea to the side table and nodded. "That was Baron's wife, Melissa. Such a tragic story. They never did find the killer."

"That's awful. Was she a friend of yours?"

Beverly shifted her position in the chair, making herself more comfortable. "More of an acquaintance. I met her a few times socially. We were already living in Frederickport when she was murdered. She wasn't really a friend of mine—in fact, neither is Baron. And if I want to be completely honest, I don't think he and Steve were on the best of terms."

"What do you mean? I got the impression they were good friends." Danielle sipped her tea.

"The two used to work together. I'm not really sure what happened, but Steve wasn't thrilled with some of the things that were going on back then. I don't really know what it was all about, and Steve wasn't big on bringing his work home. I think he preferred to think of home as his sanctuary."

"Right, while having a little something on the side," Walt scoffed.

"I just know Steve wasn't happy, and when he decided to apply for the job as bank manager here, I thought it was a good idea. Of course, my reasons were probably a little selfish. We were living on the outskirts of Portland back then, and I loved the idea of moving to a beach community. Of course, they still worked on some projects together even after Steve took the job at the bank. But over the last five years or so, they really haven't worked much together."

"When I met Mr. Huxley, it sounded like they were good friends."

"Oh, I'm not saying they weren't still friends, exactly." Beverly picked her teacup up off the end table. "Baron bought a house here about a year ago, and he and Steve would go fishing when he'd come to town. But a couple months ago, their relationship seemed to get a little strained again. I asked Steve about it, but he said it was no big deal. Maybe he was right; Baron did bring him tamales."

"Tamales?" Danielle leaned forward, one hand holding Max so he wouldn't roll off onto the floor while the other hand set the now empty teacup on the coffee table.

"A friend of Baron's, his wife makes homemade tamales. He always brings some to Steve. I'm not really fond of them myself, but Steve loved them. Anyway, Baron stopped in to see Steve the other day and brought him some tamales. So I guess whatever issue they had must have been resolved."

"So he never remarried?" Danielle asked.

Beverly shook her head. "No, but I have the feeling he enjoys playing the part of the tragic widower. From what Steve used to tell me, Baron never had a problem finding female companionship."

"That must have been pretty devastating for him, losing his wife in such a violent and senseless way."

Beverly shrugged. "I suppose it was. But frankly, he didn't seem that broken up about it at the time. Of course, the spouse is always the first one they suspect, so I guess it was lucky for him he was a couple hundred miles away when she was murdered."

"You think they suspected he was involved?"

Beverly set her cup back on its saucer. "Steve told me they questioned him for hours. But they never could find anything to link him to her murder, plus she was seen leaving that restaurant with another man. Not just leaving with him, witnesses said they were arguing."

"I read that," Danielle muttered.

"Can I tell you something, just between you and me?"

Danielle nodded. "Certainly."

"Should I leave the room?" Walt asked with a chuckle, making no attempt to leave.

"I got the most unsettling feeling when Baron stopped by to give his condolences."

"How so?"

"He was much too—well, touchy. I've never really considered him anything more than a friend of my husband's. He just made me uncomfortable." Beverly shivered.

"Like he was trying to hit on you?"

Beverly sat up straight. "Exactly! But it sounds so—well, self-absorbed of me to even consider something like that. After all, he and Steve have been friends for years, and I'm sure he only came over to give his condolences. Hitting on me was probably the last thing on his mind—but still…"

"It has nothing to do with being self-absorbed, more like self-aware. When my husband died, I was shocked at the number of friends—married friends—men who were married to close friends of mine—who hit on me."

Walt looked over to Danielle and frowned. "You never told me that."

"Really? You mean I wasn't imagining things?"

Danielle shook her head. "No. In fact, Lily said something about how Baron kept looking at you—seemed a little intimate."

"I'm glad to know I'm not crazy! What is it with men? Can't they for two minutes behave like a civilized adult without that little guy in their pants calling the shots?"

Danielle glanced briefly at Walt, stifling a grin.

"Don't look at me like that," Walt said. "I don't even have anything in my pants." Walt paused and frowned. "Wait a minute… that didn't come out right. I just meant…you know…" Flustered, Walt vanished.

"HE SAID he didn't have anything in his pants?" Lily asked with a giggle after Danielle finished telling her about her afternoon with Beverly, and Walt's parting comment. The two sat on the front porch swing at Marlow House.

"I knew what he meant. What we see is nothing but an illusion—smoke and mirrors. So technically speaking, there really isn't a body under the suit he wears."

"Was Beverly here a long time?"

"A couple hours. I made her a sandwich. We had a nice visit. I like her. Most of my dealings with Steve—aside from being a bank customer—was museum business. I really haven't talked to Beverly that many times. We discussed the open house."

"What about?"

"About my arrest for Cheryl's murder and then, later, for Stoddard's."

Lily shook her head. "Nothing like making small talk over one's murder arrests."

Danielle smiled. "Yeah, well, she said she was impressed at how I put all that behind me and how I now have a good relationship with the Frederickport Police Department in spite of it."

POLICE CHIEF MACDONALD sat behind his desk, reading the autopsy report, when Joe and Brian knocked at his open door. He looked up and waved them in, gesturing to the two chairs facing his desk.

"What is it, Chief?" Brian asked as he took a seat.

"I just got the autopsy report back on Steve Klein. The corner says he was in anaphylactic shock when he went over that rail. He was allergic to something. So allergic that he was probably disoriented when he fell off the pier. The coroner believes it was probably a food allergy."

"What was he allergic to?" Joe asked.

"I don't know," the chief lied. According to what Steve's spirit had told Hillary, he was aware of his allergy to shellfish. So aware that he normally kept an EpiPen with him. But he didn't have one with him that night.

"Do they have any idea what caused it?" Brian asked.

"According to the coroner, he had crabmeat in his stomach."

There goes the theory Danielle suggested that he touched something with shellfish and transferred it to his food.

"I know a lot of people are allergic to shellfish," Brian said. "My cousin is so allergic to fish that she can't even stay in the house if someone's cooking it. She breaks into hives."

"If it was the shellfish, then he obviously didn't know he had an allergy," Joe said. "Not that uncommon for someone to develop an allergy to a food they've eaten all their lives."

"I'd like to keep the contents of this autopsy to ourselves for now. We need to find out a few things."

"What do you need, Chief?" Joe asked.

"First, I want to find out if Steve knew he had a food allergy. Second, I want to know what he was allergic to. And then I want to find out who knew about his food allergy."

Brian frowned. "Do you suspect foul play?"

"If it turns out he was allergic to shellfish which he knew about and he had crab in his stomach, I don't see Steve as having a death wish."

"If he knew about his food allergy, it probably isn't shellfish," Joe said.

"Why do you say that?" Brian asked.

"Lots of other allergies out there. Take peanut allergies, for example. I know that can be deadly. Bite into a muffin that has a nut you don't know about and then, pow, you're a goner."

The chief stood up. "Let's not waste our time speculating. I need you to find out what he was allergic to."

Brian stood up. "That's if he was even aware of the allergy. As Joe said, it's possible to go all your life eating something before it decides to kill you."

JOE MORELLI SAT with Carla in a booth at Pier Café. "You doing okay, Carla?"

Carla shrugged indifferently, her fingers tugging nervously on a stray lock of purple hair. "Just getting used to the fact Steve's really dead. I still can't believe it." Wearing her waitress uniform, she shifted nervously and glanced over to the counter.

"I need to ask you a few questions about Steve."

Carla shifted again on the bench seat. "Yeah, I figured that.

What do you need to ask me?"

"Do you know if Steve was allergic to anything?"

She absently twisted the lock of hair around her finger. "He said he was allergic to lobster, but I think he just said that because he didn't want to take me to the seafood restaurant in Astoria."

"He said he was allergic to lobster?"

"Well, not that exactly. He said he was allergic to fish."

"Did you ever see him eat fish?"

"Steve?" Carla laughed. "He was strictly a burger guy. He told me his wife was always griping at him to stop eating red meat. But he'd eat a burger for lunch every day if he could get away with it."

"Do you know if he carried an epinephrine auto-injector with him?"

Carla frowned. "You mean one of those pins you stick yourself with to stop an allergic reaction?"

Joe nodded. "Yes."

"I know he always had one in his car. He showed me where he kept it. Told me if he ever had an allergic reaction when he was at my house, I was to run to his car and get it for him."

Joe jotted down a note on his pad of paper.

Carla studied Joe for a moment and then released the strand of hair she had been playing with. "Why are you asking me all this?"

"We're just trying to figure out why he may have fallen off the pier."

Combing her hand through her hair, she leaned forward, propping her elbows on the table. "You know, Joe, you're a good guy. How come you never asked me out?"

Joe froze a moment and glanced up, noting how Carla was leaning over the table toward him. "Well…I have a girlfriend."

Carla let out a snort and then plopped back in the seat. "Joe Morelli, I know for a fact you didn't have a girlfriend a couple months ago. How come you never asked me out back then?"

"Carla, can we stick to business, please?"

She rolled her eyes. "Whatever. I really need to get out of this town. What's wrong with me? I'm not a bad person. Sure, maybe I did get too close to a married man, but was that my fault? Can I help who I fall in love with?"

Joe arched his brow. "You were in love with Steve Klein?"

Carla let out a sigh. "No. But I could have fallen in love with him."

SIXTEEN

Officer Brian Henderson pulled the squad car up in front of Beverly Klein's house and parked. He sat in the vehicle, his hands still on the steering wheel, and studied the house a moment before getting out. It was one of the nicer homes in town. Of course, nothing like Stoddard's house—which was actually Chris's now. But Brian's modest home looked like a shack in comparison to the Klein home.

Beverly Klein was a good-looking woman. He couldn't understand why Steve had strayed with someone like Carla. *It's not that Carla is unattractive, but why forfeit filet mignon for a hamburger?* Brian frowned at the thought. *I imagine someone might jump down my throat if I said that out loud, comparing women to food.*

He got out of the vehicle and slammed the door shut behind him, making his way to Beverly's front door.

"So the coroner's report is really done?" Beverly asked Brian a few minutes later as she led him to the living room.

"Yes, they sent it over this afternoon."

"Have you read it?"

"No. The chief has. You can call and talk to him about it if you want."

"Does this mean his body will be released, and I can plan his funeral?" She gestured to the sofa for him to take a seat.

"I believe it does, but you can call down to the station and get the details." Holding his baseball cap in his hand, he sat down on the sofa.

"I can't believe you came all the way over here just to tell me the report is in. You could have called me for that."

"No, I have a few questions for you."

"Of course, can I get you something to drink, Officer Henderson?"

"No, thank you." Tossing his cap on the cushion next to him, he pulled his small notepad from his pocket.

"Then how can I help you?" Beverly asked as she took a seat facing him.

"I was wondering if your husband had any kind of food allergy?"

Wearing designer jeans and a turquoise silk blouse, Beverly settled back in the chair and crossed her legs. Her feet were bare, showing off a recent pedicure and polish. "Why, yes. Steve had a severe allergy to shellfish."

Brian looked up from the pad. "So he never ate shellfish?"

Beverly frowned. "Of course not."

"Did he keep an epinephrine auto-injector with him?"

"We keep one in the house, and he always keeps one in the car. He also kept one in his tackle box."

Brian frowned and then flipped through his notes. He looked back to Beverly. "There wasn't one in his tackle box when we found it on the pier."

Beverly shook her head. "I'm not sure what to tell you, unless he moved it for some reason. He always keeps one in there. But then, I never go in his tackle box."

Brian nodded and jotted something down in his pad.

"Officer Henderson, what is this about? Why do you want to know about Steve's allergy, about his EpiPen?"

Brian closed the pad of paper and looked up at Beverly. "We're just trying to figure out why your husband fell off that pier. Did something happen to him that made him lose his balance and fall? Maybe he had an allergic reaction to something."

"I'll admit it used to make me a little nervous when Steve would go fishing off the pier. People touch things; we put our hands in our mouth without thinking. Cross contamination in something like this could be deadly. That's why I always nagged him about keeping an EpiPen with him." Beverly paused a moment and then stood up abruptly, staring at Brian. "Oh my god, you don't think that's what happened, do you?"

"What do you mean?"

"Did he touch something down there? Did he accidently put his hands in his mouth? Oh my god!" She turned abruptly from Brian and started pacing.

"Please sit down, Mrs. Klein, we don't believe his allergic reaction—if he had one—was caused by him putting his hands in his mouth."

She turned and looked at Brian a moment, studying him. "How can you know that?"

"I just do. Now please…" He motioned to her chair.

Reluctantly she sat down.

"Do you have any idea what your husband might have had to eat that day?"

"He had breakfast that morning, cereal and toast, I think. I don't know what he had for lunch. When he got home that night, I was getting ready for the bridge girls."

"Yes, you told us before you play bridge every Thursday."

"Well…" She shifted in the chair. "To be perfectly honest, we don't actually play bridge."

"I thought you said it was bridge night?"

She shrugged. "I don't even know how to play bridge. Some of my friends started this group about five years ago. It was a way for us to get together once a week and not have to make dinner. The person who hosts the party makes the food, and we take turns. It was my turn last week."

"Did Steve eat here before he went fishing?"

"Like I started to say, he had breakfast here that morning—but that was it. I don't know what he had for lunch. I made quiche that night; it was still in the oven when he left. So no, he didn't eat anything at home that day except for breakfast."

"Do you have any idea what his plans were for dinner?"

"Just the tamales. He had two of them. Told me that was going to be his dinner. He also had a thermos of coffee, but he forgot that. Left it sitting on the counter."

"Do you know where he got the tamales?"

"His friend Baron Huxley gave them to him the day before." Beverly wrinkled her nose. "Personally, I can't stand tamales. It's the texture. But Steve even liked them cold. He liked to take them with him when he went fishing."

"Do you know where this Baron Huxley gets his tamales?"

"I believe he has a friend whose wife makes them. When he comes to town, he usually brings Steve a few. They say she makes the best tamales, but I wouldn't know about that."

Beverly watched as Brian jotted more notes down in his pad.

"Do you know anyone else who knew about your husband's food allergy?"

"It certainly wasn't a secret. Most of our friends knew."

"Would this friend who gave Steve the tamales have known?"

"Certainly. Baron and Steve go way back; they used to work together. When you go out to eat with someone enough times, something like a food allergy is bound to come up, especially when someone suggests going to a seafood restaurant."

Brian nodded and jotted something else down.

"I really don't think my husband had any sort of allergic reaction that night."

Brian looked up. "Why is that?"

"Steve was careful. Even if he didn't have an EpiPen in the tackle box, he keeps one in his car. I don't know why my husband fell off the pier that night. Maybe he had a heart attack. You wouldn't know what the autopsy report says, do you?

CHRIS JOHNSON TOSSED the steak on the grill and took a swig of his beer. It was chilly out, but not too cold to grill. As far as he was concerned, it was never too cold to barbeque a steak. He stood alone on his back patio, admiring the ocean view beyond his property. He hadn't stopped congratulating himself on purchasing his beach home.

Just as he was about to take another sip of beer, motion from the right caught his attention. He looked up. There, standing just beyond his patio, on the beach, was a man dressed in a black suit, wearing a red bow tie. Chris instantly knew who the man was. It was Antoine Paul, the ghost who had been visiting Hillary's dreams for over a decade. The man who she believed was her muse.

Chris said nothing, but simply stared at the intruder.

Antoine Paul studied Chris a moment. Finally, he said, "You can see me, can't you?"

Instead of answering the question, Chris looked away and took another sip of beer and turned to his grill, flipping his steak.

"I thought for sure you could see me," Antoine muttered. "The way you were looking at me." Instead of leaving, he walked onto the porch and took a seat in an empty chair. He continued to study Chris.

Chris turned his back to Antoine and stared back to the ocean, his gaze seemingly looking through the spot where Antoine had been standing just moments before.

"I should have known you couldn't see me," Antoine said as he leaned back in the chair, still staring at Chris. "What are the chances? You're obviously not dead. I've never seen a ghost cook a steak before, but I suppose there's a first time for everything."

Chris returned to the grill and looked down at the steak.

"That ghost girl Danielle Boatman can see me. I'm sure of it. But I'm not going to even try approaching her in Marlow House. It was risky enough going to her in a dream when the guy was hanging around. I don't need that kind of distraction. If I'm going to use her, I'll have to do it when she's away from Marlow House—and away from Walt Marlow."

Chris walked to the table and picked up a plate. He returned to the grill with it and placed the now cooked steak in the center of the plate.

"I think that other one can see me. But she seems more unreliable than Hillary. Hillary was a waste of time." Antoine stood up.

Chris walked toward his back door. From the corner of his eye he could see Antoine walking back toward the beach. When Chris opened the door, he turned one more time to face the ocean. He could see Antoine in the distance, walking away from his house.

Hurrying inside and closing the door behind him, Chris tossed his plate with the steak onto the counter and hastily picked up his cellphone and dialed Danielle.

"Hillary's muse was just here," Chris told her. "I don't have a good feeling about this."

SEVENTEEN

Cupping a steaming mug of coffee in her hands, Danielle leaned back on the library sofa, her feet propped up on the coffee table as she watched Chris and Walt. They paced the room together, each walking in the opposite direction, and then would do an about-face, turning to go the other way, where they would pass each other and then repeat. She thought it amusing how they avoided running into each other. It would be possible for Chris to walk through Walt without missing a beat, yet she didn't think either one would appreciate that.

She noticed Chris's sandy-colored hair could use a trim; it about touched his shirt's collar. Dressed casually, he wore khaki pants, a blue-striped collared T-shirt, and flip-flops. Walt was dressed more formally, wearing a three-piece suit, minus the jacket, with his sleeves pushed up. She had to admit, there was something sexy about a man wearing a suit and vest. Of course, Chris, even dressed casually, looked like he had just stepped off the pages of one of those trendy fashion magazines. Danielle sighed, appreciating the view. *Dang, I have it rough*. She sipped her coffee.

Chris had arrived fifteen minutes earlier. After they had talked on the phone last night, they agreed he should come over in the morning and the three—Walt, Danielle, and Chris—would discuss the situation regarding Antoine Paul. Lily had declined joining in on the discussion, she felt it would be a waste of time, considering she wouldn't be able to hear Walt's side of the conversation. Instead, she went across the street to have breakfast at Ian's house.

"He said he didn't want to deal with me?" Walt asked, still pacing.

"I have no idea how he even knows about you," Chris said.

"Remember, Walt was in the dream hop with me when Paul jumped in," Danielle reminded them. "And would you two please sit down. I'm starting to get dizzy."

Chris headed for the empty space next to Danielle, but Walt instantly appeared there before Chris took the second step. Flashing Walt a glare, Chris reluctantly took the chair facing the sofa. Smiling, Walt waved his hand for a cigar.

"I still don't know how Paul knew Walt was a ghost," Chris said.

"Spirit," Walt corrected.

"Same thing," Chris reminded him.

Ignoring their banter, Danielle said, "I think there's some sort of spirit information pipeline. Something beyond two spirits bumping into each other and exchanging info. Look at Angela, she knew about Walt being here. How did she know that if no other spirits had been through Marlow House to encounter Walt back then?"

"I do feel cut off," Walt grumbled.

"You know how to fix that," Chris said with a smile. "You could step outside."

"Yes. And be forced to move on." Walt frowned. "You'd like that."

Chris studied Walt a moment and then sighed. "Nahhh, who would I have to argue with?"

"Chris, do you really think this Antoine Paul is some sort of danger?" Danielle asked.

"He did warn you to stay out of his business," Walt reminded.

"That doesn't necessarily mean he's dangerous," Danielle pointed out.

"He's up to something," Chris said. "And I really don't like the fact he's managed to be on the scene of all those murders. I still think he did something to nudge the killers to act, like assisting Pete in finding that bottle at just the right moment."

Danielle glanced from Walt to Chris. "I don't like how he's hanging around Heather. You know, she really seemed depressed the other day. Although having the chief take her seriously and getting an artist to do a drawing of Paul did seem to cheer her up.

Yet the problem with Heather, she swings from one extreme to the next."

"Like be your pal one minute and then be the first one to point a finger in your direction when someone happens to find a dead body in the parlor?" Chris grumbled.

Danielle chuckled. "Well, you can't really blame her for that. Even a stable person would come unhinged after finding something like Peter Morris's body brutally murdered under the same roof they're staying at. But the thing with Heather, even when she's not standing in the middle of a murder scene, she can be nice one minute and snotty the next."

"I'm more concerned about you," Walt said. "From what Chris overheard, it sounds like this guy's looking for some way to attach himself to you when you're away from Marlow House."

Danielle glanced to Walt. "What I'm curious about, if Antoine Paul barged into Marlow House, what could you really do? It's not like you can hit him with something. It'd just go right through him. Do you have some powers you can use on another spirit?"

Walt considered the questions a moment and then shook his head. "Not that I know about. But I've never really been in the situation of having to deal with another spirit in that way. That character Stoddard never stepped inside this house, so I didn't have the opportunity to find out."

"I wonder if Hillary has really moved on," Danielle muttered. "If she was still around, would he focus back on her, or is he looking for a flesh and blood person?"

"From what I gathered from Paul's ramblings, he's no longer interested in using Hillary. He called her unreliable. I don't know if that's because she's a spirit now or if he feels she was unreliable when she was still alive."

"When he said something about the *other one*, you really think that was Heather?" Walt asked.

"That would be my bet. We know Heather saw him a few times and he even followed her back to her house. If it is Heather, he's not interested in her."

"If that's true, then maybe I don't need to be that concerned with Heather if he's going to leave her alone," Danielle suggested.

"We just have to be worried about you," Walt reminded her.

Danielle smiled at Walt. "He's a ghost, Walt, and in my opinion, the only way a ghost can be truly dangerous is if I was unaware of what he was. I still don't believe a spirit who wanders like he does is capable of harnessing a significant amount of energy to do serious damage, at least not to someone who is aware."

"But we still need to find some way to get him to move on," Chris reminded them.

"I agree. And the only way we can really do that is if we figure out what he's about." Danielle set her mug on the end table and picked up her cellphone.

"Who are you calling?" Walt asked.

"The chief. I want to see if anything's come up on Antoine Paul."

"SO YOU FOUND ANTOINE PAUL?" Chris asked as he and Danielle entered the police chief's office. He shook MacDonald's hand in greeting.

When Chris and Danielle sat down, MacDonald took a seat behind his desk. "The Antoine Paul I found, he's a dead ringer for the man Elizabeth drew."

Danielle clutched her purse; it rested on her lap. "So it is the same guy. How did he die? How long after he murdered Melissa?"

The chief shook his head. "I don't know. At the moment, our Antoine Paul is a missing person."

"No one knows he's dead? When did he go missing?" Chris asked.

"His sister reported him missing about a month after Melissa Huxley's murder."

"Did you find any connection between Melissa and Paul?"

The chief shook his head again. "No. And frankly, I really don't have the time to look into a decade-old murder that happened outside my jurisdiction. I'm afraid what I give you today is about all the help you can expect from me. I've got my hands full at the moment."

"Steve's death?" Danielle asked.

"And I can't even use you two." The chief leaned back in the chair and sighed.

"What do you mean?" Chris asked.

"Danielle here already told me what Hillary passed on from

Steve's ghost." The chief paused a moment and chuckled over the absurdity of the conversation.

Danielle looked to Chris. "As far as Steve knows, he went into anaphylactic shock and fell off the pier. If there was foul play, he didn't seem to be aware of it."

"We know the anaphylactic shock wasn't caused from a transfer of shellfish from the pier to his food," the chief said.

"How can you be so sure?" Chris asked.

The chief leaned forward and snatched up his pen, absently tapping it against the desktop. "We just do."

Danielle dropped her purse from her lap to the floor by her feet. "Are you suggesting someone did something to cause him to go into anaphylactic shock?"

"I can't say right now."

She considered the situation for a moment. "If that's true, I doubt they were trying to kill him."

Chris let out a sardonic laugh. "What, a friendly little prank?"

Danielle shrugged. "No, I'm just saying however it happened, it must have been an accident. If someone did something to make him go into anaphylactic shock, I can't see how it was part of a murder plot. After all, they had no way of knowing he'd fall off the pier or that there wouldn't be someone nearby who could help him."

"I suppose it depends how severe someone's allergy is," the chief reminded them. *And if the EpiPen isn't where it's supposed to be.*

They were all silent for a few moments considering the possible scenarios. Finally, Danielle said, "Steve's wife dropped by yesterday."

The chief cocked his brow. "I wasn't aware you were friends."

"Casual acquaintances, but I like her. She dropped by to return my dish from the casserole Lily and I took her on Sunday. Although, I think she just wanted to talk to someone. I felt so sorry for her. Oh, and I learned Steve's friend Baron Huxley is the widower of Melissa Huxley."

"It is a small world," the chief mused.

"I felt so sorry for her. I really hope she doesn't find out about her husband's infidelity. She seems so lost as it is, that would just destroy her."

"You don't think she knew he was fooling around? I've always heard a wife often knows," the chief suggested.

"I had absolutely no idea Lucas had been cheating on me. That totally threw me."

"Would it be so bad if she learned the truth of her husband?" Chris asked.

Danielle turned to Chris. "I don't know what purpose that would serve. Sometimes ignorance is bliss. And she and Steve have two kids together. Do they really need to know their father cheated on their mother? I lost my parents when I was about their age. It's rough. They really don't need to deal with anything more."

The chief let out a sigh. "I'd love to be able to accommodate you, Danielle, and keep Steve's sordid secret, but I'm afraid it's going to come out."

"Why does it have to?"

Chris glanced from Danielle to the chief. "This is a murder investigation now, isn't it?"

"Even if it is, I can't believe Beverly had anything to do with Steve's death. She seems sincerely crushed."

"Come on, Danielle, you're seeing yourself in her. You aren't being objective," Chris said.

Danielle frowned. "What do you mean?"

"Danielle, maybe you're right," the chief said. "Maybe she doesn't know anything about her husband's affair and had nothing to do with his murder. But if someone killed Steve, we have to look at motives. Top of our list, we have a wife who was being cheated on and an ex-lover who was recently dumped."

"Damn." Danielle slumped back in her chair. "If it was Carla, then the truth will come out at trial." Danielle looked up at the chief. "But I can't even imagine Carla doing something like that."

"I'm not saying it was Carla or Beverly, I'm just saying they're the two likely suspects."

"Is it possible to keep Steve's affair quiet for now? If Steve really was murdered, then maybe you'll find someone else who had more of a motive to want him dead. If so, then why heap unneeded pain on the family?" Danielle asked.

"We're going to be discreet, Danielle. But we have to do our jobs."

Danielle sighed. "I suppose."

EIGHTEEN

After Chris and Danielle left the police station, they stopped at Lucy's Diner for lunch. Sitting across from Chris, Danielle opened the file MacDonald had given her. It contained the information the chief had gathered on Hillary's muse.

"It seems our Antoine Paul was a freelance writer," Danielle said as she skimmed through MacDonald's notes. "According to this, his sister hasn't heard from her brother since right before Valentine's Day. She reported him missing mid-March."

"Melissa Huxley was killed right before Valentine's Day, wasn't she?" Chris asked.

Danielle nodded. "I wonder when he was killed—and how. Did something happen right after the murder, like when Chuck Christiansen murdered Bart Haston and ended up driving off Pilgrim's Point."

"And his body has never been found?"

"Apparently not." Danielle continued to read through the papers.

"We'd have a better chance of nailing down the time of his death if we could find anyone who saw him from the time of Melissa's murder until he was reported missing. Just because his sister hadn't heard from him, it doesn't mean he vanished at the same time as Melissa's murder."

"True. But since the guy worked from home, it's not like he went to an office each day. So there's really no one to say he hadn't shown up for work. From what the chief wrote down, I guess the police talked to some of his neighbors, but no one could recall seeing him for a couple months."

Chris picked up his glass of water. Before taking a drink, he said, "So basically, as far as we know, his sister was the last one to see him alive."

"No, Melissa and the witnesses were."

Chris started to say something but paused, still holding onto his glass of water. "You might want to close that file. Our subject of interest is standing outside on the sidewalk, looking in the window. If he decides to come in, you need to figure out if you want to ignore him or let him know you can see him."

Danielle closed the folder and then placed it on the seat next to her, under her purse. "I intend to let him know I can see him. Just not right now. I want to learn as much as I can about him first."

The server arrived at the table just as Antoine Paul did.

Order pad in hand, the waitress smiled down at Danielle and Chris, Antoine by her side. "Have you decided what you want to order?"

"I'll have a grilled cheese," Danielle told her, ignoring Antoine, who waved a hand in front of her face, trying to get a reaction.

"They said you can see spirits. Did they lie?" Antoine dropped his hand to his side and glared at Danielle.

"Do you want the French fries?" the waitress asked.

Danielle smiled. "I'll have the fresh fruit."

"And to drink?"

"What good are you if you can't see me?" Antoine disappeared and then reappeared, sitting in the booth seat next to Chris, facing Danielle.

"Ice tea, please." Danielle smiled at Chris, trying her best not to look over at the unwelcomed spirit.

Antoine let out a sigh and leaned back; closing his eyes, he shook his head back and forth. "Why me? Was I really such a bad person? Yes, I had one little lapse."

Danielle bit her tongue. *You call murdering Melissa a little lapse?*

The server looked to Chris. "What will you have?"

"I'll have the cheeseburger, fries. Ice tea. Make the burger medium rare."

When the server left their table, Chris and Danielle sat in

awkward silence, trying to decide what to say with Antoine looking on.

Danielle fidgeted with her water glass. "So how's your new office going?"

"They're supposed to install the furniture next week."

Ten minutes later, after listening to Danielle and Chris discuss the trivialities of transforming the Gusarov Estate into a new office complex for Chris's foundation, Antoine let out a groan. "This has to be absolutely the most boring conversation in the world." Antoine disappeared, yet not before Heather Donavan stepped into the diner and saw him sitting with Danielle and Chris.

Danielle glanced around, looking for Antoine. Yet it wasn't the ghost she spied, but her neighbor Heather, who stood at the entrance of the diner, staring blankly at Chris and Danielle's booth.

Chris looked toward the door and spied Heather. "Do you think she saw him?"

"By her expression, I think she did." Danielle forced a smile and waved at Heather, urging her to join them. Instead of accepting the invitation, she turned abruptly and fled the diner.

Danielle groaned. "I need to talk to her. She's going to think she's crazy."

Chris shrugged. "In all fairness, I suspect she was already partway there."

"That's not fair, Chris. You know what it's like having the ability to see spirits. And with Heather, hers is pretty hit and miss. Although, I suspect it's getting stronger."

Their conversation was interrupted when the server arrived with their order. The two sat in silence as plates were set on the table. After asking if they needed anything else, the server turned and walked away.

Watching the parting server for a few minutes, Chris finally said, "The thing is, I really don't feel comfortable having someone like Heather know I can see spirits. If she starts to broadcast that—and then people start taking a closer look at me—"

"Hey, I get it." Danielle picked up her grilled cheese sandwich. "Heather already knows about me, although I haven't gone into detail with her. She doesn't have to know about you. But I need to let her know about Antoine. Before, she thought he was a real person. And now, seeing him vanish before her eyes, I can't imagine what she's thinking now."

AFTER LUNCH, Danielle dropped Chris off at his house and then drove down the street to Heather's. She sat in her car for a few minutes, trying to decide what she wanted to say.

When Heather opened her front door a few minutes later, she carried her calico Bella in her arms, her face devoid of expression. "What do you need?"

"Hi, Heather." Danielle reached out and scratched behind Bella's ears. "Bella." Dropping her hand back to her side, she smiled at Heather. "I was hoping we could talk."

With a shrug, Heather turned from the doorway, leaving it wide open, and headed to the living room. Danielle took that as an invitation to come in and followed Heather, closing the door behind them.

She smelled lavender. Glancing around, she noticed the diffuser sitting on the fireplace mantel, a pillar of steam wafting up to the ceiling. "Mmm, lavender. It smells nice."

"Lavender is supposed to be calming." Heather plopped down on a chair, Bella now on her lap. "But I don't feel especially calm."

"I think we need to talk about something." Danielle took a seat on the couch across from Heather.

"Did you see him?"

"I assume you're talking about the man who was sitting next to Chris in Lucy's."

"And then just disappeared. Did Chris see him?"

Nibbling her lip nervously, Danielle shook her head. "No. I saw him, but Chris didn't. He can't see spirits."

"Does he know you can?"

"Heather, I've told you I really avoid discussing this with anyone. It only causes problems. But I thought it was important that you know more about the man who you saw sitting next to Chris—so you can protect yourself."

"Protect myself from what?"

Danielle considered the question a moment and then said, "Honestly, I'm not quite sure. I just know that spirit you saw, when he was alive, he murdered someone."

"Who is he? And why was he sitting with you? Why do I keep seeing him?"

Danielle leaned back on the sofa, her eyes on Heather. "When

Hillary was staying with me, she told me about a reoccurring dream she had. In the dream, the same man kept coming to her and showing her murder scenes. She called him her muse. She said those scenes inspired her stories. But the fact was, those murder scenes really happened. In fact, the last one she saw was Jolene's."

"I don't understand."

"Hillary's muse was really a spirit who regularly visited her dreams. I have no idea what his motive was. But one thing I'm fairly certain of, when he was alive, he committed the first murder he showed Hillary. When he was alive, his name was Antoine Paul."

"Why is he here now?"

"I have no idea. He doesn't know I can see him. I would like to keep it that way until I know more about him. I think he knows you can see him, since you called the police after you saw him staring in the window."

"I guess that explains why there were no footprints in my flower bed." Heather tossed Bella, who was now getting restless, to the floor.

"I'm trying to find out more about him, to figure out some way to convince him to move on."

"Wouldn't it be easier just to talk to him? Ask him why he's here?"

"I plan to. But first, I want to learn more about him. At this point, he could say anything, and I wouldn't have any idea if he was telling the truth or making stuff up. If I knew at least something about the man he was when he was still alive, I might be in a better position to deal with him."

"I guess this explains why he didn't help me when I found Steve's body. He was dead too."

"You haven't seen Steve, have you?"

Heather smiled. "I assume you're talking about Steve's ghost?"

Danielle nodded.

"No. Which is fine with me. Although, I liked Steve. I got to know him a little bit at the museum."

Danielle had forgotten Heather had been briefly involved with the museum. She had learned from Millie Samson that her neighbor had volunteered to be a docent for a brief time, yet Heather soon realized she didn't particularly enjoy chatting with all the visitors. Although, she did appreciate the fact she could make phone calls at the museum without her phone number popping up on someone's cellphone. She had used the museum's phone when looking for a diver to help her locate the Eva Aphrodite, several months earlier.

"I just wanted you to know you aren't going crazy. You did see Antoine Paul."

"I guess I should tell the police chief not to run the picture in the paper," Heather suggested.

"It's not going to hurt if he runs the picture. I wouldn't worry about it."

"But he knows about you, doesn't he?"

Danielle frowned. "What do you mean?"

"Chief MacDonald knows you see ghosts, doesn't he?"

"Heather, even if he did, if he was to acknowledge something like that, it would be detrimental to his career. Trust me, when a person starts telling others they can see and talk to spirits—or if they tell others they believe it's possible and they know someone who does—their credibility begins to crumble."

After Danielle left, Heather picked up her cellphone and dialed the Frederickport Police Department.

"May I speak to Officer Brian Henderson, please."

When Brian got on the phone a few moments later, Heather said, "Hi. This is Heather Donovan. I live on Beach Drive."

"I know who you are."

"Yeah…I suppose you do. I wanted to apologize for my outburst the other day. I'm afraid, after finding another dead body on the beach…well…I may have temporarily snapped."

"Temporarily?" he said under his breath.

"And I wanted to tell you something else. This morning I realized my alarm clock must be broken. It's not keeping accurate time. I'm pretty sure it was much earlier when I took the trash out on Thursday than I originally told you. So obviously, I saw Hillary right before she went back to Marlow House and went to bed."

NINETEEN

Joe Morelli couldn't help but wonder how someone could afford a vacation home like this. Located on the same street as the Gusarov Estate, it faced the ocean, and he wouldn't be surprised if someone were to tell him it had once been featured in an architectural magazine spotlighting seaside mansions. He couldn't help but feel a twinge of envy. He would never be able to afford anything like this, at least not on his salary.

Baron Huxley was already opening the door when he reached the front porch. Joe had called ahead and arranged the meeting. After exchanging greetings and a brief handshake, Baron led Joe to the back porch overlooking the beach. A pitcher of iced tea and two glasses waited for them on the patio table. Slices of lemon bobbed along with the ice cubes in the tea-filled pitcher.

Joe took a seat and got out his notepad as Baron poured them each a glass of tea and sat down.

"I was shocked to hear about Steve. I've known him for years."

Joe thanked Baron for the tea and then asked, "When was the last time you saw him?"

"On Wednesday morning. I had just gotten into town. Like I mentioned on the phone, I don't live here full time." He was about to take a sip of his tea but then paused mid-sip and asked, "How is it you got my number?"

"Mrs. Klein gave it to us."

Baron took his sip and then set his glass back on the table. "I'm not really sure why she would give you my number. I thought Steve's death was some sort of accident. Didn't he fall off the pier, hit his head? At least, that's what the paper said."

"Apparently Mr. Klein had gone into anaphylactic shock shortly before he fell off the pier."

"Ahhh…his shellfish allergy." Baron reached into his shirt's front pocket and removed a thin cigar and silver lighter.

"You knew about his allergy?"

"Certainly. We enjoyed a lot of dinners out over the years—yet never one at a seafood restaurant." Flicking the lighter, Baron lit his cigar and took a puff.

"I understand you gave him some tamales the day you saw him. According to his wife, that's what he took with him fishing."

"Yeah. It was sort of a custom with us. I'd bring him some tamales when I'd come to town. I'd usually bring him a couple dozen, and he'd toss them in his freezer. But I haven't ordered any lately, so I just grabbed a couple from my freezer before I headed for Frederickport. For tradition's sake, I couldn't really show up in town empty-handed."

"Was there any possibility those tamales contained shellfish?"

"Absolutely not. They were pork tamales. As far as I know, Carlos's wife only makes pork or chicken tamales."

"Who's Carlos?" Just as Joe asked the question, he got a whiff of cigar smoke. There was something familiar about the scent, yet he couldn't place it.

"My gardener. His wife makes absolutely the best tamales. I always buy some from her when she makes them."

"And there's no chance the two you gave Steve contained shellfish?"

"Carlos's wife only makes one type of tamales at a time. One month it's pork, the next chicken. The ones I gave to Steve came from a batch of pork ones I bought. So unless Carlos's wife made a batch of fish tamales and they got mixed up with mine, then I'd have to say Steve didn't have a problem with the tamales. But I'll be happy to give you Carlos's number if you want. You can check with him."

"I'd appreciate that."

Baron stood for a moment—his cigar hanging out of the side of his mouth—and dug his wallet out of his pocket. Standing, Baron removed Carlos's business card from his wallet and handed it to Joe. He then returned the wallet to his pocket, sat down, and removed the cigar from his mouth after taking a puff. "Damn, I sure as hell hope they didn't accidently give me a couple fish tamales."

"How long have you been friends with Mr. Klein?"

"We met in college. Before he took the job here, we frequently worked together. But I think Steve wanted a more stable job, something with a real salary and benefits."

Joe glanced over at Baron's house. While the Kleins had a nice home, it was nothing like this. "Looks like you did alright for yourself."

Baron smiled. "When it comes to business, I've been fortunate. But Steve came out the real winner. He had a lovely wife and two great kids. I envied him that."

"You aren't married?"

Baron let out a sigh. "I'm a widower."

"Oh, I'm sorry."

Baron shrugged. "It's been a while now. Like they say, it gets easier over time. Of course, I still miss her every day."

"I'm sorry for your loss." Joe closed his notepad.

"Thank you. I hope you find out those tamales I gave Steve didn't have any seafood. I don't think I could live with myself if I discovered I'd inadvertently gave seafood to Steve. I can't even imagine how I could tell his wife and kids."

WHEN JOE RETURNED to his vehicle twenty minutes later, he pulled out the business card Baron had given him for Carlos's landscaping service. Instead of waiting to make the call, he dialed the number on his cellphone. Less than five minutes later he had his answer. Carlos's wife never made fish tamales. Just as Baron had said, she only made chicken or pork.

Instead of putting his phone down, Joe made a second call.

"Where are you? What are you doing?" Joe asked Brian when he answered the phone.

"I'm at the station, getting ready to call it a night. Where are you?"

"I just wrapped it up with Baron Huxley."

"The tamale guy?" Brian asked.

"Yeah. What are you doing for dinner?"

"I don't know. Probably a TV dinner. Something exciting like that."

"Why don't you meet me at Pier Café. We can have dinner."

"Is this a work dinner?"

"What do you think?" Joe slipped the key in the ignition.

"SO WHAT'S THIS ALL ABOUT?" Brian asked Joe twenty minutes later. They sat together in a booth at Pier Café.

"The tamales Steve ate were pork, not fish. I spoke to the person Huxley bought them from. Some guy name Carlos, he's Huxley's gardener. Carlos's wife makes tamales, and Huxley regularly buys them from her and shares them with Steve. According to Huxley, they were pork. Carlos verified that. Said they would have to be pork or chicken; those are the only kinds his wife ever makes."

"So if there was fish in the tamales, someone had to put it in there later—intentionally."

Joe nodded. "I just wish we'd found something on the pier. According to Beverly Klein, Steve had a paper sack with him, and the tamales were wrapped in foil. But we never found the sack or the foil."

"Probably blew off the pier overnight."

"Or someone removed it later."

"So why did you want to come down here?" Brian glanced over to the waitress station. He didn't see Carla. "Did you want to talk to Carla?"

"I called after we hung up. She's not working right now. But the cook who was working that night is."

Brian frowned. "And?"

"I'm curious. Did Steve order something else to eat that night? We know he bought coffee. Did he order something else we don't know about?"

"Pier Café doesn't have shellfish on its menu," Brian reminded him.

"True. But Carla could have brought some with her," Joe suggested. "After Steve ordered his food, she slips it in. Right now, she's the only one with a motive. As far as we know, Beverly had no idea about the affair. And Carla couldn't have been happy being dumped like that."

"How did Carla even know he was coming in that night?"

"According to Beverly Klein, her husband came down every Thursday night to go fishing."

"It's a safe bet he wasn't fishing all those Thursdays he was fooling around with Carla. But I see what you mean. Carla probably figured he'd be on the pier that night."

"Obviously, if she gave him something she made at home, then the cook won't be of any help. But at least we can see if he had any take-out orders that night. Something that she could have added to."

EARL SWEENEY HAD BEEN FLIPPING burgers at Pier Café for over ten years. If it were possible to turn back the clock twenty years, his coworkers wouldn't recognize him. That Earl Sweeny had a wife, son, and a corporate job. But somewhere around his forty-first birthday something had snapped and he dropped out, leaving behind his wife, son, mortgage, and 401(k). He wasn't especially worried about the family he had left behind. His wife'd had an even better job than he'd had, and was on her way up the corporate ladder.

Now, he rented a room from an elderly woman on the south side of town. There was no way he could afford renting a house or an apartment in Frederickport, not with his wages. Below average height and slightly overweight, with thinning perpetually greasy hair, his fingernails needed a good scrubbing. He spent his money on cigarettes, cheap scotch, and used paperback books. Earl loved to read.

"How can I help you boys?" Earl asked as he took a seat next to Joe.

"We were wondering if you remember Thursday night?" Brian asked.

"You mean the night Steve fell off the pier?"

"Yes."

"Sure, what do you want to know?" Earl leaned against the table and looked from Joe to Brian.

"Do you remember Steve coming into the restaurant that night?" Joe asked.

"Sure. He came in to get some coffee. Carla waited on him." Earl lowered his voice and glanced around. "Have to admit, took a lot of nerve for him to come in here."

"Why do you say that?" Joe asked.

Earl chuckled. "I just figure, when you fool around with a waitress, you switch restaurants after you dump her. Or at least come in when she's not working."

Brian arched his brow. "You knew about Carla and Steve?"

"Sure. We never talked about it. But it was pretty obvious, the way he was always slipping his hand up her skirt when he thought no one was looking." Earl shook his head. "Would love to know what the shareholders at his bank would have thought about that."

"Did anyone else know?" Joe asked.

Earl shrugged. "The rest of the staff, we kind of joked about it. Of course, Carla denied it. But when she came in here all bitchy a while back and started trashing men, I figured her little love affair was over. And then when she screwed with his coffee that night…" Earl shook his head.

"What do you mean screwed with his coffee?" Brian asked.

"I was getting ready to go on break. It was kinda slow that night. I looked out to see if we had any new customers. I saw Steve ordering something from Carla. Figured I'd wait a minute, see what it was in case I needed to toss a burger on the grill before I grabbed a smoke. But he just ordered coffee."

"So he didn't order any food that night?" Joe asked.

Earl shook his head. "No, just coffee."

"What did you mean screwed with his coffee?" Brian asked again.

"I watched as she filled his cup; then when he wasn't looking, she grabs a pack of sugar and dumps it in his coffee."

"I don't get it? Was she not supposed to put sugar in his coffee?"

"Steve drinks his coffee black. He hates sugar in his coffee."

Joe glanced at Brian and shrugged.

"Carla's not a bad gal. But she shouldn't have been getting in his things when he went to the bathroom."

"What do you mean?" Brian asked.

"After she gave him the coffee, I went outside to have my smoke. I looked in, and Steve was headed to the bathroom. He'd left his coffee with his fishing gear on the bench up front. While he was in the bathroom, I saw Carla rushing up to the front while looking back to the bathroom, like she didn't want to get caught. She was carrying something, but I couldn't tell what it was. She started going through his things. Looked like she took something, but I couldn't tell what. If it had been any other customer, I would have jumped all over her, but I figured whatever was going on between the two of them was their business."

TWENTY

"Where's Lily off to?" Walt asked Danielle when he appeared in the dining room on Thursday morning. Danielle sat alone at the table, reading the morning paper and drinking a cup of coffee.

Looking up from the newspaper, Danielle smiled. "Morning, Walt. She's off to Portland with Ian and Chris, did you forget?"

"Is that today?" Walt took a seat at the table next to Danielle and focused his attention briefly on the newspaper. Seemingly moving on its own volition, the front page slipped from the paper lying before Danielle and slid over to Walt. He picked it up.

"Hey! Paper thief!" She didn't attempt to snatch it back. Instead, she picked up the remaining pages and skimmed the headlines.

His gaze focused on the front-page article. "I forget, why are they going to Portland today?"

Danielle turned the page she was reading. "They're going to see Kelly, and Chris is taking his new car back to the dealer for them to fix something. He's driving, and they're picking him up while the dealer has his car. So he'll hang around with Lily, Ian, and Kelly today."

Lowering the front page slightly, Walt gazed over the top of the page. "Hmmm, he's going to spend the day with Ian's sister? Kelly is an attractive young woman. I always thought she would be a good match for Chris."

Her eyes still on the paper, Danielle flipped the page. "Kelly is still dating Joe. From what I hear, it's getting serious."

"Chris has more to offer," Walt said with a shrug.

"When he comes back, I'll be sure to tell him you think he's a great catch."

Walt set the paper on the table and looked over at Danielle. "Why didn't you go with them?"

"I have a lunch date with Marie. I don't dare cancel it. I know she probably has a million questions about Hillary."

"Are you going to her funeral?"

"Lily and I were discussing that. I'd really like to talk to Antoine Paul's sister. See what she can tell me about her brother. She lives in Vancouver; that's where Hillary's service is. I thought I'd go to the service and then see if I can talk to the sister."

"What do you hope to learn from her?"

"From what the chief found on Paul, he didn't have a record. Not even a parking ticket. He was a freelance writer. One reason he didn't show up on my initial Google search, he used a pen name. I don't really see how this guy, who has no record, ends up strangling some woman in an alley."

"Maybe they were lovers? Had a fight, it got out of hand?"

"No kidding, *it got out of hand*."

"And you did say they were seen leaving a restaurant together," Walt reminded her.

"Gosh, if that's true, do all married people cheat on their spouses?" Danielle shook her head.

"I never did."

Danielle lowered the paper for a moment and flashed Walt a smile. "I know Melissa was married to a very handsome and wealthy man, but he was much older than her. Maybe she wasn't happy and foolishly let herself get involved with Paul. But why did he kill her?"

"Are you sure he did?" Walt asked.

"According to the dream hop he showed Hillary, he did. And if he didn't really strangle her, then why would he show Hillary something like that?"

Walt folded the paper in front of him and pushed it aside. He studied Danielle. "I don't believe spirits are necessarily more truthful than someone from the living world. But the difference, we no longer have a reason to lie. In fact, lying can work against us if we're ready to move on and prefer an easier road ahead."

"The difference between heaven and hell?"

Walt shrugged. "I'll leave that to your imagination. It's not necessary to have all the answers at once. Sometimes that only gets in your way."

"I just hope his sister can shed some light on his behavior. On one hand, I wish his spirit would just move on and deal with whatever the universe has in store for him, but then I keep thinking of Melissa's husband and how he deserves answers."

"If his wife was having an affair, do you think he needs to know after all this time?"

Danielle set the paper on the table and looked at Walt. "Honestly, I'm torn about that. On one hand, he deserves to know what really happened to his wife, yet if she was having an affair, what is the point in finding out now? It's been over eleven years. That will only open up new wounds."

"So why get involved?" Walt asked.

"Because I don't want Antoine Paul's spirit hanging around Frederickport."

"You know, Danielle, it's entirely possible your Mr. Huxley already knows about his wife's infidelity. After all, she was seen leaving a restaurant with a man."

"True. But we're only making an assumption about the infidelity." Danielle stood up.

"Where are you going?"

"To get ready for my lunch date with Marie."

Walt glanced at the wall clock. "Isn't it a little early for that?"

"I have a few errands to run first."

"Have a nice visit with little Marie." Walt glanced over to the papers Danielle had been reading. They drifted up, hovering for a moment over the table before floating into Walt's hands.

When Danielle reached the doorway, she paused a moment and looked back at Walt. "The heater guys are supposed to be here this afternoon. I told them I'd leave a key under the kitchen mat for them."

Glancing over at Danielle, he asked, "Do you think that's a good idea, letting them come into the house when you're not here?"

"Nahh. I have a watch ghost."

With his eyes back on the paper, he shook his head and called out, "It's watch spirit, not ghost!"

DANIELLE WAS JUST BACKING out of her driveway when her phone rang. It was Chris. She stopped the car and took the call.

"Danielle, I have a huge favor to ask you."

"What do you need?"

"There are some papers I was supposed to drop by at Adam's office today. I totally forgot about them."

"You want me to take them to him?" Danielle asked as she sat in her car at the edge of the driveway, the engine still running.

"I'll owe you big time."

"You certainly will," she said with a laugh. "Where are they?"

"They're sitting on my kitchen counter. You still have my house key, don't you?"

"Of course, I keep it on my key ring so I can snoop through your house when you go out of town."

"If that's true, I'll try to remember to leave something interesting for you to find."

Danielle laughed. "Thanks. Glad you called now, I was just leaving the house. You want me to drop them off at his office right now?"

"You're going to Marie's for lunch, aren't you?"

"Yeah."

"Adam said something about having a morning meeting, so I don't think he'll be there right now, and I really don't want the file to be sitting around his office. If you could drop it off after you leave Marie's, that would be great."

After picking up the folder at Chris's house, Danielle turned her car around and headed to town. She spied the pier ahead. On impulse, she pulled into the pier parking lot and parked her car. She hadn't been down here since Monday, and then, she had only gone into the café and hadn't really looked around on the pier. She couldn't help but wonder if Steve's spirit had returned.

The moment she saw them, Danielle was tempted to turn around and go back to her car. Curiosity had nudged her to look for Steve, but she certainly never imagined she would find both Steve and Hillary sitting side by side together along the stretch of pier he had fallen from. Someone had removed the broken railing, and it had not yet been replaced. Instead, a warning sign had been attached, noting the lack of railing.

With their legs dangling off the side of the pier, Hillary and Steve reminded Danielle a bit of Tom Sawyer and Becky Thatcher, or at least what the pair might have looked like in their twilight years. Danielle assumed Steve was wearing what he had worn the night he'd fallen off the pier, faded jeans and a blue work shirt, its sleeves pushed toward his elbows. Hillary, who had obviously mastered the spirit outfit change—also wore faded blue jeans, yet her cotton blouse was red and white gingham, and she sported a straw hat.

Contemplating her next plan of action, Danielle debated returning to the car or talking to Steve and Hillary. After a moment, she took her cellphone out of her pocket and walked to the two ghosts.

With her cellphone now to her ear, Danielle glanced around. Hillary and Steve sat chatting amongst themselves, their backs to Danielle, unaware of her presence.

"Hello, Hillary, Steve."

Both ghosts turned abruptly and faced Danielle.

"Hello, Danielle. Who are you talking to on the phone?" Hillary asked.

"She can see us?" Steve asked.

Hillary nodded. "I told you. You didn't believe me."

"I'm pretending to be on the phone," Danielle explained as she glanced around. On the other side of the pier, a fisherman cast his line out, his back to her.

"Makes sense." Hillary nodded to the empty place next to her. "Care to join us?"

"Umm, thanks. But I don't think I want to risk falling off the pier. And according to that sign, they don't want me to sit there."

"Yeah, well, that first step is a bitch," Steve said with a laugh. "I suppose one good thing about being dead is you don't have to follow signs anymore."

"So you understand you're dead?"

Steve looked up to Danielle; by his expression, he obviously thought her question was stupid.

Danielle shrugged. "Many spirits don't right away."

Steve looked back to sea. "To be honest, I didn't right away.

After I ran into Hillary the first time, I came back here to get my stuff. Tried like hell to get my things, but my fishing pole kept falling out of my hand. I couldn't hold onto anything."

Hillary looked up to Danielle. "After I left you, I came back down here to find Steve. I figured he needed to know the truth."

"So now that you know, why haven't you two moved on?"

"We have to go to our funerals," Steve said. "I'd like to see everyone one more time. My kids, and of course Beverly. She's going to have a lot on her plate now. Poor thing."

"You're going to your funeral too?" Danielle looked at Hillary.

"Yes, are you going?" Hillary smiled cheerfully.

"Umm…yeah, I was planning on it."

"Good. I'll drive with you."

"Umm…you know, that really isn't necessary. I mean…I think you can just get there on your own."

"You expect me to walk all the way to Vancouver?"

"No, of course not. But, Hillary, you're a spirit. It's like being your own airline."

"I'd rather drive with you…unless it's too much trouble."

Danielle let out a sigh. "Fine. You can drive with us. Are you moving on after the funeral?"

Hillary shook her head. "I told you. I don't want to see my husbands. Who needs that kind of drama in their life…err…I mean death?"

Still holding the phone next to her ear, Danielle glanced around. "By any chance have you seen Antoine Paul?"

"Yes, but we haven't talked to him. Grouchy spirit, if you ask me." Hillary shook her head.

"He is definitely a strange guy," Steve said.

Danielle frowned. "What do you mean?"

"After I left Hillary that first time—after falling off the pier—I ran into the guy when I was walking back here to get my stuff. Of course I couldn't, I was dead."

"What did he say that made you think he was strange?"

"He said karma was a bitch. Whatever that was supposed to mean."

"That is an odd statement," Danielle said with a frown and then asked, "Steve, are you moving on after your funeral?"

"I suppose so. Nothing really to keep me here." He glanced at Hillary, who sat to his right. "No offense."

Hillary looked down at her bare feet and wiggled her toes. "None taken."

"Umm, maybe I shouldn't bring this up…but, Steve…the police are looking into your death…they suspect there may be foul play."

Steve frowned. He glanced up to Danielle. "What are you talking about? I fell off the pier. Serves me right for being careless."

"From how the chief was talking, they must have found something in your autopsy. He didn't say what exactly, but he did say your allergic reaction wasn't caused by you carelessly transferring shellfish from the pier to your food."

"Why else would I have had the allergic reaction?"

"Hmmm…autopsy, you say?" Hillary glanced from Danielle to Steve. "I believe they check the stomach contents when they do one of those. My guess, the autopsy found seafood in your stomach. Someone must have put fish in your food. Any idea who would want you dead?"

TWENTY-ONE

Bright yellow paint had recently been brushed over the clapboard siding of Marie's bungalow and fresh white paint over its trim. It was the same color the house had been before the painters had arrived on Monday. Yet now it was clean and fresh, a fitting setting for Marie's flowers, which were already starting to bloom.

It was still too chilly to have their lunch outside, so Marie had set a table in her sitting room. She used her mother's Rosenthal Bavarian china luncheon plates. Trimmed in gold—purple pansies, gold and purple roses and other fanciful blossoms and foliage adorned the edges of the octagonal plates. Crystal goblets were already filled with iced tea, each garnished with lemon slices, while the luncheon plates waited for slices of warm quiche, and tiny bowls —from the same set of Bavarian china—sat at the head of each setting, each filled with fresh cut fruit.

"This looks beautiful," Danielle said as she took a seat at the small table. The first thing she noticed was the colorful bouquet of flowers tucked in a sterling silver pitcher at the center of the table. Gently removing the cloth napkin from its place under the fork on the left side of her octagonal luncheon plate, she placed it on her lap as she watched Marie dish up a slice of quiche and set it on her plate.

"It's spinach and ham," Marie explained.

"Oh my, you made quiche?"

Marie chuckled and scooped up a slice for herself. "I warmed it up. Adam picked it up for me this morning from Old Salts Bakery."

"Yum. I've never had their quiche before. But if it's anything like their cinnamon rolls…"

Marie set the plate with the remaining quiche on a hot pad she had already placed on the table and then took her seat across from Danielle.

"It's the only way to bake," Marie said as she picked up her tea. "Order from Old Salts!"

Danielle smiled and then took a bite.

"I still can't believe about Steve Klein." Marie shook her head and took a sip of tea. "And Hillary Hemingway too? The same night!"

"A week ago today, assuming Hillary passed away on Thursday night and not early Friday morning," Danielle said, taking another bite. "This is really delicious."

Marie nodded to the plate of extra quiche. "There's plenty more."

"Thanks. Your house looks great, by the way. Adam mentioned you were having it painted."

"I'm just glad it's done. I was a little concerned about the rain, but it all worked out. So you don't have any guests staying with you right now?"

"No. We've been having some issues with the furnace. We decided to have it replaced after Hillary left. She was supposed to check out on Friday morning—the morning we found her."

"The poor dear definitely checked out."

Danielle cringed and speared another bite of quiche with her fork. "It was a shock, that's for sure. But she went peacefully. I suppose that's what we all want."

Marie looked over at Danielle and smiled. "Perhaps, when you get to be my age. But when a body is your age, it's best to hold on tight and refuse to go out without kicking up a ruckus."

"Adam tells me your birthday is coming up."

Marie shook her head. "Please, I'm too old to keep counting birthdays. But I suppose I should be grateful. Poor Steve Klein. I think he was in his early fifties. Too young."

"I feel sorry for his wife, kids."

Marie shrugged. "It's sad to lose a parent, but I don't think those two were very close with their dad. I heard Steve cut off Steven Junior, that's why the boy joined the military. Of course, can't really blame the kids, parents spoiled them shamefully. Can't let your kids run wild and expect them to grow up into responsible adults."

"Funny, for some reason I thought they had small children. I guess because Steve's wife looks so young."

"Well, she is a good ten years younger than her husband."

"I've seen her a couple times since the accident. I feel so sorry for her. She seems devastated."

Marie let out a snort. "Beverly will do okay for herself. She's young, attractive, and I imagine Steve's insurance will set her up for life."

Danielle picked up her goblet of tea. "Yeah, but still, losing her husband like that, so sudden."

"You mean losing a husband who can't keep his zipper pulled up?" Marie shook her head. "Never understood how a woman puts up with that."

Setting her glass on the table, Danielle looked over at Marie. "Steve fooled around?"

Marie let out a chuckle. "Wasn't exactly a secret. At least not in some circles."

Danielle cocked her head slightly and studied Marie. "What circles are that exactly?"

Taking a bite of quiche, Marie chewed slowly and considered how to answer the question. After washing down the bite with a sip of tea, she said, "When they first organized the historical society, I naturally joined. Steve was one of the people instrumental in getting it going. There were a lot of meetings back then; Beverly wasn't particularly interested in the project. One of the early members—can't recall her name—she has since moved from town—but let's just say she and Steve had more than a few private meetings supposedly to work on the museum project."

"He was fooling around with another member from the historical society?"

"Oh yes." Marie nodded. "Everyone knew, but just ignored it. I think Millie Samson was relieved when the woman and her husband moved from town."

"He was fooling around with a married woman?" Danielle gasped.

"Why not? He was married."

Danielle speared a chunk of melon, looked over at Marie, and shook her head. "So you think Beverly knew?"

"Honestly, I always figured she had to have. But I suppose it's possible she didn't."

"So you think he fooled around after that?" Danielle knew he had, but she asked the question anyway.

"I'm sure it wasn't his only affair. I've heard rumors over the years."

"Hmm…" Danielle looked down at her plate and silently ate her quiche. *I suppose that's why Jolene so easily figured out Steve and Carla were having an affair. He was a serial cheater.*

"So tell me about Hillary," Marie asked.

Danielle then went on to tell Marie about how they had found Hillary on Friday morning and how she had cleaned out her room, leaving out the details involving Hillary's lingering spirit.

"You didn't even peek at her new book?"

Danielle looked up from her plate to Marie and smiled. "No. I just wanted to get the stuff sent off. And frankly, I've never read any of her books. Please don't tell her."

Marie chuckled. "Dear, I don't think you're going to have to worry about her finding out now."

You'd be surprised.

ADAM NICHOLS SAT ALONE in his office, feet propped up on his desktop, eating a meatball sandwich. He had muted the speakers on his computer; he didn't need them for what he was watching—and he certainly didn't want Leslie to walk by and overhear the heavy breathing and foul language from the nude actresses featured in the soft porn film he was currently watching on his computer.

A knock on the open office door caught his attention and he looked up, startled. It was Baron Huxley, a previous client. He stood in the hallway just outside Adam's office door.

Adam hurriedly fumbled to turn off his monitor before Huxley caught a glimpse of what he was watching. A meatball fell from his sandwich and landed in the middle of his chest. It rolled down his powder blue golf shirt, leaving a trail of tomato sauce from his chest to his crotch.

Standing up abruptly, his feet landing on the floor at the same time as the meatball, he grabbed a napkin and glanced at his now black monitor.

"I'm sorry, Adam. I didn't mean to startle you." Huxley entered the office, his eyes on the trail of sauce staining the once spotless shirt. "There wasn't anyone out front; I thought it would be okay if I just came in."

"No, that's fine." Adam glanced at the wall clock. Leslie wouldn't be leaving for lunch for another fifteen minutes. He guessed she was probably in the bathroom. Using the napkin to wipe off the sauce, he took a step and his shoe promptly landed on the meatball, smashing it into the carpet. Looking down, he lifted his foot up and glanced at the bottom of his shoe now coated with smashed red meat.

"I really am sorry," Huxley said as he looked from Adam's shirt to the meatball divided between the floor and Adam's shoe.

Adam shook his head and laughed. "No problem. Have a seat and tell me what I can do for you. Hope you don't mind if I don't shake your hand."

Baron chuckled and sat down. "Not at all."

Removing his right shoe, Adam sat back down on his chair. Reaching over to the trash can, he scraped off the shoe on the can's edge and then used another napkin to wipe off the shoe's sole.

"Can I buy you another sandwich?" Baron offered.

"Nahh, it's what I get for not paying attention." Giving his shirt another swipe with a napkin, he then picked up meatball remnants from the floor and tossed the napkin into the trash can. Sitting back in his chair, he asked, "What can I do for you?"

"I wanted to talk to you about selling my house here."

"Seriously? I thought you loved that house. I mean, hey, I'm more than happy to list it for you. I'm just surprised."

Baron let out a sigh. "I have a lot of things going on right now. I don't have the time to use it, and I don't want it to just sit."

"Have you considered putting it into my rental program? I wouldn't have a problem keeping that house rented, and I could get you a great price."

Baron shook his head. "No, I'd rather just sell it. And I'd like a quick sale."

"Quick? It's a great property, and I know I can find a buyer for it. But I can't really guarantee quick. A house in that price range takes a little longer."

"How about if we underprice it?"

"Underprice?"

"As you know, there isn't a loan on the property, I own it outright. So I can afford to price it a little lower than what it's worth."

"Exactly how far under value do you want to go?" Adam asked.

"Fifty thousand."

TWENTY-TWO

Danielle arrived at Adam's office a few minutes after his assistant, Leslie, left for lunch. None of the other property managers were in the front office, so she assumed they were all on lunch break. Adam's car was parked outside and the front door was open, so she entered and headed down the hall to Adam's office.

Standing outside his open doorway, she started to knock when she realized he wasn't alone. Hesitating a moment, she considered going back to her car and calling him on her cellphone, letting him know she had Chris's papers, when he noticed her and motioned for her to come in.

"Hey, Danielle. Did you bring Chris's papers?" Adam asked as she stepped into his office.

Waving the folder in her right hand, she told him yes, and then she glanced over to the other man. From the hallway, his back had been to her. But when he turned, she recognized him immediately; it was Baron Huxley.

Adam took the file from her. "Danielle, I'd like you to meet Baron Huxley. Baron, this is Danielle Boatman. She's the owner of Marlow House."

"I believe we've already met," Baron said graciously, accepting Danielle's hand for a brief shake.

"Nice to see you again, Mr. Huxley," she said politely.

"Please, call me Baron. May I call you Danielle?"

Danielle grinned. "Certainly."

Adam frowned. "When did you two meet?"

Danielle swung around and faced Adam. "Wouldn't you like to know—" She paused a moment, taking in the bold red trail of sauce streaking down his shirt. "What happened to you?"

"He got in a fight with a meatball, and lost," Baron said with a chuckle.

"The polite thing to do would be to ignore the stain," Adam said with faux primness.

"Kinda hard to ignore that thing," Danielle teased.

"Did I hear that right, are you the one who owns Marlow House? I think I remember Beverly mentioning that," Baron said.

"Guilty." Danielle smiled.

"You still haven't told me, when did you two meet?" Adam asked.

"When Lily and I stopped by Beverly's to give our condolences and take her a casserole, Mr. Hux—I mean Baron was there."

"Steve's the one who introduced me to Baron," Adam explained.

"Adam here sold me my Frederickport home."

"Ahh, so you're one of Adam's clients. He'll be nice to you. He's mean to me," Danielle teased.

Adam rolled his eyes. "Danielle here is a close friend of my grandmother's."

"Who I happened to have had lunch with a little while ago. Thanks for picking up the quiche, by the way, it was delicious."

"Danielle, I've always been fascinated with Marlow House. Would you mind if I stop by sometime and get a tour? I understand you turned it into a bed and breakfast."

"Yes, I did, and you're more than welcome to stop by. At the moment, they're putting in a new furnace, so you might want to wait until everything is put back together. But you're more than welcome to stop by." Danielle glanced at the clock. "Well, I should let you two get back to your business. I have a few more errands to run. It was nice seeing you again, Baron."

"SO THAT'S the one who inherited Marlow House?" Baron said after Danielle had left the office. No longer standing, he sat on a chair facing Adam, one leg casually propped over the opposing knee.

"And all that money." Adam let out a low whistle as he took a seat behind his desk.

Baron arched his brow, waving his right hand slightly. "So…are you two?"

Adam frowned. "What, me and Danielle?" Adam laughed.

"What's so funny? She's a very attractive young woman."

"No argument there. But like I said, she's close to my grandmother. Grandma considers Danielle a surrogate granddaughter."

"Ahhh…so hands off?"

Adam laughed again. "Just the opposite. If Grandma had even an inkling there was something between Danielle and me, she'd start planning the wedding."

Baron laughed.

"When I first met Danielle, we…ah…didn't quite hit it off. But for some reason, Grandma had it in her head Danielle had some sort of crush on me. Truth was, Danielle wanted to crush me alright, with a heavy object."

"Seems like you two are friends now."

"Yeah, I like Danielle. She's alright." Adam glanced down at his shirt and absently rubbed his tomato stain.

"From what I read, she found the Missing Thorndike?"

"Found it and got to keep it."

"Yeah, I remember Steve telling me how she brought it over to the bank right after she found it and put it in a safety deposit box. That thing must be worth a fortune. Does she plan to sell it? Or has she already?"

"I know she planned to sell at one time. But then she inherited all that money from her cousin, so it really wasn't necessary."

"Ahh, you mean for the taxes?"

Adam nodded. "Right. The taxes were going to kill her, and when she first found it, all she thought she had inherited was Marlow House and a little cash. Not enough to pay the inheritance tax without selling something."

"What did you mean, she thought she had *just* inherited Marlow House?"

"You didn't read about it in the paper?"

Baron shrugged. "I must have missed that."

"Apparently her great-aunt intended to leave the bulk of her estate to Danielle, which was considerable. But Clarence Renton, her aunt's lawyer, diverted the funds before the aunt died, leading Danielle and the courts to believe the estate was much smaller."

"And the aunt didn't realize what he'd done?"

Adam shook his head. "By then she had Alzheimer's."

"Renton…" Baron pondered the name for a moment. "I think I had a couple dealings with him. I do remember now hearing about how he was arrested for embezzling from his clients. He was killed a while back in prison, wasn't he?"

Adam nodded. "At first they said it was a suicide, then it came back he was murdered. Prisons can be a tough place."

"No kidding. One place I intend to avoid."

"Not sure how well Danielle did regarding her aunt's estate, but I understand she ended up with more than she first thought. And then she inherited her cousin's estate, worth millions. That might still be going through probate, I'm not sure."

"My…" Baron arched his brows. "She certainly doesn't act like someone who has that much money."

"Oh, then I forgot, there are those gold coins! Those are worth a couple million." Adam laughed and shook his head.

"Gold coins? Sounds interesting."

"This just happened about a month ago. Walt Marlow's business partner stashed some gold coins in the house across from Marlow House—which happens to be owned by my grandmother. We found them, along with a will that left them to Walt Marlow."

"Walt Marlow, the one who built Marlow House?"

"No. That was Frederick Marlow, Walt Marlow's grandfather."

"Ahh, the one the town's named after."

"Exactly. Walt Marlow left his estate to his housekeeper, who was the mother to Danielle's great-aunt."

Baron laughed. "Are you telling me that little gal that just left here also inherited the gold coins?"

Adam let out a dramatic sigh. "Much to my pain and sorrow. That's still being handled in the court, but no one's contesting, so I'm sure Danielle will get them."

"Hmmm…she sounds like a lucky little lady. I'm surprised you don't have your sights on her. Hell, if I was you, I'd let my grandmother start planning the wedding."

Adam laughed. "Even if I agreed, I seriously doubt Danielle would go along with it."

"So she has a boyfriend?"

"Not sure if I would call him a boyfriend exactly." Adam paused a moment and then said, "I want you to know, I'd never talk about a friend's—or client's—personal business. But this is public knowledge. Hell, everyone in town knows. For a while, it's all anyone would talk about. Surprised you didn't know."

Baron shrugged. "I'd heard a little bit about it—her inheriting the house, turning it into a B and B, finding the Missing Thorndike. I'd also heard about Renton, but I didn't realize he was connected to Marlow House. But I only come on weekends, and lately I haven't come that often. Which is why I need to sell."

Adam sat up in the chair and snatched his pen off the desktop. "If you want to get this rolling, we could sign the papers now. Faster we get it on the market, the faster we'll get it sold."

"That's probably a good idea."

ADAM WAS ALONE in his office, reviewing the listing contract Baron had signed thirty minutes earlier, when Bill Jones walked into his office, clipboard in hand. Without waiting for an invitation, the handyman made himself comfortable on the chair facing Adam. Tossing the clipboard on the desk, he pulled an open pack of cigarettes from the pocket of his work shirt.

Glancing up from the listing contract, Adam eyed Bill as he tugged a cigarette from the pack. "Don't even think of lighting that in here."

Letting out a sigh, Bill shoved the pack back into his pocket, yet continued to hold the unlit cigarette, fiddling with it in his hand. "It's for later."

"Yeah, sure it is." Tossing the contract on the desk, he picked up the clipboard and skimmed over it.

"What's that? You sell something?" Bill nodded to the contract.

"Not yet. It's a listing for the Huxley house."

Bill frowned. "Huxley?"

"It's down the street from the Gusarov Estate. I sold the guy the house about a year ago. I think you did some work for him."

"That guy who was into kickboxing?"

Adam paused a moment and then said, "That's right, I forgot about that."

Bill let out a low whistle. "No kidding? He's selling that place? That's going to be one fine commission. I think you need to start paying me more."

Adam rolled his eyes. "Yeah, right."

"So what's he asking?"

When Adam told him the price, Bill frowned. "I thought the houses went for a lot more over there."

"Yep. But he wants to move it fast."

"With that price, I imagine he will. Still a good commission for you—and fast. Does he owe much on it?"

Adam shook his head. "No. He paid cash, never took out a loan. In fact, I suggested he might want to carry paper. But he wasn't interested. He also doesn't want a long escrow."

"Sounds to me like he needs the money—and fast."

Tossing the clipboard back on the desk, Adam picked up the listing contract again. Flipping through it, he said, "I have to agree with you. I wonder why."

TWENTY-THREE

Joe and the police chief stood in the office next to the interrogation room, looking through the two-way mirror. Carla sat alone on the other side of the window, sitting at the table, waiting for Brian. She had abandoned her rainbow look and had recently dyed her hair dark burgundy. With her purse sitting on the table in front of her, she fidgeted nervously with a lock of hair while continually glancing to the door, waiting for someone to come in.

When Brian entered the interrogation room a few minutes later, Carla nervously removed her purse from the table and set it on the floor by her feet. Sitting up straight, she folded her hands on the table and watched as Brian silently took a seat across from her, a notepad and pen in his hands.

"Thanks for coming in this afternoon, Carla."

Carla nodded. "Sure."

"I need you to think back to Thursday night, when Steve came in to Pier Café to order coffee. I'd like you to go back and tell me exactly what happened from the first time you saw him that night to the last time."

Shifting nervously in the chair, Carla shrugged. "Not much to tell. He just came in and ordered coffee, then left."

"Did you talk at all?"

Carla shifted in her chair again and then leaned forward, propping her elbows on the tabletop. She shook her head. "Not really. In fact, it sort of pissed me off. Which kind of makes me feel crappy now. I mean, Steve is dead, and I was pretty snotty to him that night. But in all fairness, he acted like he barely knew me. Like I was just a nobody."

"So you didn't have any type of conversation? You didn't talk about the weather, what he was doing down there, anything?"

Carla shook her head. "No, he just came in, said, '*I'd like a large decaf coffee to go.*' That was it. No *please* or *how are you tonight, Carla.* Nothing. He didn't even thank me when I gave him the coffee. But I guess that sounds kinda petty now, considering everything."

"Then what did he do?"

"He took the coffee and left. I didn't see him again."

"He just left? Right after you gave him the coffee? When you say he left, did he go out to the pier to go fishing, or did he use the restroom first?"

Biting her lower lip nervously, she squirmed in the chair. "Umm…I guess he used the bathroom first."

"Where was his fishing equipment? I know he had a chair with him, tackle box, fishing pole. Did he leave that outside?"

Carla shook her head. "Umm…no. He left all his stuff on the bench right inside the door."

"Did he leave his stuff there while he went to the restroom?"

"Umm…yeah…I guess."

"Did anyone touch his fishing equipment when he was in the bathroom? Maybe look through it? Take anything? Did you?"

Carla stared blankly at Brian, her eyes wide. Finally, she let out a groan and threw her head down on the table, pillowing her face in her arms.

"What happened, Carla? What did you do?"

Carla lifted her head slightly and peeked up at Brian. "Someone saw me, didn't they?" She groaned again and re-pillowed her face as she rocked her head from side to side, moaning, "I am such an idiot!"

"Tell me what happened, Carla."

After a moment, she lifted her head up and sat up straight in the chair, her hands once again folded in front of her on the table.

"Steve just really pissed me off when he came in. He didn't even say hello."

"Did you still love him?"

Carla frowned. "No!" She let out a sigh. "To be honest, I never did. I know that sounds horrible. But it's true."

"What happened that night?"

"Steve hates sugar in his coffee."

Brian arched his brow. "And?"

"I put sugar in his coffee." She shrugged. "I figured if he was going to act like nothing ever went on between us, then screw him. So I put sugar in his coffee."

"That was it?"

"Not exactly." Carla slumped down in her chair. "When he went to the bathroom, I started to regret putting sugar in his cup. I figured that was kind of a lame thing to do, and I didn't want him to think I cared that much. You know, like I was broken-hearted or something and lashing out. So when he went to the bathroom, I poured another cup and switched it with the one I put sugar in."

"You took the coffee? You didn't open his tackle box, take anything else?"

Carla frowned. "Just the coffee. I told you that."

AFTER CARLA LEFT the police station, Brian met with Joe and the chief in the break room.

"I think she was telling the truth," Brian said when he sat down at the table with them.

"Aside from what Earl saw and Carla admitted, no one has put those two together that night. It probably was just about the coffee," the chief agreed.

Brian looked from Joe to the chief. "The problem with Carla being the killer, what did she have to gain? It's not like Steve's the first guy to dump her or that she was madly in love. Women who're vengeful toward their ex-lovers usually have a pattern of past behavior. I've never heard any talk about Carla being a stalker type. A bit of a gossip maybe, but not vengeful."

MacDonald leaned forward and absently tapped his fingertips on the table. "The coroner insists there was no way Steve accidently consumed that amount of crabmeat. I don't believe he intentionally ate it, so that leaves us with someone playing with his food. As far as we know, the only thing he ate that night was two tamales. There's no way Carla had time to put crabmeat in his food while Steve was in the bathroom. She would have had to have unwrapped them, inserted the crabmeat without him noticing, and rewrapped them. No, the only way she could have poisoned him with tamales would have been by replacing them."

"Unfortunately, we didn't find the paper sack Beverly told us Steve took with him, or the aluminum foil the tamales were wrapped in. That might have given us some clue," Joe noted.

"They obviously blew off the pier," Brian said.

"Or someone removed them," the chief suggested.

"It's possible Carla took the EpiPen, but how did she know he was going to eat shellfish?" Brian asked.

"If the killer put the crab in the tamales and removed the EpiPen from his tackle box, then Beverly is looking like our prime suspect," Joe said.

"She had motive and opportunity," the chief said. "Not just the affair, assuming she knows about it, but I imagine Steve had a large insurance policy. I'd be surprised if he didn't."

"How about the guy who gave Steve the tamales? What do we really know about him?" Brian asked.

"What's his motive? He and Steve go way back. He mentioned he'd been fishing with Steve before, so he'd probably know Steve kept an EpiPen in his tackle box. I imagine removing an EpiPen from the box would be easier than shoving crabmeat in a couple of tamales so someone wouldn't notice," Joe said.

The chief let out a sigh. "Carla isn't totally off the hook. It's remotely possible she switched his tamales with fish tamales and took the EpiPen. But then we'd have to figure out how she knew he'd have tamales."

Brian stood up and glanced at the clock. "I think we need to call it a night. As for motives, I vote for the widow."

"I GUESS we won't be going to Hillary's memorial service," Danielle told Ian and Lily when she walked into her library on Thursday evening. They had returned from Portland thirty minutes earlier. Sadie, who had been napping at Ian's and Lily's feet, lifted her head and looked at Danielle, her tail now wagging.

A moment later Walt appeared in the room, sitting in a chair directly across from the sofa. Seeing Walt, Sadie started to stand, but when Marlow House's resident ghost pressed his finger against his lips, telling her not to bark, she stilled. The golden retriever stared at him a moment and then dropped her chin back on her front paws and closed her eyes.

Lily reached down and patted Sadie and then asked Danielle, "What do you mean?"

"I just got off the phone with Melony." Danielle took a seat in the empty chair next to Walt and flashed him a quick smile.

Lily glanced at the clock. "Isn't it kind of late in New York right now?"

Danielle shrugged. "I think it's about three hours ahead of us. Anyway, they've decided to have the memorial service a week from tomorrow, in New York."

"Why New York? She lived in Vancouver, Washington." Lily glanced to Ian. "Do you know if she was from New York?"

Ian shook his head. "I don't think so. But I could be wrong."

"I guess she didn't have any family in Vancouver. Her estate was left to some niece she has in Rhode Island. Her publisher and agent are in New York. They want to have it there. I got the feeling it has more to do with promoting her last book. From what Melony told me, the publisher is paying for the memorial service, and it sounds more like a prerelease party." Danielle looked at Ian. "Do they call it a prerelease party?"

Ian shrugged. "Close enough."

"What about Hillary's friends in Vancouver?" Lily asked.

"I imagine the publisher figures her friends will be buying the book anyway, so they probably don't care."

"I suppose we could fly to New York." Lily grinned over at Ian. "I've always wanted to go. And for once in my life, I can actually afford to buy the ticket."

"This late, it would cost a fortune," Ian told her.

"So? I can afford it. I'll even buy yours. The only thing I've spent money on since my settlement is paying off the medical bills and a new car." Lily grinned.

"I wouldn't rush out and buy any plane tickets right now, big spender," Danielle told Lily. "A week from Friday is also the date of Steve's funeral. I got off the phone with the chief right before Melony called. They're releasing his body tomorrow, and Beverly has already called the funeral home and set the time."

"Why is she waiting so long?" Ian asked. "I understand Hillary's situation. After all, sounds like they're trying to make her service into a promotional event."

"Has something to do with Steve's family. If they have it earlier, it'll be difficult for his sisters to get here. While I wouldn't mind going to New York—and we don't have any guests scheduled, so we actually could go—I think if we have to choose between attending Hillary's or Steve's service, we need to go to Steve's."

Lily let out a sigh and leaned back, propping her bare feet on the coffee table. "You're right. A funeral isn't for the person who died, it's for those they left behind. We wouldn't know anyone at Hillary's service. It won't matter if we go or not."

"Yeah. I wouldn't feel right not going to Steve's. I consider Beverly a friend. And Steve and I did work together at the museum." Danielle glanced from Lily to Ian. "There's also something else."

"What?" Lily asked.

"Even though they're releasing his body, his death is still under investigation."

"Are you saying they suspect foul play?" Ian asked.

Walt looked at Danielle and frowned. "According to Hillary, Steve fell off the pier on his own. No one pushed him. That's what he said himself."

Glancing briefly to Walt, Danielle looked back to Ian and Lily. "I guess it'll be in the paper tomorrow. They're releasing the coroner's report. According to the coroner, Steve's body had all the signs of going into anaphylactic shock prior to hitting the water. Crabmeat was found in Steve's stomach. He was allergic to shellfish, and they don't believe he would have intentionally eaten it. Which means someone slipped it in his food."

"Steve was murdered?" Ian asked.

TWENTY-FOUR

Taking her time, Joanne Johnson reverently moved the damp dust rag over the mahogany frame surrounding Walt Marlow's massive portrait, paying special attention to the intricate carving along the frame's edge. When she reached the top portion, she stood on her tiptoes. After she finished the frame, she shoved the rag in her apron's pocket and pulled out the feather duster, the handle of which she had tucked under her apron's belt. Using the feather duster, she gently swiped the surface of Walt's portrait and then Angela's.

After completing the task, she stepped back a moment and studied the paintings—focusing her attention primarily on Walt's, not Angela's. Joanne smiled.

Thinking back on her history with Marlow House, Joanne imagined she must have been about Walt Marlow's age—at the time of his murder—when she first came to work for Danielle's aunt. That had been almost twenty-six years ago.

When she first had accepted the job, she assumed it would be a little eerie, taking care of a house that had been empty for decades. She had always known Walt Marlow had died in the attic, but back then, she heard it was a suicide, and now she understood he had really been murdered. As it turned out, there was nothing spooky about tending Marlow House.

She had always thought Walt Marlow was an exceptionally

handsome man, and she wondered if his eyes were as blue as the artist portrayed them. In the days before Danielle Boatman's arrival —when she believed his death had been a suicide—Joanne had often stood in front of the portrait and wondered what demons had driven such a beautifully handsome man to end his own life.

Now, when she looked at his portrait, she thought it so tragic his wife's greed had ended his life. Shifting her gaze over to Angela's portrait, she frowned. If Joanne had her way, she would burn Angela's painting. It didn't deserve to be displayed next to the man she had plotted to kill. While it was all just speculation—no one could prove Angela had really conspired with her brother to murder her husband or that Angela's twin brother had been the one to place a noose around the unconscious Walt Marlow's neck, and some in the historical society still clung to the old story that Marlow had ended his own life—Joanne preferred to believe it was murder.

"Here you are," Danielle said as she walked into the library and found Joanne standing before the two life-size portraits.

"I was just finishing up," Joanne said as she tucked the handle of the feather duster back under her apron's belt.

"Everything looks spotless." Danielle smiled.

"I thought they were supposed to be here today to work on the furnace?"

"They called me this morning, something about a part on back order."

"I suppose you were wise to wait until the work's completed before you start taking guests."

Danielle handed Joanne a sealed envelope. "I wanted to give you this."

Without comment, Joanne accepted the envelope and opened it. Inside was a check. She looked from the check to Danielle and frowned. "I thought you wanted me to come in just on Fridays until you start taking guests again in May?"

"Consider it a paid vacation." Danielle smiled.

Shaking her head, Joanne tried to hand the check back, but Danielle wouldn't accept it.

"I want you to take it. It's not your fault the furnace went down and we had to close up until we get a new one installed." Danielle glanced around. "And if this house wasn't so old, installing a new heater and air conditioner wouldn't be such a production."

"Air conditioner? I didn't know you were putting in an air conditioner too."

Danielle shrugged. "I know it's something we won't use very often, but I figure this is the time to do it since we have to install a new furnace. And hey, with global warming, we might start experiencing warmer summers. Might as well be prepared."

Joanne looked at the check. "This is generous of you, but you don't need to do this."

Danielle shook her head. "No. I really appreciate all you do around here. I can't expect you to take a cut in pay just because we're closed down a while."

Joanne tucked the check in her apron pocket. She smiled at Danielle. "I can come in every day, make meals for you and Lily. Do your laundry, keep things picked up."

Danielle laughed. "No. Don't be silly. You take this time and go do something fun. Lily and I will be fine."

"You really need to take lessons on how to be a wealthy woman of leisure," Walt told her after Joanne left the library.

Danielle turned around to face Walt; she hadn't realized he was in the room. Before responding, she stepped to the doorway and peeked out into the hallway. Joanne was just leaving out the front door.

Turning back to Walt, she asked, "How long were you standing there?"

"Long enough to see you give Joanne her check. That was generous of you."

Danielle took a seat at the desk. "I think you only get points for generosity if you can't afford to give and still do."

"Are you saying that because it's no real sacrifice for you—you'll never notice the money you just gave Joanne because you have so much of it—that you don't deserve praise?"

Danielle shrugged. "Pretty much."

Walt laughed and then pointed to Angela's portrait. "Danielle, if my dear wife Angela was in the same situation, she would have insisted Joanne earn every penny, even if it meant polishing already spotless silver."

Before Danielle had time to respond, the doorbell rang. Standing up, she looked at Walt and said, "I suppose I should have made Joanne stay. Must I really be forced to answer my own door? I need a butler!" Danielle let out a dramatic sigh and then headed for the door.

Chuckling, Walt followed her down the hall.

BARON HUXLEY STOOD on the front porch of Marlow House. He had noticed a car drive off just as he had pulled up in front of the house a few minutes earlier, but he didn't think Danielle Boatman was its driver. Glancing down, he brushed a minute piece of lint off his tan slacks with one hand while the other hand held a bottle of wine. While looking down, he noticed his shoes—real Italian leather. He'd had them polished just last week and he was happy to see they still looked perfect.

He had considered calling first, but he didn't want to give her an opportunity to make an excuse to postpone the visit. As it was, she had already suggested he wait until some work was completed on the house. But since he didn't see any construction workers or trucks in the area, he could easily pretend to have forgotten what she had said.

Looking at his reflection in the window, he admired the view. He might be a good twenty years older than the lovely Ms. Boatman, but he was fully aware of the fact many women her age found older men—especially one who took care of himself, as he did—desirable.

From what he'd learned about Danielle Boatman, she had lost her father a number of years ago—which likely meant she was seeking a father figure. *I'll be your daddy, poor little rich girl.*

Baron chuckled. He found himself highly amusing.

When Danielle swung the door open a moment later, Baron smiled. She was even lovelier than he remembered. He wasn't overly fond of her braid. It wasn't a normal braid. *What is it called?* He couldn't remember. But it didn't matter. He would convince her to wear it down. Baron liked women with long hair. Beverly wore her hair too short.

While his height—over six feet—made it possible for him to date taller women without feeling uncomfortable, he preferred women of Danielle's stature. His wife, Melissa, had been about Danielle's height—five feet five would be his guess.

He wouldn't call Danielle fat—but she could afford to lose some weight. He knew a diet doctor who could take care of that with a few pills. Her bust size wasn't impressive—he had a doctor for that too. From what he understood, Danielle could easily afford a nice set of double-Ds. He was confident in his ability to convince her to make those *minor* changes.

"Baron…hello," Danielle said in surprise, one hand holding onto the door's edge.

"I hope you don't mind that I just stopped by, but you promised me a tour, and I'm not sure how long I'll be in town." With a wide smile—his straight white teeth fairly sparkling—he raised the wine bottle up, offering it to her. "I thought perhaps I could bribe you."

Danielle wasn't a wine connoisseur, but she immediately recognized the red and gold label on the bottle Baron offered her. She had seen that label's distinctive chateau before. It was the same brand of wine Adam had purchased for Chris as a closing gift—and she knew it cost over three hundred dollars a bottle.

Reluctantly accepting the wine, Danielle stepped back, opening the door wider for Baron to enter.

"This was really sweet of you." Danielle glanced down at the expensive bottle of wine and then looked back to Baron. "But you really didn't need to bring me anything. I'm happy to show you the house."

"Who is this dandy?" Walt asked as he circled Baron, looking him up and down.

Resisting her urge to smile at Walt, Danielle shut the front door and then set the bottle on the entry hall table. "I suppose we can start the tour downstairs." She pointed to the parlor door.

"Do you have guests staying here now?" he asked, his voice low and even.

"No. We're closed for a few weeks until we complete some work."

Baron followed her into the parlor. Instead of allowing a comfortable distance between him and Danielle, Baron walked so closely behind her that should she suddenly stop, he would find himself pressed along her body. The man's hovering presence did not go unnoticed by Walt, who took it upon himself to place his hand in front of Baron's belly and give him a firm shove back, widening the distance between Danielle and Baron.

Baron let out a grunt and stopped walking, his hand flying to his stomach. Danielle, whose back had been to Walt and Baron and had missed Walt's intervention, turned and looked curiously from Walt to Baron.

"The man needs to know when to give a lady her space," Walt grumbled, giving Baron the evil eye.

"Is everything okay?" Danielle asked, wondering what had just happened.

Baron absently rubbed his stomach and glanced around the room nervously. "It must have been something I ate."

"Can I get you something? A Tums maybe?" She glanced over to Walt, wondering why he was smirking.

After a moment, Baron shook his head and seemed to regain his composure. He smiled at Danielle and glanced around the room. "Did you decorate this yourself?"

"Most of the furniture was here when I moved in. We really haven't made many changes other than reupholstering and refinishing some pieces."

"We?"

"When I say we, I mean me and Lily. You met Lily at Beverly's. She helps me run the bed and breakfast. Lily's the one responsible for a number of the improvements in the garden—with the help of a great landscaper."

"This is a quaint little room." While glancing around, he took a step closer to Danielle.

"This is our parlor," Danielle said politely, taking a step back just as Walt was preparing to give Baron another jab in the gut.

From the parlor, they moved to the library, kitchen, downstairs bedroom, and living room. As they made their way up the staircase, Danielle held onto the rail while Baron walked next to her. When his hand moved to her lower back, in a seemingly gentlemanly and protective gesture, Walt reached out and swatted the man, causing Baron to stop a moment and stare at his hand, a look of confusion on his face.

When they reached the second-floor landing, Baron asked if he could use the restroom—a look of confusion still clouding his features as he continually glanced down at the hand Walt had swatted.

"You have to stop that!" Danielle hissed when Baron went into the bathroom.

"Stop what?" Walt asked innocently.

"You smacked his hand. I saw you. And what did you do to him in the parlor?"

"The man is trying to climb all over you!"

Danielle rolled her eyes. "No, he's not. Granted, he's one of those people who have no clue about respecting a person's private space. But I think he's harmless."

"Harmless?" Walt practically choked on the word.

"He's old enough to be my father."

"Maybe you should tell him that. Might work better than a bucket of ice."

"Come on, Walt, behave. He just wants to see the house."

Now it was Walt's turn to roll his eyes.

When Baron returned from the bathroom, they continued the tour without incident. That was primarily because Baron was still a little preoccupied with the odd sensation he had experienced in the parlor and then again when coming up the steps—as if someone had hit him.

But by the time they returned to the first floor, Baron had regained his composure. If Danielle assumed her uninvited guest was about to leave, she was wrong.

Standing by the entry table, Baron picked up the wine bottle and said, "Let's have a glass of wine and we can toast our new friendship." When Danielle didn't respond immediately, he asked, "I hope we can be friends."

"Isn't it a little early for wine?" Danielle asked awkwardly.

"Don't tell me you're one of those people who believes they have to wait until five to have a drink?"

"Umm…I guess not…"

"And I'd love to see how you like this wine. It's absolutely my favorite."

Knowing how expensive the wine was, Danielle felt a little guilty just keeping it. She supposed the least she could do was share it with him. Reluctantly, she flashed Baron a smile and led him into the kitchen.

TWENTY-FIVE

"So you're closed down for a while?" Baron asked as he watched Danielle open the bottle of wine.

"Yes. We'll be open again for sure in May." She filled two wineglasses and handed Baron one.

"A toast," Baron said, picking up the other glass off the counter and handing it to Danielle. "I hope this is the beginning of a rich friendship."

Feeling awkward, Danielle tapped her glass against Baron's and took a sip. She paused a moment and looked at her wine. "Wow, this really is good."

He smiled. "I told you."

Walt shook his head in disgust and sat down at the table. He watched Danielle and Baron, who stood next to the counter, each with a glass in hand.

"So tell me, Ms. Boatman, do you like to be spontaneous?"

"Spontaneous, how?" She took another sip.

"Why don't you fly to San Francisco with me tonight? I know a great little restaurant I'd love to show you."

Danielle choked on her wine. After a few unfeminine sputters, she caught her breath.

Placing a hand on her shoulder, he asked, "Are you okay?"

"Yeah, I'm afraid it went down the wrong way. I think your offer to fly to San Francisco caught me off guard."

Walt was just about to smack Baron's hand off Danielle's shoulder when Baron moved it on his own.

"It's just dinner out, Danielle. Can't two friends enjoy dinner together?"

Danielle looked in Baron's gray eyes. "But fly to San Francisco?"

Smiling, he reached out, the back of his hand gently grazing the side of her face. "I felt something the first moment I saw you. We could be so very good together, I just know it. I want to take care of you."

The only thing that stopped Walt from breaking Baron's hand was the fact he spied Chris coming up the walkway leading to the kitchen door. The only reason Danielle didn't swat Baron's hand herself, she was in shock. Walt had warned her what the man was up to, but she hadn't taken him seriously. She should have.

Danielle took a step back and set her wine on the counter, preparing to tell Baron she wasn't interested, when the kitchen door suddenly flew open. Both she and Baron looked to the now open door at the same time. It appeared that Chris, who now stood just inside the kitchen, had just opened the door, when, in fact, it was Walt who had flung it open.

"For once I'm glad to see you," Walt told Chris.

"Oh, Chris, hi," Danielle called out.

"I'm sorry, I didn't realize you had company." Chris looked as if he was about to turn around and leave.

"You aren't going anywhere." Walt snatched Chris's arm and yanked him farther into the kitchen, slamming the door behind him.

Confused, Chris glanced from Walt to Danielle and then to the strange man standing in the kitchen with a glass of wine.

"Would you like some wine?" Danielle asked, sounding more cheerful than she felt.

Chris glanced at the kitchen clock and frowned. "Umm…no, that's okay."

"Baron, this is a good friend of mine and neighbor, Chris Johnson. Chris, this is Baron Huxley. He was a good friend of Steve Klein's."

Still a bit confused, Chris walked to Baron and shook his hand.

"Don't get too friendly with the palooka. He was all over Danielle a moment ago," Walt said with disgust.

Danielle flashed Walt a glare while Chris looked from Danielle to Baron.

Baron started making small talk with Chris, who wasn't paying attention to what he was saying. It was too difficult to concentrate with Walt talking—especially considering what Walt was telling him.

"This guy comes over here with the pretense of wanting to see the house, and the next thing you know, he's trying to get Danielle to fly off to San Francisco with him. I warned her what he was up to, but no, Danielle insisted he's old enough to be her father, as if that means he's harmless." Walt fairly growled. "Harmless like a rattlesnake."

"What is it you do?" Baron asked Chris for the second time.

Trying to process what was going on, Chris finally caught Baron's question. Flashing him an uneasy smile, he said, "I'm sort of in between jobs right now."

"Really?" Baron looked Chris up and down. "I have a friend who does property management in town—Danielle knows him—Adam Nichols."

Chris grinned. "I know Adam."

"You should talk to him. He mentioned something to me today about his handyman needing help. He might be able to use you. It could work into something."

Unable to suppress a giggle, Danielle picked up her wine, took another sip, and then said, "Chris is not really the handyman type."

Chris looked over at Danielle. "I just stopped over to see if you wanted to go out and get something to eat a little later."

"I'm afraid I got to her first," Baron said with a wink.

"If you won't hit him, I will," Walt said.

Chris frowned at Baron. "Excuse me?"

Noting Danielle's startled expression, Baron quickly added, "I just meant I already asked Danielle to go out to dinner with me. We were just in the middle of negotiating where we should go."

"He's lying," Walt said. "He told Danielle he wanted to fly her to San Francisco for dinner. She never agreed." Walt looked at Danielle. "Am I wrong?"

"I appreciate your offer, Baron, but I'm not interested in going out to dinner with you."

"Maybe we should discuss this after your friend leaves?" Baron suggested.

Walt groaned and gave Chris a little shove in Danielle's direction. "Are you just going to stand there like an idiot? Tell the guy to take a hike and keep his hands off your girl."

Startled by his comment, both Danielle and Chris looked to Walt.

Baron started to say something, but in the next moment, Walt pushed Chris again, sending him colliding into Danielle. Walt grabbed Chris's right wrist, forcing his arm around Danielle's shoulder, almost knocking the glass out of her hand. Danielle couldn't help it, she giggled. Chris, now standing next to Danielle with his arm casually draped around her shoulder, snatched the wineglass from her hand and took a sip.

"You see, Mr. Huxley, Danielle here is my girl."

Danielle could swear Chris had suddenly taken on a hillbilly accent.

Chris took another sip of the wine and paused. He turned to Danielle and said in a serious voice, "Wow, this wine is really good."

Danielle nodded. "I know. It's the same brand Adam got you."

"The one that was stolen?"

Danielle nodded again.

Chris took another sip. "Damn. I should have filed charges against that vagrant."

"I…I think I'll be going now," Baron Huxley stammered. Setting his still-full glass on the counter, he hurried out the kitchen door.

"So what was that all about?" Chris asked, his arm still draped over Danielle's shoulder. It didn't stay there long. In the next moment, Walt knocked it off and gave Chris a shove away from Danielle.

Ignoring Walt's last outburst, Danielle picked up the bottle and suggested they move it to the library. Before leaving the kitchen, Chris grabbed a clean glass for himself.

In the library, Chris managed to beat Walt to the sofa, where he sat with Danielle. Walt stood by the fireplace, smoking a cigar, while Danielle told Chris about her odd encounter with Baron Huxley.

"So you met him once and then he hit on you?" Chris asked after she finished telling her story.

"Twice. I met him first on Sunday, when Lily and I stopped over at Beverly Klein's and then again at Adam's when I dropped those papers off for you."

Chris looked at Walt. "Was he really that bad?"

Walt nodded. "Worse."

"I thought he was interested in Beverly, the way he was looking at her the other day. To be honest, when Lily and I met him, he really didn't give either of us a second look. His attention was completely on Beverly. And when I met him the second time at Adam's he was just polite. I really did think he just wanted to look at the house. I'd like to believe I could have handled him without your guys' help, but my radar was really off. When he asked me to go to San Francisco with him and started saying all that stuff…" Danielle cringed.

"He certainly didn't seem overly concerned about Chris being competition," Walt smirked.

Chris shrugged. "He figured I was just a beach bum."

"Well, you are." Walt took a puff off his cigar.

Chris shrugged again and then took a sip of the wine. He looked over at Danielle. "Are you sure this is the same brand Adam bought me? The one that's over three hundred bucks a bottle?"

"I'm positive."

Chris frowned and looked at the wine. After a moment, he set it down on the coffee table and pulled out his cellphone.

"Who are you calling?" Danielle asked.

"Adam."

For the next few minutes, Walt and Danielle silently listened to Chris's side of the conversation. When he was off the phone, he turned to Danielle. "Adam owes you an apology, which will be delivered tonight in the form of filet mignon, which I've offered to barbeque."

Danielle frowned. "I don't understand."

"Danielle, you know I adore you." Chris glanced over at Walt and back to Danielle. "And you know Walt adores you. But I think Baron Huxley is just after your money."

Walt paused mid-puff and looked at Chris. "Her money?"

"What are you talking about? I got the impression he has his own money. Heck, he wanted to fly me to San Francisco for dinner."

"After you left Adam's office, your Mr. Huxley started asking Adam about you—and Adam being Adam, they talked about your two inheritances and the gold coins. In Adam's defense, he figured everything he was saying was public knowledge."

"So why jump to the conclusion he's after my money? Not that I'm remotely interested in the guy, but still…"

"The reason Huxley was in Adam's office is he's listing his beach house. He wants to dump it, and fast. He's so anxious to sell that he's having Adam list it way below market value and he won't carry paper or consider a long escrow. It's pretty obvious the man needs cash. And if that's true, why bring over a three-hundred-dollar bottle of wine unless he figured he'd be seeing some return."

"You mean he wasn't just interested in my sunny disposition and wholesome good looks?"

TWENTY-SIX

Saturday afternoon cartoons were playing on the television, yet Edward MacDonald suspected he was the only one listening to them. Sitting in his recliner, he looked up from the newspaper and glanced over to the breakfast bar. His sons had abandoned their cereal bowls on the counter. A half-eaten slice of toast was trapped on the linoleum floor, impaled by the barstool Evan had been using not five minutes earlier.

He could hear the boys. They were in Eddy's bedroom, playing. Picking up the remote from the side table, he aimed it at the television and turned it off. Setting the remote down, he focused his attention back on the newspaper and turned the page.

Looking up at him from the next page was the drawing of Antoine Paul. MacDonald regretted not pulling the drawing after Danielle had informed him Heather understood Paul was a ghost, not a living man. He hoped running the drawing wasn't going to cause any problems.

SHIRLEY PAUL WAS JUST ABOUT to pour herself another cup of coffee when her phone began to ring. Setting the empty cup on the counter, she walked to the kitchen table and picked up the phone. Looking at the caller ID, she saw it was her brother's old girlfriend, Alice, who she hadn't talked to in over six months. Taking a seat at her kitchen table, she answered the phone.

"Hey, Alice. Long time. How are you doing?" Glancing over at the counter where she had left her cup, Shirley stood up and went to pour herself that cup of coffee she had intended to get before the phone rang.

"Hi, Shirley. Have you heard anything from Antoine?"

With one hand holding the phone to her ear, she used her other hand to pour herself a cup of coffee. "Nothing's changed."

"I saw him!" Alice blurted.

Just about to pick up the now full cup of coffee, Shirley froze. "What do you mean you saw him?"

"Well, not him, exactly. But a drawing of him and I swear it looks exactly like Antoine. It ran this morning in the Frederickport newspaper."

Shirley frowned. "Frederickport? Where's that?"

"It's a little Oregon beach town south of Astoria. I have a friend who lives there. She saw the drawing in this morning's newspaper and she thought he looks exactly like your brother. She took a picture of it and emailed it to me."

Abandoning the coffee on the counter, Shirley returned to the kitchen table and sat down, her full attention on what Alice was telling her.

"What kind of drawing are we talking about?"

"It's one of those police sketches, you know, when they're looking for a person of interest. He was seen in Frederickport, looking in people's windows."

Shirley shook her head. "Antoine in Frederickport? Looking in people's windows?"

"Shirley I never believed Antoine would just disappear like that. I know you think he ran off with that woman he was seeing, but I can't believe he wouldn't contact you. That wasn't the Antoine I knew."

"I'd rather think that than the alternative," Shirley said in a dull tone.

"I know you believe if he didn't run off with her, then it means he's dead, but maybe there's another possibility. I always wondered, perhaps something happened, he had an accident, he lost his memory. That would explain him doing something out of character like looking in windows."

Shirley could feel her heart race. "When was he sighted?"

"I tell you what, let me email you the article and picture. You can read it yourself."

ADAM SAT with Bill at Pier Café's lunch counter, waiting for their breakfast. Next to him on the counter was a newspaper a previous diner had abandoned. He snatched up the paper just as Carla came to refill their cups.

"How you doing, Carla?" Bill asked. "I like your new hair color."

Setting the coffee pot on the counter, she reached up and tugged on a lock of hair. "Do you? I thought I needed something more serious."

Adam set the newspaper on the counter and looked up at Carla. "Why's that?"

In response, Carla shrugged. She leaned down, resting her elbows on the counter as she propped her chin on one balled fist while her other hand fidgeted with the newspaper's edge. "I heard Steve Klein's funeral is on Friday."

Bill picked up his cup and took a sip, his eyes on Carla. "You going? He was a regular in here."

"I doubt it. I have to work that day."

Adam picked up the paper again. "I'll probably go."

"I hate funerals," Bill grumbled.

ADAM TURNED the newspaper's page, his eyes skimming over the articles. "Great, now we have a peeping tom running around."

"Peeping tom? Where?" Carla leaned over the counter to get a glimpse of what Adam was talking about.

INSTEAD OF A MORNING JOG, Heather sat on her bed, casually leaning against her headboard, methodically dissecting a cinnamon roll from Old Salts Bakery. Tugging off one curled layer at a time, she popped each one into her mouth and then licked her fingers before removing and eating another sweet hunk.

She felt a little guilty filling up with carbs and sugar when she should be out giving her cardio a workout, but she'd had a rough week. After consuming the roll, she licked her fingers one more time, removing any remaining sugary residue.

Reaching to the nightstand, she grabbed the glass of almond milk and took a swig before picking up the newspaper from the mattress. That morning she'd only gotten out of bed to bring in the morning paper, pour herself a glass of almond milk, and snatch the sack with the cinnamon roll she had purchased yesterday.

Bella slept soundly on the foot of the mattress. With a sigh, Heather skimmed the front of the newspaper and then turned the page. There, looking back at her, was Antoine Paul.

"So you're a killer?" Heather asked the drawing.

Cocking her head slightly, she studied the picture. "I guess having Elizabeth come in to draw your picture and running it in the newspaper was a major waste of time."

BEVERLY KLEIN SAT in her husband's recliner, the open newspaper in her lap. It was turned to the obit section. Steve's obituary had come out in this morning's paper; she had already read it three times. The picture they had used was fairly recent, taken for his new business cards last month. Reaching out, she ran a finger over her husband's image—captured in newsprint. Beverly reminded herself she needed to stop by the newspaper office and pick up some additional copies of the paper. She was certain Roxane and Steven would each want a copy.

Closing the newspaper, Beverly leaned back in the chair and stared up at the ceiling. There was so much she needed to do before Friday. She wondered if she should buy a new dress for the service, or perhaps she had something in her closet that might do. She wasn't going to wear black. With a smile, she remembered how Steve insisted mourners attending a funeral should wear colorful clothes to celebrate the deceased's life.

Looking back to the newspaper, she skimmed the front page and then turned to the next page. There, looking at her, was a drawing of a handsome young man. There was something faintly familiar about him, but she couldn't figure out what it was.

Just as she was about to read the article accompanying the drawing, her phone began to ring. Tossing the newspaper to the floor, she got up from the recliner and went to find her phone.

"I HOPE this isn't going to cause the chief a bunch of grief," Danielle said as she stared at the drawing of Antoine Paul in the morning paper. She sat at the kitchen table, reading the article while Lily stood nearby, making French toast.

Turning the slices of French toast over in the pan, Lily glanced over to Danielle and then looked back to what she was doing. "I thought you told the chief Heather understood Antoine was a spirit. Why did he bother running that?"

"At first we just wanted to get a likeness of Paul so we could use it to figure out who he was. But then Hillary gave me his name, so it wasn't really necessary. But then, Heather's morale seemed bolstered believing someone was taking her seriously, so the chief figured he'd go ahead and let it run—and then when I explained to Heather who Paul really was, running the piece seemed a moot point."

Lily flipped the French toast onto a plate. "So why is it in the paper?"

"Actually, it was supposed to be in Wednesday's paper, and then there was some mix-up—and then after Heather learned the truth, the chief wasn't going to run it, but then someone at the station got their signals crossed and sent it down to the paper, and here it is."

Dropping the plate of French toast on the table, Lily sat down. "Well, the guy is a missing person, so maybe that drawing will stir up some memories and help figure out what really happened to him."

Helping herself to a slice of French toast, Danielle glanced across the table at Lily. "Yeah, but he's dead. He's been dead for about eleven years. Anyone who reads this article will assume he's still alive."

IF BARON HUXLEY hadn't cleaned out his refrigerator the night before, he wouldn't be standing by the front entry of Lucy's Diner, waiting for a table. Last night he'd hope to be doing something more exciting than cleaning out his refrigerator and getting his house ready to go on the market. He'd had high hopes of convincing Danielle Boatman to go out with him—and then that surfer kid had showed up and spoiled it all. Baron shook his head.

While waiting for a table, he dug a couple quarters out of his pocket and purchased a copy of the morning newspaper. He didn't normally read the local paper; what was the point? It wasn't as if he lived full time in Frederickport, and he didn't really care what went on locally unless it affected the property values. But Baron was bored, and when eating alone, he preferred to read something.

By the time he finished reading the articles on the front page, a booth opened up. After removing his reading glasses, he refolded the newspaper, slipped it under his arm, and then went to the booth. Sitting down, he tossed the paper on the seat next to him.

A few minutes later, the server took his order and brought him some coffee. While waiting for his breakfast, he picked the newspaper back up and turned the page. Absently glancing over it, he almost missed it—preparing to turn another page—and then he saw it. Antoine Paul.

Baron felt as if someone had just kicked him in the gut. Momentarily frozen, he stared at the smug face staring back at him. Adjusting his reading glasses, he moved the paper closer and read the accompanying article.

According to the piece, the nameless man in the drawing was a person of interest—the Frederickport Police Department was looking for any information on his identity. According to the article, he had been looking into the windows of a local resident—someone on Beach Drive.

Baron set the paper on the table and removed his glasses. Staring off into blank space, he frowned. *Marlow House is located on Beach Drive…*

Before he picked the paper up again, a couple teenage girls, who had been sitting at the booth behind him, stood up and were preparing to leave. As they passed Baron, one glanced down at the open paper on his table and looked at the drawing of Antoine Paul.

"Oh, there's the picture of that creepy peeper I was telling you about!" the girl told her friend. Both teenagers were now standing over Baron's table, gawking at the paper.

Baron looked up at the girls. "Have you seen this man?"

The teenager who'd pointed out the article shook her head.

"No, but my mom showed me that article this morning. Told me to look out for the guy. What a creep!"

"Do you know anyone who's actually seen him?" Baron asked.

The girl shook her head. "No."

"Hey, I bet Elizabeth drew that!" the other girl said to her friend.

"Who's Elizabeth?" Baron asked.

"Elizabeth Sparks," the girl who had mentioned Elizabeth said. "She teaches art classes. She's really good. Sometimes she does police sketches, you know, like in the movies where someone describes the bad guy and the artist draws him. Isn't that cool?"

TWENTY-SEVEN

It was surprisingly easy for Baron to locate Elizabeth Sparks. As it turned out, there was an art show at the museum, and she was one of the local artists being featured. When he arrived at the museum, he was happy to see the artists in attendance were all wearing name tags. It would make his task easier.

There were about twenty or more people already milling around in the museum when he arrived. According to the name tags of some, they were members of the Frederickport Historical Society, while others were members of the local art guild and participating artists. Those without name tags, he assumed, were patrons who'd come to view the display.

Taking his time, he leisurely strolled through the exhibits. By all appearances, he was taking in each piece of art, when in truth, his goal was to work his way to Ms. Sparks's section and then strike up a conversation. The museum was not large, so it didn't take long for him to arrive at his destination.

"You're the artist?" Baron asked the attractive brunette. The answer to his question was obvious, considering her name tag and the signature on the painting.

"Yes, I am. Thank you for coming." Elizabeth smiled brightly.

Baron made an obvious show of reading her name tag. He then smiled at her and asked, "Are you the one that sometimes works as a police artist for the local police department?"

Elizabeth blushed. "How did you know that?"

With a broad smile, Baron showed off his straight white teeth. "I saw your drawing in this morning's newspaper. You're very talented."

"Thank you." Elizabeth smiled and glanced down briefly and then looked up into his gray eyes.

"It's always amazed me how an artist can do something like that. To draw a likeness of a person you've never seen before." Baron shook his head. "Of course, I have absolutely no artistic ability whatsoever. I'm in awe of people like you."

"I'm sure you have more artistic ability than you realize."

Baron grinned. "You're just being kind."

"Well, maybe you should take one of my art classes, and you'll see I'm telling the truth."

"Maybe I'll do just that," Baron said with a grin. "So tell me, do you think your drawing looks just like the man they're looking for?"

Elizabeth shrugged. "Heather seemed to think so."

"I assume that's the one who saw him. The article said the guy was looking in windows over on Beach Drive. Sounds like a sicko, if you ask me."

"In all fairness, he's only a person of interest. One of the officers told me that she caught him looking in her window, but it's possible he was an overeager tourist, looking in a house he assumed was vacant. You know, checking out a possible rental or maybe something to buy."

"Has anyone else reported seeing him looking in windows around town?"

Elizabeth shook her head. "Not that I've heard of."

"So no one else has seen this guy?"

"As far as I know, it was just that one time."

Baron frowned. "Really? Isn't it a little unusual, doing a composite sketch over something so minor?"

Elizabeth shrugged. "Maybe there's another reason they want to get ahold of this guy. Frankly, they really don't tell me much."

IT WAS ALMOST noon when Baron arrived at Frederickport Vacation Properties. When he walked into the office, he found Adam sitting behind his desk, eating a sandwich. The moment

Adam spied Baron, he set the sandwich down and wiped his mouth with a napkin.

"I got some great pictures this morning. I just finished loading them in MLS."

"That was quick." Baron took a seat facing the desk.

Adam picked up the sandwich, yet instead of taking another bite, he set it back down again and looked at Baron. "I understand you stopped at Marlow House yesterday."

Baron leaned back in the chair and crossed one leg over the opposing knee. "I wanted to take Danielle up on her offer to see the house before I head back to Vancouver. How did you know?"

Adam shrugged and picked up his sandwich. "I saw her last night. Some of us got together for a barbecue at a mutual friend's house. She mentioned it."

"I met one of her friends while I was there…a Chris?"

Instead of commenting, Adam took a bite of his sandwich.

"Do you know him?" Baron asked.

"Yeah." Adam took another bite.

"So are those two an item?"

Adam shrugged. "Nothing official, why? You're not interested in Danielle, are you?"

Baron smiled. "Would that be so bad?"

"I just don't think she's really your type." Adam set what was left of his sandwich on a napkin and picked up his soda.

"So what does this Chris do?"

"Chris?"

"He mentioned he was between jobs. I didn't realize he knew you. I suggested he talk to you about that handyman opening you mentioned when I was in here."

Adam couldn't help it, he let out a short laugh and then took a drink of his soda.

Baron frowned. "What's so funny?"

Adam set his soda back on the desk. "Chris isn't exactly the handyman type. Unless it has something to do with waxing a surfboard or something." Adam laughed again.

"So what is this guy, a beach bum or something?"

"He's alright. Don't you want to hear about your listing? Want to see the pictures I took?" Adam picked up a paper napkin and wiped off his mouth.

Baron shook his head. "No. I trust you. Hey…did you read about that peeping tom in the paper today?"

Adam wadded up the napkin and tossed it aside. "Yes. Read about it this morning. I hate crap like that. We've had our share of bad press the last couple months."

"I understand the guy was looking into someone's house over on Beach Drive. Someone named Heather."

"Heather, Heather Donovan? She was the one who reported it?"

"You know her?" Baron asked.

"Yeah. A little. She lives a couple doors down from Marlow House."

"You haven't seen this guy, have you?" Baron asked. "Does he look familiar?"

"You mean the peeper? No. I've never seen him before. At least not if he looks like the drawing. In fact, I haven't heard anyone else in town talking about a peeping tom. But to be honest, I wouldn't be surprised if Heather's imagination is working overtime."

"Why do you say that?"

"She's a little different." Adam shrugged.

ADAM HADN'T TOLD Baron which exact house on Beach Drive belonged to Heather Donovan. But knowing it was a couple doors down from Marlow House helped narrow the search. What was especially helpful was the *Donavon* printed on her mailbox.

Newspaper in hand, Baron made his way up the walkway to Heather's front door. There was a car in the driveway, so he assumed she was home. After ringing the doorbell, he noticed the front windows were open, something he found odd for someone who had recently reported a peeping tom. *Heather Donovan must not be overly concerned with her safety*, he thought.

"Yes, can I help you?" Heather asked when she opened the door.

"I'm sorry to bother you. My name is Baron Huxley, and I read in the paper this morning about the man you saw." Baron opened the newspaper and showed Heather the picture of Elizabeth's drawing. "I was wondering if I could talk to you for a moment."

"Exactly how did you know it was me who reported seeing that man?"

Baron smiled. "It's a small town. Does it really matter?"

"What do you want?" Heather eyed him coolly.

"Like I said, I was wondering if I could talk to you for a moment about the man."

"Why?"

Growing frustrated, Baron forced a smile. "You see, he looks like someone I once knew. Someone I haven't seen for a long time."

Heather stood silently at the doorway for a moment, considering the request. The silence was broken by a meow near her feet. She looked down. Bella weaved around her ankles.

"Back, Bella," Heather said gruffly. With one foot, she gently shoved Bella back into the house. She then stepped onto the porch, closing the door behind her. Reaching out, she took the newspaper from Baron and opened it to the subject of the conversation. She sat down on the porch and looked at Antoine's image.

With a reluctant shrug, Baron sat down on the stoop next to her.

Staring at the picture, Heather asked, "What's his name?"

"Excuse me?"

"Your friend. The guy in the picture. What's his name?"

"Well…" Baron stammered. "I'm not really sure it's the same person. It just looks like him."

Heather handed the paper back to Baron and looked at him. "When was the last time you saw him?"

"Ummm…a few years."

"So what is his name?" Heather asked again. "If he's your friend, I'd think you'd know his name. After all, he's a person of interest; the police are obviously looking for him. Knowing his name would help the police. That's why they ran that picture."

"I understand that. But to be honest with you, I don't really remember his name. Like I said, it was someone I knew a long time ago."

Without expression, Heather studied Baron for a moment. Finally, she asked, "So what did you want to ask me?"

"When did you see him?"

"Last weekend."

"According to the article, he was looking in your window."

"Yeah, my living room window. I screamed, and he disappeared."

"Disappeared?"

Heather shrugged. "Well, he wasn't there anymore."

"Have you ever seen him before?"

"Yeah. The day before he looked in my window, I saw him on the beach."

"Did you talk to him?"

Heather shook her head. "No, I never talked to him. Do you want to find this guy or something?"

"Like I said, it's someone I knew a long time ago. I always wondered what happened to him."

"Well, maybe you should go talk to the police about it."

Baron stood up. "Thanks for your time, Ms. Donovan." Baron turned and made his way down the walk to his parked car.

Heather remained on the front stoop and watched as Baron got into his vehicle. After he drove off, she pulled her cellphone out of her jacket pocket and dialed Danielle Boatman.

"Hey, Heather, what's up?"

"I just had an interesting visitor."

"Don't tell me it's our ghost Antoine Paul."

"No, but it's someone who's looking for him. Some older guy named Baron Huxley."

TWENTY-EIGHT

Danielle didn't call the chief until the next morning to tell him what Heather had said about Baron Huxley stopping by. Reluctant to bother him on the weekend when he was with his boys, she figured she would wait until Monday to tell him. Yet, by mid-morning Sunday, she broke down and called him.

"Sorry to bother you at home, Chief," Danielle said when he answered her call.

"What's going on, Danielle?"

She then went on to tell him everything Heather had said about Baron Huxley stopping by and inquiring about Antoine Paul.

"I suppose I should have expected that. That was one reason I tried to pull the article."

"What do you mean?" she asked.

"It's entirely possible there was a police composite sketch done back then of the man seen leaving the restaurant with his wife. One I didn't come across in my brief search on Paul. Huxley probably recognized it."

"I figured it was probably something like that."

"Thanks for telling me. I suppose I should expect a visit from Huxley tomorrow. I need to be prepared and come up with something. I feel terrible dredging up all those memories for the poor guy. I hate giving someone false hope. If I was in his situation, I couldn't stop looking for my wife's killer."

BEFORE LEAVING VANCOUVER, Shirley Paul went online and looked up Frederickport motels. She found the Seahorse Motel, it was located right on the ocean. But she didn't care about her room's view. This wasn't a vacation. It had taken some fast talking to get a few days off at work. But she had to come.

It was late Sunday afternoon when Shirley pulled into Frederickport. With the help of her car's GPS, she drove directly to the Seahorse Motel. She found the rooms clean but well used, with the basic necessities. It was too chilly to open her sliding door, but she pulled back the curtain, exposing the ocean view. Exhausted both physically and emotionally, she kicked off her shoes and laid down on the queen-size bed, not bothering to pull back the bedspread.

When Shirley woke up several hours later, it was dark outside. Getting up from the bed, she rubbed her eyes and glanced at the alarm clock sitting on the nightstand. It was almost 9 p.m. She wondered if there was someplace still open where she could get something to eat. She hadn't eaten since breakfast, and then it was only cereal and a piece of fruit. After slipping her shoes back on and running a brush through her hair, she grabbed her purse and car keys.

Heading downtown, she found a little diner that was still open: Lucy's Diner. She hoped she wasn't too late to order something. It was a quarter past nine.

When Shirley entered the restaurant, the first thing she asked, "Are you still serving?"

The waitress, clutching several menus to her chest, smiled and said, "We sure are. We're open until ten. Sit anywhere you like."

Shirley chose a booth not far from the entrance, her back to the door.

BARON HUXLEY HAD a lot on his mind. Just when things seemed to be working out, another obstacle would be thrown in his way. Antoine Paul wasn't an obstacle exactly, but a major distraction.

When Huxley entered Lucy's Diner shortly before 10 p.m. on Sunday evening, he paid no notice to the other diners as he made his way to an empty booth at the back of the restaurant. Just as he sat down, his cellphone began to ring. Before answering it, he looked to see who was calling.

"What does he say?" Baron asked when he answered the phone. "Can he explain how Paul was seen in Frederickport? I sent you that picture. If that's not him, he has a twin brother."

Baron listened to the caller's reply. Shaking his head, he leaned back in the booth seat, still holding the cellphone to his ear.

"I just don't need this. Klein's out of the way. Everything should be smooth sailing from here on out."

Baron's phone call was interrupted when the server showed up at his table. Covering his phone briefly, he looked up at her. "I'm on the phone. Come back in about five minutes and take my order."

A pad and pen in hand, the waitress let out a weary sigh, yet she didn't acquiesce to his request. Clearly annoyed, the waitress—who should have retired ten years earlier and wanted nothing more than to take her shoes off and soak in a hot tub—shook her head.

"I'm sorry, it's after ten, and if you want something, you're going to have to order now," she said stubbornly.

Glaring at the server, Baron knew instinctively she was not going to budge. Turning his attention briefly to his phone, he said, "I'll have to call you right back."

Baron proceeded to give the waitress his order, and while doing so, his eyes wandered past her to a young woman at a booth facing him. The woman had just stood up and tossed money on the table. When she looked up in his direction, he almost jumped from his seat. Knowing he had to follow her, he attempted to get out of the booth, but the waitress was blocking his way. He almost told the waitress—who hadn't noticed his sudden shift of interest due to the fact she was busy scribbling his order on the pad—to get out of his way, when he realized it was too late. The woman had stepped out of the diner.

Sliding to the far side of the booth's bench seat, he looked out the window into the dark night. He couldn't see where she had gone, but he had to find her.

The waitress, who now noticed her customer's odd behavior, looked up from her pad and frowned. "Is something wrong?"

"That woman who just left—I think it's an old friend of mine. She didn't happen to say where she's staying, did she?"

"What woman?"

Baron pointed to where the woman had been. "She was sitting there. She just left."

The server glanced around and looked at the now empty booth. With a shrug she said, "No. She didn't say anything."

After the server finally left his table to put in his order, Baron promptly called back the person he had just been talking to.

"Antoine Paul has to be in Frederickport. I just saw his sister."

ON MONDAY MORNING, Police Chief MacDonald sat at his desk, reviewing his file on Steve Klein's death. He was halfway through the file when Brian showed up at his door with a cup of coffee in each hand.

Glancing up from his desk, MacDonald smiled. "Please tell me one of those is mine."

"You left your coffee sitting in the break room." Brian walked to the chief and set one cup on his desk. "I poured you a fresh cup."

"Thanks." MacDonald picked up the coffee and took a sip.

Sitting down in a chair facing the desk, Brian nodded to the folder MacDonald was looking at. "Is that on Klein?"

"Someone fed him crabmeat, and we need to find out who it was."

"The obvious suspects, Carla or his wife. They both had the opportunity. The motive." Brian took a sip of his coffee.

"I keep thinking of Baron Huxley."

"The tamale guy?" Brian asked.

"He gave Steve the food he supposedly ate that night. According to Beverly, they had some issues. And according to Danielle, Mr. Huxley may be having some money problems."

"How would Danielle know that?"

MacDonald smiled sheepishly. "Don't repeat this."

"Certainly not." Brian's grin widened.

"Danielle called me yesterday morning. She told me Huxley stopped by Marlow House, supposedly wanting a tour of the place. While he was there, he asked her to fly with him to San Francisco for dinner."

Brian arched his brows. "Wow. Likes to sweep the ladies off their feet, doesn't he? I didn't even know she knew him that well."

"She doesn't. Only met him at Beverly's when she stopped by to give her condolences, and again at Adam Nichol's office."

"Fast mover. I take it she didn't accept his offer. So why does she think he has money problems?"

"Because the reason he was at Adam's office, he listed his beach house here—at a significantly reduced price. He wants a fast sale. She suspects he has a cash-flow problem."

"If he does, then why is he offering to fly Boatman to San Francisco for dinner?"

MacDonald smiled. "Why do you think?"

Brian considered the question a moment and then said, "Ahhh…he was after the lady's money."

"That's what Danielle thinks."

Brian shrugged. "Maybe she's selling herself short. She's an attractive woman. I could see why Huxley would hit on her."

Before MacDonald could respond, the phone on his desk rang. It was the receptionist at the front of the office.

"Yeah?"

"There's a woman who insists on seeing someone regarding that picture we had in the paper. Her name is Shirley Paul. She says the man in the drawing is her brother. Who do you want me to have her talk to?"

MACDONALD NOTICED the striking resemblance between Shirley Paul and the drawing of her brother the moment she walked into his office. He guessed she was about Danielle's age, which meant she was probably around twenty when her older brother went missing.

The night before, he had decided what he would tell Baron Huxley about the man in the drawing—should he show up in his office and make an inquiry. While Huxley hadn't yet shown up, MacDonald decided he would give Shirley Paul the same story he had concocted for Huxley.

Standing up from behind his desk, MacDonald shook Shirley's hand, they exchanged brief introductions, and he asked her to take a seat while he closed the office door.

"Like I told the woman at the front desk, I'm here about the picture that ran in Saturday's paper—about that person of interest you're looking for." Opening her purse, she pulled out a photograph of her brother, stood up, and handed it to the chief, who now sat behind his desk. He accepted the photograph and she returned to her chair.

Studying the picture in his hand a moment, he looked up at Shirley and smiled. "He does look a little like the man in the drawing."

"He looks *exactly* like the man in the drawing," she insisted. "I believe the man you're looking for is my brother, Antoine Paul."

Setting the photograph on the desktop, MacDonald looked at Paul's sister. "I really appreciate you coming in, and I'm sorry for wasting your time. But, we've already located the man we're looking for. It wasn't your brother. His name isn't Antoine Paul."

Shaking her head in denial, she said, "Then my brother must be using another name. I don't think he knows who he is."

"Are you saying you believe your brother has lost his memory?"

"It's the only thing that makes sense. He went missing about eleven years ago. I haven't heard from him. Antoine wouldn't just disappear without letting me know where he was."

MacDonald noticed the tears welling in the young woman's eyes. He felt it inhumane to give her false hope.

"Ms. Paul, how old would your brother be now?"

Shirley frowned a moment and then said, "Late thirties.'

"You see, the man in this drawing—the man who was seen looking into someone's window—is just twenty. I saw his driver's license, and I've no reason to doubt he is who he says he is. So you see, he can't be your brother." Picking up the photograph from his desk, he stood up and handed it back to her.

"I don't understand…" she said numbly, standing up briefly to take back the photograph. Sitting down in the chair, she stared at her brother's picture.

"I'm really sorry it isn't your brother. You see, the man in the drawing was a visitor in town and thought the house was empty, and he was a little overcurious and peeked inside. When he saw his picture in the paper, he came forward immediately—contacted me personally at my house. It was all a misunderstanding."

TWENTY-NINE

"Antoine Paul's sister is here? In Frederickport?" Danielle asked excitedly after MacDonald told her who had stopped in his office less than an hour earlier. Danielle had dropped by to see if Baron Huxley had come in to ask about the man in Saturday's newspaper. She was curious to find out what the chief intended to tell him.

Leaning back in his office chair, he frowned at Danielle. "Why do you sound so excited?"

"I intended to look her up when I went to Hillary's funeral in Vancouver."

"I thought they were having her services in New York now."

Sitting down, Danielle tossed her purse to the floor. "Exactly. I was thinking I was going to have to drive into Vancouver just to see her, and now I won't have to. Do you know where she's staying?"

"She mentioned she got a room at the Seahorse Motel, but I imagine she's checked out already. Anyway, you don't want to bother the woman. I felt so sorry for her clinging to hope that her brother is still alive."

"We already agreed I should talk to her," Danielle insisted.

"You didn't see her."

"I'll be sensitive. I promise."

Picking up the pen from his desk, he absently fidgeted with it.

"I've already convinced her the man in the newspaper isn't her brother."

"What did you say to convince her of that?"

MacDonald went on to tell Danielle the falsehood he had fed Shirley Paul.

When he was done explaining, Danielle leaned back in the chair and crossed her legs. "Not a bad story, but what if she mentions it to someone?"

"What do you mean?"

"Isn't Joe the one who took the call at Heather's? Isn't this technically his case? How will you explain what you told her?"

MacDonald smiled. "Brian was in my office when Ms. Paul showed up, wanting to talk to someone about the picture in the paper, insisting the man was her brother. I already knew what I intended to tell Huxley, so I decided to stick to the same story. Basically, I lied to Brian. It's the same story I'll tell Joe."

"What do you mean you lied to Brian?"

"Before I talked to Paul's sister, I told Brian some guy stopped by my house on Saturday, he had found out where I lived, and I was out in the front yard. He confessed he was the one in the paper; I figured it was all just a mistake and let him go. He was a tourist, of course."

"Umm…isn't someone going to wonder why you didn't do something more…I don't know…official…like take the guy's name for some report?"

"Well, I did write it all up—but damn, something happened to the papers. And I can't seem to remember the man's name—it might have been John. I'm fairly confident the citizen who made the initial report—Heather—is not going to push it."

Danielle chuckled. "Who woulda thunk it? Police Chief MacDonald making up stories."

"Until I met you, I never had to."

DANIELLE PULLED her car into the parking lot of the Seahorse Motel and turned off the ignition. Instead of getting out of the vehicle, she sat in the driver's seat, hands still on the steering wheel, and looked up at the motel.

Before leaving Chief MacDonald's office, they had argued about the wisdom of her still seeking an interview with Shirley Paul. Danielle wanted to get more information on Antoine, and she couldn't imagine a better source than his sister. But the chief was right, it wasn't fair to give the woman false hope. Whatever Antoine's sins might have been, they weren't his sister's fault. At least, that was what Danielle assumed.

Sitting in the parking lot, Danielle racked her brain to come up with a plausible story to give the woman.

"Oh, come on, Danielle, if the chief was able to come up with a cockamamie story, surely you can come up with something."

Still running possible storylines through her head, Danielle noticed a young woman matching the description MacDonald had given her of Shirley Paul. The woman stepped out of a room on the first floor, a suitcase in her hand.

"Oh crap. She's going to get away!" Hastily, Danielle snatched her keys out of the ignition and grabbed her purse off the passenger seat. After getting from her car, she hurried toward the woman, who appeared to be headed for the front office, Danielle assumed, to check out.

"Excuse me, are you Shirley Paul?"

Upon hearing her name, the woman stopped abruptly and faced Danielle.

"Do I know you?" she asked when Danielle reached her.

"Hello. My name is Danielle Boatman; I live in Frederickport. I own Marlow House Bed and Breakfast."

The woman frowned. "I don't understand? Do you hang out at motels, trying to drum up business for your bed and breakfast? If so, I'm going home, so you're wasting your time."

Danielle smiled. "No. I wanted to know if I could talk to you about your brother—Antoine."

SHIRLEY TOSSED her suitcase on the unmade bed of her motel room and then went to open the blinds on the sliding door to let in the sunshine. Danielle, who had followed her into the room, closed the door and then took a seat on one of the two chairs.

A moment later, Shirley sat down and looked at Danielle. "What do you know about my brother? How did you know I was here?"

Taking a deep breath, Danielle prayed she could pull off the elaborate tale. According to Walt, there were times she lied brilliantly—yet other times she was transparent.

"I saw the drawing in Saturday's paper." It wasn't a lie; she had seen the drawing in the paper. "I thought it looked like your brother."

"You knew my brother?"

Danielle shook her head. "No. But a friend of mine knew who he was. She showed me a picture of him—from an article after he went missing." That was only half a lie. She considered Hillary her friend, and Hillary had known Antoine, at least his spirit. As for the photograph from an old newspaper article, she had also seen that, yet Hillary hadn't shown her.

"I don't understand. They told me that drawing wasn't my brother. Are you saying it is—was he in Frederickport?"

"No. It wasn't him. Like you, I thought it was. When I went down to the police station, they told me who it really was—but they mentioned I wasn't the first one to think it was Antoine Paul. They said his sister had come in—that you had come in—asking about the picture. We both thought the same thing. But it wasn't him."

"Did someone at the police station tell you where I was staying?" She sounded upset.

"Oh no!" Danielle lied. "But I'm in the hospitality business, so I figured the Seahorse Motel was probably where you'd be if you were staying in town. In fact, this is where I stayed when I first arrived in Frederickport." Most of that statement was true. She and Lily had stayed at the Seahorse Motel when she had first moved to town.

"How did you know it was me?"

"I didn't. But when I pulled up into the parking lot and saw a young woman around the right age of Antoine's sister, I figured I'd give it a shot." That was totally true.

Shirley quietly studied Danielle a moment. Danielle assumed the woman was trying to decide if she should believe her or kick her out of the motel room.

"What do you know about my brother?"

"I know he's missing. That he's been missing for about eleven years."

"Why are you interested in him? You said you never knew him."

"Do you know who Hillary Hemingway was?" Danielle asked.

"Certainly, she was one of my favorite authors. Didn't she just pass away?"

Danielle nodded. "Hillary had been staying at my bed and breakfast for the last month. Over a week ago, she had a heart attack in her sleep, and we found her the next morning."

"She died at your bed and breakfast?"

"Yes."

"What does she have to do with my brother?"

"Hillary was working on a story about a real-life unsolved crime about a woman who was murdered in Portland around the time your brother went missing. The night before they found her body, she was seen with a man who matched your brother's description."

"What does my brother have to do with this murdered woman?"

Now comes the tall, tall tale. Hope I can pull it off. "When researching the story, Hillary came across a picture of a man who went missing around the same time as the murder. That man was your brother. She thought he looked like the man the police were looking for. The man who had been seen with the woman hours before she was found dead. When Hillary was telling me about the story she was researching, she showed me your brother's picture. So when I saw that drawing in the paper the other day, I thought the same thing as you did."

"If Hillary's dead—why are you looking for Antoine?"

"I suppose I was curious. And a part of me wanted to help solve Hillary's mystery."

Shirley stood up, walked to the sliding glass door, and looked out. "Who was the woman my brother was seen with? The one who was murdered?"

"Her name was Melissa Huxley."

After a moment of silence, Shirley turned from the window and faced Danielle. "I've never heard of her before."

"She was murdered in Portland about eleven years ago."

"Sorry, the name's not familiar." Shirley walked back to her chair and sat down.

"Would you tell me about your brother?"

Shirley smiled wistfully. "He was a good brother. He always took care of me, especially after our mom died. Our father took off not long after I was born. I never knew him. But mom was always there. At least she was until she got sick. I was in high school at the time. When she died, I moved in with Antoine. He was eight years older than me. I lived with him until I went off to college."

"How old were you when he went missing?"

"I'd just turned twenty. We normally talked at least once a week. But after a few weeks when he didn't call and he didn't answer his phone, I realized something was wrong."

"What did you think happened?"

"I knew he had started seeing someone. Someone new. But he wouldn't introduce me to her, said it was too soon, that it was complicated. Finally, he admitted he was seeing a married woman."

"You didn't know who she was?"

"No. But he told me if he disappeared suddenly, not to be worried. He said they might have to run away together, that was the only way they could safely be together. He told me once he got settled, he would contact me."

"If you thought he'd run away with his girlfriend—that he had gone into hiding—why did you report him missing?"

Nervously fidgeting with her hands, Shirley looked down. "I really didn't know what else to do. Part of me didn't believe he'd really just take off like that. And I had this gut feeling something was wrong. After all, everything was still in his apartment. I thought, if he was going to run off, why not take his things with him? It didn't make sense."

"Then what happened?"

"I waited. Months went by. Then years. I'm still friends with my brother's old high school girlfriend. She never believed he would just take off without letting me know where he was. She's the one who saw the picture in the paper."

"Your brother was a writer?"

"Yes. He was a freelance writer. He did investigative reporting about politics and stuff. Although, I think he always wanted to be a mystery writer."

"Was your brother ever—violent? Did he have a temper?"

"Antoine?" Shirley frowned. "He had a temper, but he was never physical or violent. I mean…well, he could get sarcastic and maybe a little verbally insulting when he'd get mad. But he never threw stuff. Nothing like that."

"He never hit you?"

"Hit me?" Shirley stared at Danielle. "No…do you think this

woman who was murdered was the woman he was seeing?"

"I think it might be. They were seen coming out of a restaurant together—arguing."

Shirley shook her head. "If you think my brother murdered this woman and then ran off, you're wrong. Antoine would never do something like that."

IT HADN'T TAKEN LONG for Baron Huxley to find out where Shirley Paul was staying. After returning from Lucy's Diner the night before, he started calling all the local motels, asking the same question. *"Hello, I'm just checking on my sister, Shirley Paul. She's supposed to have arrived there from Vancouver this evening, and I wanted to make sure she arrived safely."*

It was his second call—to the Seahorse Motel—that gave him the answer he wanted. When they asked him if he wanted them to put the call through to her room, he simply said, *"No, I don't want to disturb her if she's already gone to bed. I know it's late and she needs her rest. I just wanted to make sure she arrived safely."*

He had been in his car all night, keeping an eye on the motel—waiting. When Antoine Paul arrived at his sister's motel room, Baron would do what needed to be done. When Antoine didn't arrive that night, Baron was certain he would show up the next day. But it wasn't Antoine Paul who showed up at his sister's motel room—it was Danielle Boatman.

THIRTY

After Susan Mitchell finished her shift at the bank on Monday, she stopped at the Frederickport Police Department. Officer Brian Henderson had asked her to stop in; they needed to ask her some questions about her former boss. She had to admit, she was curious to see what they intended to ask her.

"Thank you for coming," Brian told Susan when he led her to the interrogation room. "I thought you might be more comfortable if we talked here rather than at the bank."

"It is sort of a fishbowl down there." After draping her purse's strap over the back of a chair, she sat down.

Brian took a seat across from her at the table, a pad of paper and pen sitting before him.

"What did you want to ask me?"

"I understand the week Steve died, you worked every day at the bank?"

"Yes. Like always. Five days a week. I don't do Saturdays anymore."

"How long have you worked at the bank?" he asked.

"Gee…five years, I guess." She shrugged.

"So Steve was the manager when you started working there."

"Yes."

"Do you know if Steve had any food allergies?"

"You mean like his allergy to shellfish?"

"So you knew about that?"

"Sure. Anyway, it was just in the paper. I imagine the whole town knows."

"Did you know about it before you read it in the paper?"

"Sure. Everyone at the bank knew." She shifted in her chair to get more comfortable. "Sometimes we'd make jokes about it."

"How so?"

Leaning over the table, she placed her hands on the tabletop. "Well, it doesn't seem so funny now. Especially considering what happened to him. According to the paper, he had some allergic reaction and fell off the pier, hit his head."

"What kind of jokes?"

"It was nothing. You know how it is. Even if you like your boss, sometimes you get mad at him. If he called someone in his office to jump all over them, sometimes the person would later make a joke about bringing crab cakes to the next employee potluck. It was sorta a standard joke. No one was serious."

"Did Steve know about the…joke?"

Susan shook her head. "No, I don't think so."

"Do you know of anyone at the bank who had an issue with him?"

"Not that I know of."

"Did you ever have a problem with him?"

Susan glanced down at her hands and then looked back up at Brian. "Does it really matter? I mean, Steve's dead now. And it's not like I fed him shellfish or anything."

"Did you have a problem with him at one time?"

"Sort of, but that was a long time ago."

"What kind of problem?"

Susan considered the question for a minute before letting out a deep sigh. "I really don't want his wife to know. I really like her."

"Did you have a relationship with Steve Klein?"

Susan gasped, "Oh, gawd no!"

"Then what was it?"

"Well, when I first went to work there, he sort of…well…I think he hit on me."

"You think?"

"Yeah. I guess he did. I told him I wanted to keep our relationship professional and if he ever made another advance, I'd go over his head and talk to his boss. After that, he left me alone. I never had a problem with him again."

"Do you know if he was seeing anyone else at the bank?"

She shook her head. "No. I don't think so."

"Do you know of anyone who had a problem with Steve?"

"Aside from the normal employee-management conflicts, not really." She paused a moment and then said, "Although, the day before he died, he got into a bad argument with that friend of his. I was sort of surprised."

"Which friend was that?"

"Mr. Huxley. He would come into the bank about once a month. He'd go into Steve's office with him; they'd close the door and talk for about an hour. I don't know if it was business or personal."

"How do you know they argued?"

"I had to ask Steve a question, and it couldn't wait. I hated to interrupt him, but I had no other choice. But when I got to the door, I could hear them shouting at each other in Steve's office."

"Did they say anything to you?"

"You mean when I heard them shouting?"

"Yes."

"No. I don't think they knew I heard them. I went back to my desk and tried to figure out the problem on my own. I wasn't about to walk in on that."

"How did Mr. Huxley seem when he came out of the office?"

"Actually, he seemed fine. Like nothing had happened. They both seemed perfectly calm. It was weird."

"Had you ever heard them fight before."

"No…but…"

"What?"

"I usually answer the phones at the bank. Not always. If I'm with a client and one of the tellers is free, they will. But over the last couple of months there's been a few times when Steve told me that if Mr. Huxley called, to tell him he was in with customers—even when he wasn't. I thought that was odd, since I knew they were friends."

"But you only heard them argue that one time?"

She nodded. "Yes."

"You mentioned you liked Mrs. Klein. Did you see her often?"

"Just when she'd come into the bank, or we'd have some

company get-together. She's really nice. Everyone at the bank likes her. She's nice to all of us."

"Do you think she ever knew her husband hit on you?"

Susan groaned and scooted down in her chair, embarrassed. "I sure hope not. I would hate for her to think I ever did anything to encourage that. And I did nip it immediately."

"Do you think Steve cheated on his wife…after he hit on you?"

Sitting back up straight in the chair, she pondered the question a moment. "I don't know. Maybe they were just having problems back then, and I sent the wrong message. Who knows? I was new at the bank at the time, and maybe I was trying too hard to be friendly and fit in. Maybe he got the wrong impression."

"So Steve didn't have a reputation around the bank for fooling around on his wife?"

She shook her head. "Oh no. And I certainly never said anything to anyone. I was too embarrassed."

"Did they seem like a happily married couple, Mr. and Mrs. Klein?"

Susan smiled. "Yeah, actually, they did. Which is one reason I wonder what was going on back then when I first started working at the bank. When that happened, I hadn't met his wife yet, so I didn't know what to expect. And when I finally met her, she was nothing like I imagined."

"What do you mean?"

"They seemed so happy together. When we'd get together for bank functions, they'd often hold hands, stuff like that."

"Did you ever get the feeling Mrs. Klein suspected her husband might be fooling around?"

"I don't think he was. I mean, I know that one time he made a pass at me. But generally, Steve was always very professional. He did everything by the book at the bank. And they did seem happily married. I always got the feeling his wife adored him, and if he ever cheated on her, I really don't think she ever knew. She acted like a woman who loved and trusted her husband."

"But you said he hit on you when you first went to work there?"

"I never heard any of the other women at the bank complain about him. So maybe it was my fault. Maybe something was going on in his life back then, and I sent the wrong message."

"WHY DOES it bug the hell out of me that Susan Mitchell makes excuses for Steve?" Brian asked the chief after Susan left the station. "We know he was a player."

"You think she was right? Did his wife have any idea he was seeing Carla?"

"I don't know."

"If I hadn't talked to Steve about his affair with Carla after Jolene's murder, I might start to wonder if maybe Carla was a midlife-crisis thing. His first affair."

"If he hit on Susan when she first went to work for him five years ago, then it obviously wasn't his first time," Brian reminded him.

"I know it wasn't. Not how Steve talked to me."

"How wouldn't his wife know her husband was a player? Don't wives often turn a blind eye to their husband's infidelity to make their marriage work? How wouldn't you know?"

"When did you figure out your wife was cheating?"

Brian didn't answer immediately. "Okay, you got me. I was clueless. I had absolutely no idea she'd been fooling around for over a year until she filed divorce papers."

"So maybe we need to take a closer look at this Baron Huxley. We know he gave Steve the tamales, and we know he argued with him the day before Steve died. Why don't you find out what they argued about."

BRIAN STOPPED by Baron Huxley's house on the way home Monday night. But Huxley's car was not in the driveway, yet there was a new for sale sign in front of his house. He tried calling Huxley's cellphone, but there was no answer, so he left a message for Huxley to call him.

THIRTY-ONE

Lily paused at Danielle's open bedroom door a moment, looking in, before making her presence known. She watched as Danielle stood at the dresser, looking into the mirror, weaving her hair into a neat fishtail braid.

"It always amazes me how you make that look so easy," Lily said as she entered the room.

With both her hands holding onto strategic strands of hair, Danielle glanced to Lily and smiled, and then looked back in the mirror. "After doing it for so long, it's almost second nature. I'll confess, I've been considering getting my hair cut."

Now standing next to Danielle, looking into the mirror with her, Lily frowned. "You wouldn't. You have beautiful hair."

"I would hope she wouldn't," Walt said when he suddenly appeared. He sat on the foot of the bed, watching the two young women.

Danielle glanced over her shoulder to see where Walt had landed. "Morning, Walt."

"Where is he?" Lily glanced around the room.

"He's sitting on the end of the bed."

"Hmmm…" Lily looked to the bed. "Do you always just barge in Danielle's room like that?"

"He does. I have no privacy." She sighed melodramatically. Putting the final touches on her braid, Danielle looked into the mirror. She could see her bed, but she couldn't see Walt. It didn't surprise her. Ghosts had no reflections.

"Do you think Antoine Paul's sister left for Vancouver yet?" Lily asked Danielle a few minutes later when the two women walked into the hallway, Walt trailing behind them. They headed for the staircase.

"She told me she was going to leave this morning. Yesterday, when I first saw her, she was getting ready to check out."

"Yeah, I remember you saying that." Lily held onto the railing as she started down the stairs.

"But I guess she felt emotionally drained after our talk yesterday and decided to spend another night and take off this morning."

"Do you think it helped, talking to her?" Walt asked. "Did you learn anything that might put you in a better position to convince her brother's spirit to move on?"

"I'm not sure." Danielle paused a moment, her hand on the railing. She considered Walt's question and then started walking again. "He didn't sound like a horrible person. Not like someone who would strangle a woman in an alley. He took in his sister when their parents died, helped her get into college."

"And she said he wasn't violent?" Lily asked as she stepped onto the first-floor landing, followed by Danielle and then Walt. The three headed for the kitchen.

"He had a temper, but she said he was never violent, but he could get really sarcastic."

"As I recall, he did call you *ghost girl*," Walt reminded her.

"Considering everything that's going on, I'm not even sure I should be worried about his spirit anymore. Chris saw him just that once, and Heather hasn't been bothered again. He mentioned something in front of Chris about wanting to get to me when I was away from Marlow House, but I've been all over town this last week and never saw him once. I would have figured he would have showed up at the Seahorse Motel, with his sister there."

"Maybe he's moved on." Lily led the way into the kitchen.

IAN JOINED Lily and Danielle for breakfast that Tuesday morning. The three sat at the kitchen table while Walt lounged by the counter on the other side of the room, smoking a cigar. Initially he had been sitting at the table with them, but the glare Danielle flashed him after a lit cigar appeared in his hand made it very clear to him she did not want cigar smoke at the table while they were eating.

"I learned something interesting last night," Ian said as he spread peach jam over his toasted English muffin.

"Yes? What's that?" Danielle asked.

"You know that guy who wanted to take you to San Francisco for dinner?"

In response, Danielle groaned and then popped a piece of bacon in her mouth.

"You know how we talked about Hillary basing her murder scenes on real-life crimes?"

Danielle and Lily stopped eating for a moment and exchanged glances.

"Yeah, what about it?" Danielle asked.

"When you told me his name, I knew it sounded familiar. So I looked him up last night. His wife was the first victim. The woman who was murdered in *Beautiful Rage,* so to speak."

Danielle glanced at Lily. Obviously, her housemate hadn't shared that bit of information with her boyfriend. *And we say Lily can't keep anything to herself.*

Lily flashed Danielle a grin while taking a sip of her coffee.

"You know he was a friend of Steve's. He was at Beverly's when Lily and I stopped over there on Sunday."

"I remember you telling me that. You obviously made quite an impression on him." Ian took a bite of toast.

"According to Chris, it was my money he was impressed with," Danielle scoffed.

"Chris might be right," Ian agreed.

"Hey!" Lily reached over and gave Ian's forearm a light smack. "Why wouldn't he be interested in Dani for herself?"

Ian blushed. "I didn't mean that."

About to take a bite of her English muffin, Danielle arched her brows and looked coolly at Ian. "I am so abused around here."

Ian chuckled. "I'm sorry, Danielle. I didn't mean it like it sounded. It's just that when I looked up the guy last night, I was a little curious. By some of the articles I came across and a few things I saw on social media, looks like a number of his past clients are pretty upset with him. I wouldn't be surprised if he has a serious cash-flow problem like Adam suggested."

"Then he shouldn't be going out and buying wine for three hundred bucks a pop." Danielle took a bite out of her English muffin.

"He's also the one who gave Steve the tamales. That's supposedly what Steve ate the night he had the allergy episode and fell off the pier," Lily told him.

Ian looked at Lily. "How do you know that?"

"Beverly told Danielle that when she dropped over here the other day."

"I guess he and Steve were old friends. According to Beverly, they used to work together. But she seemed to think they weren't as close as they used to be," Danielle explained.

IT WASN'T QUITE 11:00 a.m. on Tuesday when Beverly Klein opened her front door for Officer Brian Henderson. She hadn't yet dressed for the day, but instead wore a floor-length terrycloth bathrobe, tied at the waist with a terrycloth belt. What she had underneath the robe, he had no idea. There were no pajama bottom cuffs peeking out below the robe's hem. Her face was free of makeup, but her hair was damp, as if recently shampooed.

"I was hoping I could ask you a few questions," Brian asked, still standing on the front porch.

Beverly opened the door wider and welcomed him in.

After she showed him to the living room, he said, "If you'd feel more comfortable slipping into something else, I can just wait down here."

Beverly let out a heavy sigh. "I'm afraid this is all I've the energy to put on today." She plopped down on a chair facing him. "Although I suppose I should be flattered anyone might consider me in terrycloth even remotely racy."

"Oh…I didn't mean—" Brian blushed.

Beverly cut him off, waving her hand dismissively. "I was just teasing. Thank you for making that offer, but frankly, I don't really care who knows I haven't gotten dressed yet. Hell, considering everything, I may never get dressed again."

"I'm sorry to have to bother you, under the circumstances, but there are still a lot of unanswered questions."

"I understand. Would you like me to get you a cup of coffee first? Some tea? Water?"

Brian smiled. "No, thank you, I'm fine."

Leaning back in her chair, she folded her hands on her lap and looked at Brian. "Well then, what did you want to ask me?"

"Have you seen Baron Huxley in the last couple days?"

"Baron?" She shook her head. "No, why?"

"We've been trying to contact him. There are a few more questions we'd like to ask him. But he wasn't at his house, and he hasn't been answering his cellphone."

"Perhaps he went back to Vancouver. Baron doesn't live here, you know."

"I understand. But we found his car this morning in the pier parking lot. The cook at Pier Café said he noticed it parked there last night when he got off work. But there is no sign of Mr. Huxley."

She frowned. "That's odd."

"I noticed the for sale sign in his front yard—"

"For sale sign? What are you talking about?"

"Mr. Huxley put his Frederickport house up for sale."

"Really? He never mentioned anything to me about that when he stopped over here the other day."

"I dropped by Frederickport Vacation Properties and spoke to Adam Nichols—that's who's listing the property—and according to Adam, Mr. Huxley should still be in town. He told Adam he'd talk to him before he left for Vancouver."

She shook her head. "I don't know what to tell you. But then, Baron was more my husband's friend—and my acquaintance. We never really did anything socially—not since his wife was killed."

"If you hear from him, I'd appreciate it if you'd call me."

"Certainly." Beverly smiled. "Was that it?"

"No. As I said, there are still a number of unanswered questions."

"Like why Steve had crabmeat in his body?"

Brian nodded.

"I've been asking myself that same question over and over again. I can't come up with any logical reason for Steve eating crab. He just would never do that."

"The only other explanation—your husband ate something that had crab in it, and he didn't know. Did your husband have any enemies?"

"Enemies?" Beverly frowned. "Are you saying someone intentionally gave my husband something with crab in it? Without his knowledge?"

"We're looking into all possibilities. Did he have any enemies?"

"Absolutely not. Not everyone loved Steve, but I don't believe anyone hated him. Certainly not enough to kill him."

"Do you know if your husband had any sort of problem with Mr. Huxley?"

"Baron? You're asking because Baron's the one who gave Steve those tamales, aren't you?"

"Do you know of any problems they may have had? Did your husband mention anything to you about Mr. Huxley?" Brian already knew Beverly had confided in Danielle about problems between Steve and Huxley. He wondered what Beverly would tell him.

Beverly sat silently in the chair a few moments, considering the question. "To be honest, Steve and Baron have had issues off and on for as long as I've known them. But I never really knew the details, and they always seemed to work out whatever problems they had."

"Do you know what kind of problems?"

"A difference of opinion in how to conduct business. Steve took his job very seriously, and while he didn't make a habit of discussing his work in depth with me—he often told me it would just bore me—he did suggest a few times over the years that Baron wasn't especially ethical. I suspect that's why he cut ties with him."

"Cut ties with him? I thought they were friends."

"I meant professionally. Years ago they started a business together, and not long after Baron's wife died, Steve and Baron dissolved their partnership."

"But they remained friends?"

"Yes. It was better when they separated their business and personal lives. After Baron bought his beach house here, they'd often go fishing together. I think they enjoyed each other, as long as they didn't have to work together."

"Do you know if they've had any recent disagreements? A falling out?"

"Certainly you don't believe Baron did something to those tamales, do you?"

"You don't believe Baron Huxley is capable of something like that?"

Beverly considered the question a moment. Finally, she said, "To be honest, I really don't know Baron that well. I have no idea what he might be capable of."

"Do you know if he and Steve had any recent issues?"

"Actually, they did. About a week before Steve's death, I walked into the bedroom and Steve was on the phone with Baron. They were obviously in a heated argument."

"Do you know what about?"

She shook her head. "No. As soon as I realized Steve was on the phone—and in the middle of an argument—I turned around and left the room and closed the door behind me."

"How did you know he was talking to Huxley?"

"When he came out of the bedroom after he finished the call, I asked him who he was talking to; he said Baron. I asked him what was going on, and he just said *you don't want to know.*"

"And you didn't press him?"

She shook her head. "No. But they've argued before and then the next day everything's fine again."

THIRTY-TWO

Both Danielle and Lily moved their cars to the street so the truck belonging to the heating and air-conditioning company could park along the side of the house. Inside Marlow House, Walt was following the workers around, keeping an eye on them and making sure they were doing a good job. Not that he actually knew anything about installing a heater and air conditioner, but it was keeping him busy and he seemed to be enjoying himself.

After parking her car on the street along the sidewalk in front of Marlow House, Lily went with Ian to go shopping. Danielle stayed home; there was a book she wanted to finish. Wearing jeans and an oversized pullover sweater, Danielle sat on the front porch swing, reading.

When Danielle looked up from her book thirty minutes later, she wondered how long he had been there. It was Steve Klein's ghost standing on the sidewalk, watching her. She looked at him for a moment and then glanced around. She didn't see anyone else. When he kept staring at her, she finally waved him over.

The next moment he was no longer standing on the sidewalk, but sitting next to Danielle on the swing. His instantaneous change of venue made her lurch in surprise, dropping her book to the ground.

"You startled me!" she scolded, leaning down, slightly annoyed to see the book had closed, causing her to lose her page.

"Sorry. No one sees me, so I forget something like that might scare someone."

"I'm not scared." Danielle set the now closed book on her lap and looked at Steve.

Turning to her, he studied her for a moment. "I'm a ghost, aren't I?"

"I thought you already went through that with Hillary."

"I did." He looked out to the street and leaned back in the swing. "It's just that I grew up believing people are afraid of ghosts."

"I think most are—but they generally can't see them, so it's sort of a nonissue."

"It's quite amazing to me that you can see ghosts. I never knew. Hell, I never even believed in ghosts when I was alive."

"Where's Hillary?"

"I don't know. I left her on the beach. She's trying to decide if she wants to stick around here or move on. It seems the prospect of seeing both her husbands at possibly the same time is a bit overwhelming to her."

Danielle chuckled. "I suppose that could be awkward."

"I think I'm ready to move on," he said.

"I thought you were going to go after your funeral?"

He shook his head. "No. I can feel something pulling me—a constant tug from the other side. It's time. But I can't yet. Something's bothering me."

"The police are looking into your death. They think it might be murder. Perhaps that's what's bothering you."

Turning back to Danielle, he frowned. "I wasn't murdered. I was careless."

"No. According to the coroner's report, you had crabmeat in your stomach. We're not talking about some cross contamination; we're talking crabmeat."

He shook his head. "That's impossible. I didn't eat anything that night except for the tamales."

"If that's true, then those tamales were tampered with. Who would do that?"

"I guess the obvious would be Baron; he gave me the tamales. But I don't see why he'd want to make me sick. We had our disagreements, but nothing that would make him want to hurt me."

"He did more than hurt you. You're dead."

Steve shrugged. "That's only because I couldn't find my EpiPen. I panicked and stumbled off the pier. It was stupid of me."

"Did you take the EpiPen out of your tackle box? Maybe leave it somewhere?"

"No. I remember seeing it Wednesday night when I put some new hooks in the box."

"Then someone removed your EpiPen and fed you crabmeat. What about your wife?"

"Bev? Absolutely not. I may not have been a perfect husband—but she was the perfect wife."

"Then why did you cheat on her?"

Stunned by her question, Steve just stared at Danielle. Finally, he asked, "How did you know?"

"It doesn't matter. I just do. Maybe your wife found out about Carla—or maybe Carla tampered with the tamales?"

With a groan, Steve leaned back in the swing and closed his eyes, rocking his head back and forth. A moment later, he lifted his head again and looked at Danielle. "You have to promise me something."

"What?"

"If Bev finds out about Carla, please let her know that I loved her. That I never had feelings for Carla. She was the one I loved."

Narrowing her eyes, Danielle glared at Steve. "Why do some men say crap like that? You cheat on your wife and then have the audacity to declare, *gee, it was you I always loved*. Sheesh." She shook her head in disgust.

"Does that mean you won't tell her?"

"I don't know," she grumbled.

After a few moments of silence, Danielle asked, "Tell me who had access to those tamales after you got them from Baron."

"I was at the bank when he gave them to me. I put them in the refrigerator in the lunchroom. So basically, anyone who was at the bank had access to them. It's not like the room is locked, and the hallway to the public restroom is right near the door to the break room."

"Did you take them home that night?"

"Yes. Put them in our refrigerator at home. And then I took them fishing with me."

"Did Carla have access to them?"

"I suppose she did when I went into the restaurant to get coffee.

But there was no way she had time to tamper with them. Anyway, I don't think Carla would do something like that."

"Someone did!"

Steve let out a sigh. "I suppose it would be possible if she switched the tamales Baron gave me with crab tamales."

"That seems pretty farfetched too. Where would she get her hands on crabmeat tamales?"

"They do sell them at Beach Taco."

Danielle glanced at Steve. "They do?"

"I stopped by there a couple weeks ago to pick up some takeout for me and Carla. I saw them in the cooler. Crab tamales. I never heard of such a thing."

"So you were getting takeout for you and your girlfriend?" Danielle snarked.

"Yeah…I was. We really couldn't go out and eat together in town. I remember telling her I'd never buy tamales at that place; they might give me the wrong ones." He laughed.

Danielle flashed Steve a scowl. "Amazing you can joke about it, considering they did kill you."

He shrugged. "Nothing I can do about it now."

"I'm curious about something."

"What?"

"Was it common for you to take tamales with you when you went fishing?"

"Yeah. Beverly can't stand them. So we never have them at home. Baron usually comes into town at least once a month, always brings me some. Easier than making a sandwich."

"Did the tamales taste different that night?"

Steve frowned and considered the question a moment. "Now that you mention it, they did taste a little different. But not like they had crabmeat. The sauce was different. It was a different sauce."

"Perhaps your tamales weren't tampered with—per se. Instead of someone replacing the meat, maybe someone switched your tamales."

"STEVE HAS MOVED ON?" Police Chief MacDonald asked. He stood with Danielle in the Frederickport Police Department parking lot.

Casually leaning against her Ford Flex, Danielle nodded. "Yeah, after he told me all that about the crabmeat tamales they sell locally."

"Did he have any idea who'd want him dead?"

"No. He insists his wife didn't do it. And he didn't believe Carla would, either. I asked him about Baron Huxley and he said while they had some issues over the years, it was nothing that would end up with one of them killing the other one."

"We do know Carla was poking around in his things when he went to the restroom that night, and she did have a motive."

"I'm not sure she had a motive exactly. I keep going back and forth about Carla. I like her, and I can't imagine she'd do something like that, but she did have the opportunity, and she *might* have had a motive."

"What I need to do is see if any of our suspects have recently purchased crab tamales."

GEORGE MARTINEZ STOOD behind the counter in his restaurant, Beach Taco.

"Sure, we sell crabmeat tamales. The tourists love them."

"I was wondering if I could look at your credit card records to see who might have purchased any in the last month."

Martinez laughed. "I guess you missed the sign in the window, Chief. Cash only. We don't do credit cards."

The chief took out an envelope and removed several photographs. He placed them on the counter. "Do you recognize any of these people?"

Martinez nodded. "Sure, they're all customers. I don't know all their names, but I've seen them all in here at one time or another."

"Do you remember selling any of them crabmeat tamales?"

Martinez carefully studied the photographs for a moment, but then shook his head. "Sorry, Chief. I couldn't tell you."

"How about any of your other employees? Do you think they might remember who bought some recently?"

"It's just me and my wife and one employee. Wife works in the kitchen, never waits on customers. The girl who works for us just started yesterday, so I don't imagine she'll be of much help."

"What about the employee she replaced?"

"She moved out of town. I have no idea where."

Picking up the photographs, MacDonald slipped them back in the envelope. He looked up at Martinez. "Any chance you have any cameras set up?"

"You mean like those surveillance cameras that capture hold ups, like we see on the news?"

"Yeah…"

Martinez laughed. "What would I need those for? You take good care of us, Chief. I don't think any restaurant in town has ever been robbed."

THIRTY-THREE

Brian Henderson drove into the Frederickport Police Department parking lot at the same time as the chief. They parked their cars next to each other. When MacDonald got out of his vehicle, he was carrying a sack from Beach Taco.

"Lunch?" Brian asked as he slammed his car door shut.

"I figured since I was at Beach Taco, I might as well pick up some tacos. I bought enough for everyone. Have you eaten yet?"

"No. I just left Beverly Klein's. Why were you at Beach Taco?"

"Did you know they sell crabmeat tamales?"

"Any of our suspects purchase any recently?" Brian asked.

"Martinez didn't know. The girl who usually works the front counter quit a few days ago and moved out of town. Since the girl who replaced her started after Steve was killed, she won't be of any help."

Now at the entrance to the building, Brian opened the door and let the chief go in first.

While going through the doorway, MacDonald asked, "How did it go with Beverly Klein? Did you learn anything new?"

LATER THAT AFTERNOON, after MacDonald returned to his office, he was surprised by two unexpected visitors from the FBI.

They looked like FBI, MacDonald thought, as the two men walked into his office. He guessed they were in their forties. Each wearing a dark suit they were clean cut with closely cropped hair and firm handshakes. They identified themselves as Agents Thomas and Wilson. After each took a seat facing MacDonald's desk, they explained they were there to discuss Steven Klein's death.

MacDonald gave them a brief summary of the investigation to date and then asked, "Why exactly is the FBI interested in this case?"

"It involves one of your suspects, Baron Huxley," Wilson told him.

"How so?"

"We've been investigating Huxley for over six months," Thomas explained. "It involves one of his companies, a mortgage consultant company that supposedly helps at-risk homebuyers who've fallen behind on their mortgage."

"Supposedly?" the chief asked.

"We believe he's used the company to take advantage of his clients, many of whom have lost their homes after dealing with him," Thomas explained.

"What does Klein's death have to do with this?" MacDonald asked.

"Klein was Huxley's business partner when the company was initially set up, but they had some sort of falling out and Klein left the company," Wilson told him.

Agent Thomas then said, "Recently we came across some information we intended to use to convince Klein to work with us in exposing his former partner."

Are we talking blackmail? MacDonald wondered, yet he kept the thought to himself. Instead, he asked, "What is Huxley facing if charges are brought and he's convicted?"

"Considering his age and the number of charges, it could send him away for the rest of his life," Wilson said.

"You think Huxley is the one who murdered Klein?"

Wilson shrugged. "He had the motive."

"Did he know Klein was going to roll on him?" MacDonald asked.

"We hadn't spoken to Klein yet." Wilson glanced to his partner and shifted in his chair. "You see, Chief MacDonald, this is very sensitive, and it can't leave this office."

MacDonald nodded. "Understood."

"We believe there was a leak in our office—someone Huxley has been paying off—and we're fairly certain he tipped Huxley off about us going to Klein."

"So Klein had no idea you were going to talk to him?" MacDonald asked.

Wilson shook his head. "Not unless Huxley told him, which we don't think he did. If Klein knew everything we did about him, I imagine he would be calling us, considering his past history."

"What do you want from me?"

"Were you intending to bring murder charges against Huxley?" Smith asked.

"I'm not there yet. In fact, we can't find Huxley."

Wilson bolted up straighter in his chair. "What do you mean?"

"We've been trying to locate him since yesterday afternoon. No one's at his beach house, and his car was parked overnight at the pier. Of course, it's always possible he had car trouble and left it down there overnight. It hasn't even been twenty-four hours yet."

"You said he wasn't at his beach house last night, have you checked this morning?" Thomas asked.

"He wasn't there this morning, and we know he didn't return last night. My officer left a note on his door, and it was still there this morning. Plus, he hasn't been answering his cellphone."

Thomas looked at his partner. "Did he skip town?"

"I spoke to Adam Nichols about Huxley," the chief said. "He's Huxley's Realtor. According to Adam, Huxley was planning to stop by the office before he left town. The last time I spoke to Adam, he still hadn't heard from him. So as far as Adam is concerned, Huxley is still in Frederickport."

"Maybe his car broke down at the pier, and he called a friend," Wilson suggested. "If it was a lady friend, it might explain why he didn't return home, but stayed with her. Not so unusual he wouldn't be answering his phone if that were the case."

Thomas flipped through his notes and shook his head. "There's nothing on any women he was seeing locally."

Wilson looked at MacDonald. "Do you know if he was seeing anyone in Frederickport?"

MacDonald shook his head. "Not that I've heard of. I know he wanted to take Danielle to San Francisco for dinner, so that would lead me to believe he wasn't seeing anyone seriously in town."

"Danielle?" Wilson asked.

"I spoke to Danielle today. I know she hasn't seen him since he stopped over to her house on Friday night."

Thomas took out his pen and looked up at the chief. "What's this Danielle's last name? Where does she live?"

"Danielle Boatman, she owns Marlow House. But really, if she had seen him, she would have told me."

Thomas jotted down something in his notepad and then looked up at the chief. "Do you have her address and phone number?"

EDWARD MACDONALD SAT ALONE at his desk and stared at his phone. The temptation to call Danielle and give her the heads-up was overwhelming, but the FBI agents had been crystal clear—he was not to inform her they were on their way to her house. If he did tell her, it could backfire, should she slip and let them know she had been tipped off about their impending visit. With a sigh, MacDonald shoved his phone aside. He wished to maintain his good relationship with the FBI.

THE HEATING and air-conditioning people had just left. Yet the installation of the new unit looked like it was going to take a few more weeks. They had mentioned something about a problem with the ductwork and back-ordered parts.

While she should be annoyed with what appeared to be a larger project than she had initially anticipated, Danielle figured that in the big scheme of things it was really a minor bump. Considering what other people were dealing with, she figured she should just be grateful she could easily afford the new unit. She told herself, until it was installed, she would simply put on a sweater if it got too cold or open a window if it got too warm.

Danielle headed for the front door, car keys in hand. She was going to move her Flex and park it back in its spot next to the house on the side drive. Danielle swung the front door open and came face-to-face with two serious-looking gentlemen, one of whom was preparing to ring her bell.

"Oh, hello," she greeted them. Without thought she blurted out,

"Are you Jehovah Witnesses?" Several days earlier, two men—much older and not as attractive—had shown up on her porch, wearing suits. They had been Jehovah Witnesses. She wondered briefly if the church was in the midst of some spring membership drive.

The man who had been about to ring the bell pulled out an identification badge and showed it to Danielle. The second man then showed his badge.

"The FBI? Wow, I guess you aren't Jehovah Witnesses," she mumbled. "Although, I suppose an FBI agent could be a Jehovah Witness…What in the world do you want to talk to me about?" Still holding onto the edge of the door, Danielle had not yet welcomed the officers inside.

"We'd like to come in and ask you a few questions about a friend of yours."

"What friend?" Danielle asked, still not budging from the doorway.

Walt suddenly appeared next to Danielle, looking the men over. "So these are G-men?"

"Can we come in, please? It would be best if we discussed this inside, in private."

Walt glanced over the men's shoulders. "It's just you two out there. Isn't this private enough?"

Ignoring Walt, Danielle gave the agents a nod and opened the door wider so they could come inside.

"You know, it wasn't called the FBI when I was alive. Back then, it was just called the Bureau of Investigation. And they didn't call their agents G-men," Walt told Danielle as he followed her to the living room, the two FBI agents trailing behind them.

"I was watching a movie," Walt explained, "and heard the expression. I wondered why they were calling them G-men. Then I saw a special on the FBI. It's quite fascinating how much one can learn from the television."

"We can talk in here," Danielle said as she showed them into the living room. Glancing over at Walt, she wished he'd stop talking.

"The use of G-man originated after they arrested Machine Gun Kelly. According to folklore, Kelly shouted, *'Don't shoot, G-men.'* Meaning, don't shoot, government men. Of course, many believe that was fabricated by the press, and Kelly never said that."

As the agents each took a seat, Danielle briefly turned their backs to them and faced Walt, hissing under her breath, "Hush!"

"Excuse me?" Agent Wilson asked from his place on the sofa.

Blushing, Danielle turned to the officers. "Umm…I heard my cat meowing for dinner. It's too early."

"That cat?" Thomas asked, pointing in the opposite direction to the fireplace, where Max was stretched out on the hearth, sleeping.

"Umm…" Danielle glanced to Max.

Walt chuckled. "You're usually quicker on your feet than that."

Taking a seat facing the sofa where the two agents sat, Danielle perched at the edge of the seat cushion, anxious to learn why they were here.

"I still say it's Chris." Walt sat down on the chair next to Danielle.

"We'd like to ask you a few questions about your friend Baron Huxley," Wilson began.

"That's who they want to talk about?" Walt shook his head and summoned a cigar.

"Baron Huxley? I know who he is, but I don't really consider him a friend. More of an acquaintance. A new acquaintance."

"Do you often fly off to dinner in other states with new acquaintances?" Wilson asked.

Danielle frowned. "What are you talking about?"

"Isn't it true that Mr. Huxley asked you to fly to San Francisco to have dinner with him on Friday night?"

"Yeah, but I didn't accept his offer." Still frowning, Danielle asked, "Who told you that?"

"Does it matter? Was it supposed to be a secret?" Thomas asked.

"Not a secret, but it's my personal business." Danielle sounded less friendly than she had been when she had first answered the door.

"How long have you and Mr. Huxley been seeing each other?" Wilson asked.

"I'm not seeing Mr. Huxley," Danielle snapped. "I barely know the man. I just met him."

Agent Wilson was about to say something but paused and took a deep breath. He glanced around and then stood up. Looking at Danielle, he asked, "When was the last time Baron Huxley was here?"

Danielle shrugged. "He's only been here one time, this past Friday."

Wilson's gaze locked with Danielle. In a menacing and threatening tone he said, "You're lying."

Walt bolted up from his chair and glared at the agent. Without pause, he waved his hand and in the next instant Wilson flew backwards, crashing into the sofa with such force it bounced him off again, sending the agent toppling to the floor by the foot of the sofa.

THIRTY-FOUR

Agent Thomas managed to get off the sofa before his partner landed on the cushion next to him and bounced to the floor. Standing over Wilson, he offered him a hand and asked, "What just happened?"

Taking the offered hand, Wilson stumbled to his feet while shaking his head in disbelief. "I don't know. It almost felt like someone hit me."

Danielle flashed Walt a reproving glare.

"He shouldn't have called you a liar. Very ungentlemanly like. And this is your home, Danielle. It's never acceptable to come into someone's home and insult them." Taking a drag off his cigar, Walt didn't appear the least bit sorry for his action.

Sitting back on the sofa, Wilson looked at Danielle. If she was startled or surprised with his recent collision into her sofa, she didn't show it. The way she looked at him would make one believe she was quite used to seeing men flying across her living room and crashing into the furniture.

"Why did you call me a liar?" Danielle asked calmly.

"If Mr. Huxley hasn't been here since Friday, why is it I can smell his cigar?" Wilson asked.

Agent Thomas stood and looked around. "You're right! I thought I smelled something."

Narrowing her eyes, Danielle glanced over to Walt.

Walt looked from Danielle to the cigar in his hand. "Huxley smokes the same brand?"

Still looking at Walt, Danielle arched her brows briefly and then looked back to the agents and smiled sweetly. "I don't know anything about the cigars your Mr. Huxley smokes. But this is an old house, and I've been told before that it sometimes smells a little like cigar. I'm sure that's what you smell."

Agent Wilson stood up. "Then you wouldn't mind if we look through your house."

Danielle let out a sigh. "Well, you don't have a search warrant, but since I don't have anything to hide, go for it."

"We'd appreciate if you'd stay in this room while we look around," Thomas told her.

"Why certainly." Had either agent been diabetic, Danielle's hyper-sanguine tone might have sent him into a diabetic coma.

As the agents headed for the hallway, Danielle looked to Walt and gave him a little nod toward the doorway.

Grinning broadly, Walt stood up. "I'll keep an eye on the G-men. Make sure they don't get in trouble."

Walt couldn't help himself. As he followed the agents around the house, he randomly poked, tripped, and at one point grabbed Agent Wilson's right earlobe and gave it a playful tug. Haunting, Walt decided, could be rather fun.

He was careful not to hurt either man—after all, they were simply doing their jobs, and just because one had spoken rudely to Danielle didn't justify breaking any limbs—or necks.

By the time the two men returned to the library, Danielle thought they looked frazzled, reminding her of two little boys who'd just taken a tour of the haunted house on Halloween and had gotten far more than they had bargained for.

"Do you believe me now?" Danielle asked.

"We didn't find Mr. Huxley, but that doesn't mean he wasn't here. We could smell his cigar smoke all through the house."

"Like I said, that is the way the house smells. You can ask anyone. What I don't understand, why are you looking for Mr. Huxley? I'd assume you could find him at his house."

"Mr. Huxley has been missing since yesterday."

"I still don't know why you think I might know where he is."

The agents sat back down on the sofa.

"When you saw Mr. Huxley, did he say where he was going?

Who he was meeting?" Wilson asked.

Danielle uncrossed and recrossed her legs while resting her elbows on the chair's arms. "As I told you, I barely knew the man. I first met him a little over a week ago when I stopped by to give my condolences to a friend who recently lost her husband."

"Beverly Klein?" Wilson asked.

"Yes…" Danielle paused, suddenly hit by an aha moment. "That's what this is about. You think he killed Steve Klein, don't you?"

"Why do you say that?" Wilson asked.

Danielle shrugged. "Huxley gave Steve the tamales he ate on the night he died."

"How do you know about the tamales?" Wilson asked. "I thought you weren't that close to Huxley?"

"I think everyone knows about the tamales. So Huxley is really missing? You think he took off? Why did he kill Steve? I thought they were friends?"

"We're here to ask you the questions," Thomas reminded her.

With another shrug, Danielle uncrossed and recrossed her legs again. "I just figured it was my turn to ask a question."

Thomas asked another question regarding her relationship with Huxley. In turn, Danielle went on to tell them exactly when and how they had met, about their second brief meeting at the real estate office, and finally about Huxley's uninvited visit and dinner invitation.

"If you had just met Huxley, why did he offer to fly you to California for dinner? A rather extravagant first date for a woman he just met, especially considering his recent financial difficulties," Thomas asked.

"Other than the obvious, my charm and beauty?" Danielle flashed them a grin and then with a more serious tone added, "Although it probably has more to do with my bank account. At least, that's what one of my friends suggested."

Thomas frowned. "I don't understand."

"You're the FBI, I thought you knew everything."

"What did you mean, your bank account?" Wilson did not sound amused.

"It's just that I…well, I have a lot of money." Danielle let out a sigh. "That's probably the real reason Mr. Huxley wanted to sweep me off my feet."

"That's why you didn't accept his offer?" Wilson asked. "You suspected he was after your money."

"No…actually I really thought he was after my charm and beauty," Danielle said with a pout. "But I wasn't interested. Heck, he is old enough to be my father. And yuck, the first time I met him he was all over—figuratively speaking—poor Beverly Klein. We talked about it afterwards. She thought she was imagining things, the way he seemed to be hitting on her. I didn't think she was. So really, why in the world would I accept a date from a man like that?"

BEFORE THE AGENTS LEFT, Thomas handed Danielle a business card and asked her to call them if Huxley contacted her, to which she agreed.

Standing at the front door, Danielle watched the two men make their way back to their car and drive off. Taking her cellphone out of her back pocket, she dialed the police chief.

"Was it you?" she asked when he answered the phone.

"Were they there?" he asked.

"Why didn't you warn me?"

"I couldn't."

"Why in the world did you tell them about Huxley asking me out for dinner?"

STILL TALKING to the chief on the phone, Danielle closed the front door and walked back to the living room to continue her phone call. What she failed to notice were the two spirits standing across the street in front of Ian's house: Hillary and Antoine, who stood watching as the FBI agents drove away.

"You need to go talk to her," Hillary told Antoine after Danielle shut her front door.

"What's the point, she can't see me."

"Certainly she can. I told you Danielle can see spirits like us."

Antoine shook his head. "No, I told you I tried. She was sitting in the restaurant with some guy and acted like I wasn't even there."

"Of course she did. If she was sitting with someone, she couldn't let him know she could see you. He'd think she was crazy!" Hillary laughed.

"This isn't going to work."

"I'm sorry I was never able to help you." Hillary reached out to touch Antoine's shoulder, but her hand simply moved through his arm as if it were air.

"It's not your fault. I was limited by the restrictions placed on me. If I could just settle this, I could finally move on." Antoine looked at Hillary. "I'm so exhausted. I just want to move on."

"Then let's go talk to her," Hillary insisted.

LOUNGING ON THE SOFA, her feet up on the cushions, Danielle had just gotten off the phone and was about to tell Walt about her conversation with the police chief when Walt bolted out of his chair and stood, facing the doorway.

Sitting up, Danielle turned around and looked over the back of the sofa. There, standing in the doorway, were Hillary and Antoine.

"Hello, Danielle," Hillary cheerfully greeted her. She looked at Walt. "Please be nice, Walt. I don't care for that nasty look you're giving poor Antoine."

"Poor Antoine?" Danielle squeaked.

"He didn't want to come over here," Hillary explained. "And seeing Walt's expression, I can't say I blame him."

Antoine stared at Danielle. "You can see me?"

With a sigh, Danielle stood up from the sofa. "Yes. I can. I met your sister, by the way."

"Shirley, she's here?"

Danielle shook her head. "I don't think she is anymore. She told me she was leaving this morning. She stayed two nights at the Seahorse Motel, not far from here."

"Why was she in town?" Antoine asked.

"You looked in Heather's window. She saw you and didn't know you were a ghost. When she reported it, the police had a composite drawing done. Your picture was in the local paper. She saw it."

"Oh no," Antoine groaned. Dejected, he slumped down in a nearby chair. "I didn't want to drag Shirley into this…give her false hope. I don't want her hurt any more than she already is."

"Danielle, you need to help Antoine," Hillary insisted.

"Absolutely not!" Walt roared. "I don't appreciate how he just barges into her dreams, threatens Danielle—"

Hillary looked at Antoine. "Did you threaten her?"

Antoine shrugged. "I just told her to leave you alone. But in my defense, you were still alive at the time."

Hillary let out a sigh. "He has a point, Walt."

"He does?" Danielle and Walt said at the same time.

"Please, Danielle, do this for me. I've decided it's time for me to move on—but I can't do it unless you agree to help Antoine."

"You're ready to go?" Danielle asked.

Hillary smiled. "Oh yes!"

"What about your husbands?" Danielle asked.

"Well, I suppose I'll have to deal with them when I get there—wherever that may be—assuming, of course, they are there. Who really knows?"

"So why are we stuck with Antoine?" Walt asked.

Hillary frowned at Walt. "You're not stuck with Antoine. In fact, Walt, you don't have to do anything. Just let Danielle help him, I know she can. I believe the universe sent me to Marlow House in my last days to put these two together."

Walt cocked his brow at Hillary. "The universe?"

"Or a guardian angel…or God…something did." Hillary smiled.

"What I don't understand, what's changed since the last time we spoke?" Danielle asked Hillary.

"Antoine explained everything. He couldn't before, not when I was still alive. But now I understand, but unfortunately I'm not in the position to help him, you are."

"Why should she help someone who is a killer?" Walt asked.

"We aren't really sure he is actually a killer," Hillary said.

"I thought that's what you saw in your dream?" Danielle looked from Hillary to Antoine. "Is she suggesting you showed her a dream where you were killing someone when, in fact, you didn't kill anyone?"

"Not exactly," Antoine said in an unsure voice.

"Well, what is it exactly?" Walt snapped.

"The thing is…" Antoine explained, "I don't know if I killed Melissa or not."

THIRTY-FIVE

"How could you possibly not know if you killed that poor woman?" Walt's tone wasn't the least bit sympathetic.

Antoine stood and faced Walt. "Hillary told me you didn't know if you committed suicide or were murdered. So how is that any different?"

"That's patently untrue," Walt insisted. "I knew I didn't kill myself. I simply didn't know *how* I died. That is entirely different."

"Perhaps you need to sit down and explain what you do know," Danielle told Antoine.

Antoine looked to Hillary, who returned a nod of encouragement. They both sat down.

"I was researching a business owned by Baron Huxley and Steve Klein," Antoine began. "Their company claimed to help homeowners who were struggling to pay their mortgage payments or were behind in their payments. I had reason to believe it was really a scam."

"So you didn't really know Baron's wife, Melissa?" Danielle asked.

Closing his eyes briefly, Antoine let out a groan and leaned back in the chair. In the next moment, he opened his eyes again and looked at Danielle. "Oh, I knew Melissa. I met her when I first started investigating her husband's business—but she had no idea who I was. I never meant for it to happen…but…well, we fell in love."

"Did she know you were investigating her husband?" Danielle asked.

Sitting up in the chair, Antoine shook his head. "No, not until that night. Her husband was out of town. It was right before Valentine's Day. She was talking about leaving her husband, and I knew I had to tell her everything."

"How did she take it?" Danielle asked.

"She was furious with me." Antoine paused a moment and fidgeted with his red bow tie.

Danielle leaned closer to Antoine. She hadn't noticed before, but his red tie was embossed with tiny red hearts. "Are those hearts?"

Releasing hold of his tie, Antoine smiled sadly. "We were celebrating Valentine's Day. I saw the tie a couple days before, thought it would be fun to wear when we went out. But our Valentine's Day celebration didn't go as planned."

"What happened?" Walt asked.

"I came clean with Melissa. I told her everything. She was furious with me. She didn't understand. Melissa thought I had used her, that I really didn't love her."

"That's why you were arguing when you left the restaurant?" Danielle asked.

Antoine nodded. "Yes. We'd each driven there in our own cars. She was furious. As we were walking to the parking lot, she wouldn't listen to me. I knew she was just going to get in her car and drive off—drive out of my life. I grabbed her by the arm and dragged her into the alley. I just wanted her to listen to me."

"And when she wouldn't listen, you killed her," Walt snapped.

"No!" Antoine shook his head. "I…I don't think so."

"What happened in the alley?" Danielle asked.

"We were arguing, and I remember grabbing her by the forearms—I shook her. I just wanted her to listen to me. When I let go, she stumbled and fell down. And then…then…"

"Then what?" Danielle asked.

"I knelt down next to her…and the next thing I remember, I'm at her funeral. She's in her coffin, and people are walking by, looking at her. I hear them talking…whispering. I piece together what they're saying." Looking down, Antoine buried his face in his palms, unable to continue.

"He learned she had been strangled," Hillary continued for him. "The people at the funeral believed whomever Melissa had left the restaurant with—a man wearing a red bow tie—a man she had been arguing with—had strangled her in the alley."

"I'm assuming Melissa's spirit wasn't at her funeral?" Danielle asked.

Antoine didn't answer immediately. Finally, he lifted his face from his palms and looked at Danielle. "If she was, I never saw her there. I haven't seen her since that night in the alley."

"What did you want from Hillary?" Danielle asked. "Why have you been going into her dreams all these years…why have you been showing her murders?"

"I just wanted answers. I needed to know what had happened that night. I wandered around, looking for someone to help me. Then I saw Hillary, and I recognized her."

"Apparently Antoine and I attended the same writing seminar," Hillary explained. "I was exploring other genres—at the time I was burned out writing romance. It was a mystery writing seminar."

"I just assumed she was a mystery writer. I thought maybe someone like that could help me. I followed her back to her room. I tried to communicate with her, but of course she couldn't hear me. When she went to bed, I watched her sleep, and the next thing I know, I'm in her dream. I tried to explain to her what I needed, but the words wouldn't come—they never came. But I was able to show her what I remembered—and what I thought had happened."

"So you took her to the alley, and you showed her how you believed you had strangled Melissa?" Danielle asked.

"I didn't know what else to do. I was limited in how I could communicate with her. But when we were in the dream together, and I thought back to that night—everything appeared as I remembered."

"So you remembered strangling her?" Walt asked.

"No, not that. I just remembered what they said I had done. I just wanted Hillary to help me."

"I'm afraid I wasn't much help. I didn't really understand what he was trying to tell me—and then a story came to me."

"What about the other murders?" Danielle asked.

"After that night, I just wandered. I didn't know what else to do, where to go. Then one day I witnessed a man being murdered. I tried to save him—but there was nothing I could do. It was chilling.

I asked myself, if I was responsible for Melissa's death, perhaps this was my punishment. And then I began to wonder, perhaps I was supposed to do something. That killer was still alive. He was going to get away with what he had done. I needed to do something."

"So you went into Hillary's dream again? Did you really imagine showing her that murder would help catch the killer?" Danielle asked.

"I didn't know what else to do. It didn't work—but then it happened again—I tried again—and it still didn't work."

"I'm curious," Walt asked. "If you knew Danielle could talk to spirits—after all, you did call her ghost girl—why didn't you simply reach out to her and see if she could help you? Why did you tell her to stay away from Hillary?"

Antoine shook his head. "I don't know exactly. It was almost a compulsion. I'd witness a murder, show it to Hillary, expect something to happen—and when nothing did, it started all over again."

Walt frowned. "So you just kept doing the same thing over and over again, with the same failed results?"

Danielle leaned back on the sofa. By her pensive expression, it was obvious she was considering Antoine's explanation. Finally, she said, "Don't be too hard on him, Walt. I don't think it's that unusual."

The three spirits—Walt, Antoine, and Hillary—turned to her.

"What do you mean?" Walt asked.

"I've heard stories of other hauntings where a spirit does the same thing over and over again. Sort of a…loop. Take Harvey Crump, for example. He was in a loop. Each Halloween he'd show up at Presley House and look for something that hadn't been there for years. But each Halloween, he'd return and do it all over again. I suspect my interaction with Harvey and the fire broke the cycle." She then added under her breath, "At least I hope so."

"My dying broke the cycle," Hillary suggested.

"I believe so. But Antoine is still here, and I suspect he needs to know what really happened that night," Danielle said.

"But how?" Antoine asked. "I don't know what else to do."

Danielle sat up on the sofa. "I think another dream hop is in order."

"What do you mean?" Antoine asked.

"You need to take me on a dream hop—show me that night—what you remember, not what you think may have happened. At the point in the dream where you can't recall what else happened, you need to step back and let it simply play out."

Antoine shook his head, clearly confused. "I don't understand."

Hillary frowned. "Neither do I."

Walt let out a groan. "I'm afraid I do."

Hillary and Antoine turned to Walt, waiting for an explanation.

"If you take her on a dream hop where you're showing her something that actually happened when you were still alive—like you did with Hillary in the first dream—it's possible for the dream to play out as it really happened, even if you don't remember. As long as your physical body was still present in the alley, you should be able to see what happened after you knelt down next to Melissa."

"I REALLY DON'T LIKE THIS," Walt told Danielle as she climbed into bed that night.

"You agreed it would work." Wearing her pajamas, Danielle pulled the covers and sheets over her.

"I know I did. But I don't like you going off with that man. He could be a killer."

"It's just a dream." Danielle reached to the light on the nightstand and turned it off, sending her room into darkness.

"I still don't like it."

"Good night, Walt. You need to leave. No way can I fall asleep with you hovering about."

Walt didn't answer immediately. Finally, he said, "Alright. I'll go. But you be careful. And remember, if you need to wake yourself up, focus and scream."

FALLING asleep on demand was even more difficult than Danielle had imagined it would be. Curled into a fetal position facing the window, she hugged her pillow and closed her eyes. A few minutes later she rolled over, her back now to the window, the pillow still in her arms. And so it went for the next three hours—tossing and turning, taking numerous trips to the bathroom and one trip downstairs to drink a glass of warm milk. She remembered reading somewhere that warm milk would help her sleep. It didn't. It was past 2:00 a.m. when Danielle finally succumbed to sleep.

Opening her eyes, she found herself standing on the sidewalk outside a restaurant. It was nighttime and Danielle was alone. Just as a couple stepped out from the restaurant onto the sidewalk, Antoine appeared by her side. It was in that moment Danielle recognized the man who had just stepped outside—he was also Antoine. The woman by his side, Danielle had seen her picture in the news articles.

"That's you and Melissa, isn't it?" Danielle stated the obvious.

"She was so beautiful," Antoine murmured.

"Yes, she was," Danielle agreed.

"Let's get this done," Walt said when he appeared a moment later, standing between Danielle and Antoine's spirit.

"Walt?" Danielle said in surprise. "What are you doing here?"

"You didn't seriously think I was going to let you do this by yourself?"

"You can't be here!" Antoine protested.

"I certainly can!"

Antoine stamped a foot in protest. "This may not work if you're here!"

"You don't know that. There is absolutely no reason why I can't be here."

"I don't know why you had to come!"

"Hey, guys, stop arguing!" Danielle interrupted. "We need to follow them!"

Walt and Antoine stopped arguing and turned to the young couple, who were hastily making their way toward the parking lot.

Flashing Walt a glare, Antoine said, "Fine. If you insist. Let's go. We need to keep up with them."

THIRTY-SIX

The three—Danielle and the spirits of Antoine and Walt—followed the couple away from the restaurant. Melissa, who was walking at a good pace, was several feet in front of her companion, who kept shouting at her to slow down and listen to him. Just as they reached the entrance to the parking lot, he grabbed her.

"Let me go!" Melissa hissed just as Antoine—not the spirit Antoine—clutched her forearm and jerked her to the right, pulling her toward the alley.

"You're not leaving until you listen to me!" Antoine countered, his hand digging into her arm as he forced her to follow him.

"There is nothing you can say! Let me go!" Melissa shouted as Antoine continued to hold on tight, dragging her away from the parking lot.

After several stumbles, Melissa stopped resisting and silently followed him into the dark alleyway, their pace faster than a walk yet not quite a run. Once there, Antoine jerked her around so that they faced each other.

Just as Antoine—not the spirit—was about to say something, Melissa began shrieking obscenities in his face, refusing to listen to what he had to say. Frustrated, he grabbed hold of Melissa's shoulders and began shaking her, telling her to listen to him. Melissa managed to push away, yet then stumbled and fell to the ground.

"You practically shoved her down!" Danielle turned to Antoine the spirit and glared at him.

"I didn't mean to," Antoine muttered helplessly.

Walt shook his head in disgust. "There is never reason to manhandle a woman. Such a cowardly thing to do."

"I just wanted her to listen to me," Antoine explained. "I loved her."

Danielle looked back to the couple. Antoine—not the spirit—knelt by Melissa, who crouched on the ground, yet there was no motion. Like statues, the couple appeared to be frozen.

Danielle glanced to Antoine the spirit. "Why did you stop? What happened next?"

Antoine shook his head. "I don't know. This is all that I remember. After I attended Melissa's funeral and heard what I had supposedly done to her, I couldn't get the image of me strangling her out of my head. So when I showed Hillary what had happened that night—what I remembered happening—when I came to this part, I couldn't help but think about what I had heard. I didn't mean to show her that—"

"Unfreeze it," Danielle said. "Let it just happen without you interfering."

"What good will that do?" Antoine asked.

"I thought we already explained this to you," Walt said impatiently. "You don't need to remember what happened next—you don't need to improvise—simply let it happen. As long as you were present, we'll see what happened next."

Antoine didn't quite believe Walt, but he turned to the couple—the woman he loved and the man he had once been—and watched as they came to life again.

In the next moment the three observers learned why Antoine could not remember what had happened after Melissa had fallen to the ground and he knelt by her side. Some might have mistaken the sound they heard next as a car backfiring—as a bullet hurled through the air and hit its intended target: Antoine Paul.

Surprised by the sound, Danielle let out a gasp as the Antoine by Melissa's side crumpled to the ground. Looking in the direction from which the bullet had been shot, Danielle watched as three men stepped out from the darkness. One was Baron Huxley. She did not recognize the other two men.

"They shot me!" Antoine the spirit cried out. "I couldn't have killed Melissa, they killed me."

Walt shook his head. "I suspect you aren't dead, at least not at this point."

Watching the three approaching men, Danielle dismissively waved a hand at the two spirits. "Shhh, let's watch what happens next."

The scene reminded Danielle of an old gangster movie—three men dressed in dark suits, stepping out from the shadows while two people sprawled on the ground—one recently shot, blood spilling from his back, while the woman on the ground tried to grasp the reality of the man now dying just inches from her.

When Melissa looked up, she looked into the eyes of her husband. Baron towered over not just her, but his two companions. Tears ran down her cheeks as she tried to form the right words.

Looking coolly from the woman by his feet to the man to his right, Baron said without emotion, "Finish the job."

To Danielle's horror, the man on Baron's right knelt down and grabbed hold of Melissa by the neck and proceeded to strangle the life from her. Her eyes bulged, looking up pleadingly to her husband, as her hands clutched the wrists of the man who now had her by the throat.

"Oh my god!" Danielle gasped. Unable to watch the grizzly scene, she turned to Walt, who wrapped his arms around her as she closed her eyes. Holding Danielle tightly, Walt shielded her from the scene as he watched it unfold.

The dying Antoine groaned in pain, his eyes fluttering open. Just as that happened, Baron knelt down and grabbed hold of Antoine's face, forcing him to look at what was happening to Melissa.

"You caused this. Watch her die. That might as well be your hands on her throat. You killed Melissa," Baron hissed.

When Baron's henchman finished with Melissa, Baron stood and looked down at the pitiful pair. "Leave her there. But get rid of him." Baron turned and walked away, once again disappearing into the darkness. The next moment, the scene froze.

"I suspect you just died," Walt announced.

"I thought you said as long as I was still there, we'd be able to see what happened next. I'm still there."

Opening her eyes again, Danielle turned back to the lifeless bodies. "We're not really sure how all this works. We're pretty sure as long as you were alive back then and still present, the event will replay in a dream like this. But once a person dies? Spirits don't always grasp what's happening around them right after death. Walt, for example, has no memory of the events immediately following his death. He didn't know they had found him hanging in a noose."

Walt cringed. "Please, Danielle, you know I loathe thinking about that."

"Sorry, Walt." Danielle turned to face Antoine's spirit. "In some cases, a spirit will clearly remember what happened as they left their body—they remember what was going on, what people said. But obviously, you don't. Which isn't unusual when a death is especially traumatic. At least, that's been my experience."

In the next moment, Danielle found herself sitting on her bed. Walt and Antoine stood nearby in the darkness.

"Wow, that was quick." Danielle reached over and turned on her nightstand light.

"I couldn't stay there." Antoine shook his head.

"I hope you don't mind, I decided to wake you up after we left," Walt explained. "I was afraid it might be too confusing for you in the morning when you did wake up."

Danielle yawned. "Now we know what really happened. Baron had his wife killed—and you."

DANIELLE SLEPT in on Wednesday morning. When she finally woke up, she glanced at the clock on her nightstand and groaned when she saw the time. It was almost 10:00 a.m. There was also something else on her nightstand, something that hadn't been there the night before. It looked like a letter.

Sitting up in the bed, Danielle snatched the piece of paper off her nightstand and looked at it. It was from Lily.

Leaning back on her pillows, Danielle read the note.

Call me when you get up. Went to Portland. Lily.

Tossing the note back on the nightstand, Danielle grabbed her cellphone.

"Hey, sleepyhead, so you finally decided to get up?" Lily greeted her when she answered Danielle's call.

"I had a rough night," Danielle explained.

"You feeling okay? You were already in bed when I got home last night, and I heard you get up a few times."

"It's a long story. I assume Ian is with you?"

"Yeah. He's driving. So what's up?"

"I'll explain later."

"Okay. By the way, Chris stopped by when we were leaving. I told him you were still in bed."

"Did he go back home?"

"No. He was on his way to the Gusarov Estate." Lily chuckled. "So weird to think he owns that place now."

"What's he doing over there?"

"I guess he had to meet the electrician. He told me to tell you he'd probably be over there the rest of the day."

"LILY LEFT WITH IAN. I heard them saying something about going to Portland," Walt told Danielle when she walked into the kitchen twenty minutes later. He sat at the kitchen table, reading the newspaper.

"I just talked to her." Danielle glanced around. "So where's Antoine?"

Walt set the paper on the table and looked up at Danielle. "I must say I'm relieved you didn't go out with that Huxley fellow. I assume you're planning to tell the chief?"

Danielle joined Walt at the table and sat down. "Yes, but without any evidence—aside from what we saw in a dream hop—I don't see how the chief can do much."

"Maybe that's why those G-men are looking for him. Maybe they know something about Melissa's murder."

"According to those *G-men*, Huxley is missing. So maybe you're right." Danielle sipped her coffee. "Although, I've a feeling it has more to do with Steve's death."

"You think Huxley killed Klein?"

Danielle shrugged and took another sip of her coffee. "If he was capable of killing his wife—or ordering her killed, I imagine he'd be perfectly capable of killing Steve. I don't know what his motive was, but considering what we saw last night, he's now on the top of my list."

"Last night was rather chilling. And I'm dead!"

"No kidding." Danielle shivered. "I hope Antoine didn't move on yet."

"I thought you wanted him gone?"

"I need to talk to him. See if he can remember anything about Huxley that might help expose him for the monster he really is."

Walt picked the newspaper back up off the table and turned its page. Skimming it, he said, "He told me he needed to think. He went down to the beach to take a walk." Walt turned the page and grumbled, "It hardly seems fair."

Danielle frowned. "What do you mean?"

Lowering the paper, Walt looked over it at Danielle. "That he can come and go at will. I wouldn't mind taking a walk along the beach."

Danielle stood up and smiled at Walt. "I tell you what, on our next dream hop, let's do that."

"What do you think about fishing?" he asked.

"Fishing? What do you mean?"

"I wouldn't mind doing a little fishing off the pier."

"Okay." Danielle set her coffee cup in the sink and headed for the back door. She paused a moment and looked back at Walt. "But you have to clean whatever we catch."

Walt started to respond, but frowned instead, watching Danielle leave the house. Now alone in the kitchen, Walt shook his head and looked back at the paper. "Clean the fish? From a dream hop?" Walt snickered under his breath and turned the page.

THIRTY-SEVEN

Wave after wave crashed, sending seawater rushing upwards onto the shore before retreating back again, only to be pounced by another breaker—and then another. Antoine sat alone on the beach, his arms wrapped around his bent legs while his chin rested atop his knees. Staring out to the endless horizon, he wondered what he might have done differently—how he might have saved Melissa and himself those many years ago.

"There you are," came a voice from behind him. He recognized it immediately. It was Danielle.

"I'm trying to figure out what I should do now."

Before sitting down beside him, Danielle took the cellphone from her back pocket and held it by her ear.

"Who are you calling?" he asked as Danielle sat next to him.

"If someone comes by, I don't want them to think I'm talking to myself." She flashed him a smile, still holding the phone by her ear.

Antoine said something, his voice almost a whisper. The sound of the breakers combined with the gusty wind made it difficult for Danielle to hear what he was saying. She shook her head and told him in a loud clear voice, "You need to speak up, I can't hear you."

In a louder voice he said, "You'll never know how much I regret my part in Melissa's death…the danger I put her in. I'm as responsible for killing her as her husband is."

BARON HUXLEY HADN'T RETURNED home since he had started watching the Seahorse Motel. So obsessed with finding Antoine Paul, he had spent two nights sleeping in his car, watching Paul's sister, and one night in some bushes across from Marlow House.

He was convinced Antoine Paul was in Frederickport and his sister was waiting for him to show up. But then Danielle Boatman had showed up instead. He watched as Shirley followed Danielle to her car to say goodbye. The two women hugged, and then Danielle drove off.

He waited around until the next morning, but Antoine Paul still had not shown up. After Shirley Paul checked out that morning, Huxley began wondering if he had been watching the wrong woman.

Baron's men in Vancouver, reported back to him later that day. Shirley Paul had arrived home, and there was no sign of her brother. By that time, Baron was already keeping an eye on Danielle.

According to Huxley's men, they had disposed of Paul's body by dropping it off a cliff into the ocean. Even if he had been alive, they insisted, there was no way Paul could have survived the fall. Obviously, his men had been wrong. He must have washed up on shore —still clinging to life—hiding out all these years—a smart thing to do considering Huxley would do what was necessary to finish the job.

Keeping a safe distance from Danielle, Baron followed her to the beach. He watched as she sat down on the sand alone, looking out to sea. His plan was to engage her in conversation and perhaps try to figure out her connection to Antoine Paul.

He was about ten feet from Danielle when he noticed she was talking on the phone. Pausing a moment, he considered retreating and then changed his mind. With measured steps he slowly approached Danielle, stopping when he heard her say, "It's not your fault, Antoine."

Baron froze.

"Maybe you were wrong to have an affair with a married woman, but you certainly didn't deserve to die—and neither did Melissa. Maybe Baron didn't strangle Melissa himself, but he ordered her hit."

Baron stayed frozen for only a moment. As his attention focused on Danielle's back, he moved his hand into the right pocket of his jacket and pulled out a small revolver. Pointing it at Danielle's head, he pulled back the hammer; it made a clicking noise.

The sound of the gun's hammer being engaged was not muted by the ocean or breeze. Startled, Danielle jerked around and found herself looking into the end of a revolver.

"Tell him you have to go now, and hang up. Or you know what I'll do," Baron said in a low voice.

Before Baron had issued the order, Antoine was already on his feet, his hands futilely swinging at the revolver, trying to knock it out of Baron's grasp. Unfortunately, Antoine's hands moved through Baron without so much as a nudge felt.

"I have to go now," Danielle said into the cellphone, her eyes never leaving Baron's. She went through the motions of turning off the phone, briefly wondering if Baron might notice her phone hadn't been on.

"Where is he?" Baron asked after grabbing the phone from Danielle's hand and shoving it in his pocket.

"Who?" Danielle managed to squeak.

"I know who you were talking to, Antoine Paul. Where is he?"

"He thinks I'm still alive?"

Trying to focus on the danger at hand, Danielle ignored Antoine, who began to rant, threatening Huxley—impotent threats considering the fact not only Baron couldn't hear him, he couldn't feel the blows Antoine was now pounding on his chest. Or more accurately—into his chest. Each time Antoine threw a punch at his killer, his fists moved effortlessly through the man's body.

Possible escape scenarios flashed through Danielle's mind. If she still had her cellphone, she might be tempted to knee Baron in the groin. Unfortunately, even if she did have her phone, she was still sitting on the sand, and even if she wasn't, he would probably manage to pull the trigger and blow her brains out before she got two feet away. The only other option she could think of—*Walt.*

"I can take you to him," Danielle offered.

"That was quick," Baron smirked. "And just where do you intend to take me to, the police station?"

Danielle shook her head, her eyes nervously watching the revolver still aimed at her head. "He's hiding at Marlow House. Antoine Paul, he's there."

"And why would you give him up so easily?"

"I guess…because you have a gun pointed at my head?"

IF SOMEONE HAPPENED to notice Danielle walking along the beach with the attractive older man, they would assume they were a couple, the way the man protectively wrapped his left arm around her shoulder. What they probably wouldn't notice was his right hand tucked into his jacket pocket, clutching the revolver now pointed at Danielle's midsection.

"You're taking him back to Marlow House?" Antoine asked excitedly as he walked alongside the pair.

"He better be there," Baron hissed.

Danielle refrained from conversing with Baron. Her primary objective was to get back to Marlow House without being shot. When they reached the front door, Baron gave her a little jerk backwards, stopping her from reaching for the front door.

"You need to let me unlock it," Danielle told him, her voice wavering. "The key is in my pocket."

"Who's all in the house?" he asked in a gruff voice, his left hand now clutching her forearm.

"Just Antoine. Lily went to Portland with her boyfriend."

"Good." He gave her a little shove toward the door. "Now open it."

With a shaky hand, Danielle removed the house key from her pocket and unlocked the door. She paused a moment and glanced around. She didn't see Antoine and assumed he had already gone inside.

"YOU'VE GOT to get out here and do something!" Antoine shouted when he found Walt in the library, lounging on the sofa.

Looking up from the book he was reading, Walt's expression was more bored than concerned. "What are you rambling on about? Do something about what?"

"He has Danielle!"

Dropping the book—it fell through him and onto the sofa—Walt stood. "Who has Danielle?"

"Baron Huxley. They're entering the house now—he has a gun!"

The next moment Danielle and Baron stepped into the front entry just as Walt appeared. When she saw Walt, Danielle physically relaxed. In the next moment, Baron gave Danielle a shove farther into the house as he slammed the front door shut and locked it behind him.

"What in the world is going on?" Walt demanded.

Removing his hand from his pocket, Baron aimed the gun at Danielle. "Where is he?"

Before she had time to answer, the gun flew from Baron's hand. Just as it took flight, Baron managed to pull the trigger, sending a bullet to a copper umbrella stand.

After hitting the umbrella stand, the bullet ricocheted across the entry—zigzagging along its course, briefly touching down along a bronze statue, sending the statue to the floor before moving to the next solid object and then the next until finally embedding itself into the wood banister, splitting the wood. The gun itself landed on the overhead light fixture, where it teetered precariously.

Danielle barely had time to take in the damage caused by the rogue bullet when Baron flew across the room, slamming face-first into a wall.

"Don't kill him, Walt!" she shouted.

Walt stood over the crumpled man, who moaned pitifully. "He's still alive. Don't worry, Danielle; I've no intention of killing him." Walt glanced over to Antoine, who silently watched. "We don't need another annoying ghost hanging around Marlow House."

SPRAWLED ACROSS THE WOOD FLOOR, Baron managed to flutter open his eyes. He wasn't sure where he was—everything was blurry. He lay there a moment, blinking his eyes, when the room came into focus, but now it was spinning—round and round. Closing his eyes again, he took a deep breath and could feel the rapid rate of his heartbeat. Then he heard it, a woman's voice. It was Danielle Boatman. She was talking to someone. But who? He could only hear her voice.

Telling himself to focus, Baron opened his eyes again. The room was no longer spinning. Taking a deep breath, he rolled onto his side, placed the palm of his right hand against the hardwood floor, and gave it a little shove. He sat up, still dizzy, and looked around. He was still in the front entry of Marlow House—alone with Danielle Boatman. She stood about six feet away, her arms folded across her chest as she watched him, a smug smile plastered on her face.

Licking his lips and feeling suddenly parched, he sat up straighter and glanced around the room before looking back at Danielle.

"Where's my gun?" he asked.

Danielle pointed to the overhead light fixture. He saw it—his gun perched overhead, on the verge of falling down and landing on his head—or in his hand, if he was lucky enough.

"What happened?" he asked, making no move to stand.

"You killed your wife. You killed Steve too, didn't you? Did you kill your wife because she was cheating on you or for another reason? Did she know too much about your dirty deals?"

"I don't know what you're talking about. I didn't kill either one." Baron tried standing up, but Walt gave his shoulder a shove, sending him back down onto the floor.

Danielle shrugged. "It doesn't really matter, they're both dead and you're responsible. Oh…and I forgot, Antoine Paul. You killed him too."

"What are you talking about?" Baron looked around the room frantically, as if he expected someone—probably Antoine Paul—to come jumping out of the woodwork. "Where is he? Where is Antoine Paul?"

"Don't you know? Walt, please get me my cellphone. It's in his coat pocket."

"Walt?" Again Baron looked around frantically, but when Danielle's cellphone floated out of his coat pocket and drifted across the room to Danielle, Baron let out a yelp and scooted back until his back hit the wall.

"Make sure he doesn't move, okay, Walt?"

"He's not going anywhere." Walt smiled down at the trembling man.

THIRTY-EIGHT

"Seems a lot of people are looking for you, Mr. Huxley. The FBI, the police," Danielle said when she got off the phone.

"You can't keep me here." Baron started to stand up, but Walt pushed him down again.

"Yes, I can." Danielle smiled.

"I don't understand. What's going on?" Looking around frantically, Baron scooted backwards until he hit the wall again. *I'm imagining things,* he told himself. *I must have fallen, hit my head. That's why the room was spinning a few minutes ago. I must be hallucinating.*

"The police are going to be here in a minute. I guess you haven't been home for a few days. That must be why you look—well, kind of like a hot mess."

"I know what happened to me—I remember!" Antoine blurted out. He had been standing silently by the parlor door, staring at his killer, when it came to him.

"What happened, Antoine?" Danielle asked.

"Antoine?" Again, Baron looked around. But there was no one else there—just Danielle Boatman.

"They threw me off a cliff. Figured it would take me out to sea. But it didn't. My body washed up into a cave. I know where that cave is."

Danielle looked from Antoine to Baron and cocked her head.

"So your men tossed poor Antoine off a cliff into the ocean. You know, he didn't wash out to sea. He ended up in a cave."

"Where is he?"

"I just want to know why you didn't just divorce your wife. Why kill her and her lover?"

Baron laughed. "You think I had them killed because she was cheating on me? You actually think I cared about her that much? Stupid woman, getting close to someone like Paul. He could have ruined me."

"Ahhh, so it was the story he was working on." Danielle smiled.

Slumping back against the wall, Baron glared at Danielle. "I didn't kill anyone."

"No. But you ordered the hit."

"You don't know what you're talking about."

Walt saw the police car pull up in front of the house. When he remembered Huxley had locked the front door, he promptly unlocked it.

WHEN JOE and Brian entered Marlow House, their guns drawn, they found Baron Huxley sitting on the floor, leaning against the wall. On his forehead was a rapidly developing goose egg. Without pause, Joe rushed to Baron and took out his handcuffs. When he instructed Baron to put his hands behind his back, the man started to comply and then paused and winced.

"I don't think I can. Something's broken," Baron moaned.

Joe started moving Baron's hands behind his back, but the man cried out in pain, begging him to stop, insisting his arm was broken.

Joe looked to Danielle. With a shrug she said, "He did hit that wall pretty hard, so I guess it's possible."

"How did he hit the wall?" Brian asked.

"He sort of stumbled and fell into it," Danielle lied.

Gingerly, Joe handcuffed Baron's wrists in front of his body. The man winced, but he didn't cry out again.

"Where's the gun?" Brian asked. "The chief said something about a gun. He had you at gunpoint?"

Danielle pointed to the overhead light fixture.

Looking up, Brian frowned at the precariously perched weapon.

"Interesting how guns around here always seem to end up on a high shelf…on the roof…in a light fixture…"

Danielle smiled sweetly.

"Is it loaded?"

"I know it had at least one bullet. You'll find that in my banister. I have to assume there are more."

"I don't like how it's sitting up there. If it fell down—"

Before Brian could finish his sentence, the gun slipped from the fixture. What he couldn't see was Walt, who reached out and snatched the gun in midair, assisting in its descent so as not to release a second bullet.

Without thought, Brian dove for the gun, taking hold of its barrel and ripping it from Walt's hold.

"That was close," Brian said in a rush, his breathing elevated. "It could have gone off again."

Walt glanced over to Danielle and chuckled.

WALT AND ANTOINE stood by the open doorway and watched as the two police officers led the handcuffed man from the house. Danielle trailed behind them as they took Baron to the patrol car. According to Brian, more officers were arriving shortly to process the scene. She wondered if they intended to dig the bullet from her banister, and if so, how much damage would they do?

Had Danielle not witnessed what happened next with her own eyes, she might have assumed the person who was telling the story had embellished the tale. Even after she witnessed it, she questioned what she had just seen.

Brian and Joe had reholstered their guns. Baron, whose wrists were now handcuffed in front of his body, was being led out to the patrol car by Joe, who clutched the arrested man's forearm. Brian was trailing closely behind them when Heather Donovan came driving down the street. Pulling up along the sidewalk, her passenger window down, she was about to ask what was going on when Baron suddenly kicked out his foot in two sharp jabs, nailing Joe in the groin and then Brian, sending both officers bending at the waist in pain.

In the next instant, Baron literally dived into Heather's vehicle, and before she had time to react or jump out of the running car, she found herself pressed painfully against the driver's car door as Baron took control of the wheel and sped off—with Heather still trapped in the car, sandwiched between him and the car door.

After planting his right foot soundly on the gas pedal, Baron used his left foot to keep Heather's feet from successfully making their way to the brake pedal. Unable to move her left arm, which remained firmly trapped between her own body and the car door, held in place by Baron's weight, she used her right hand to ineffectively rail against Baron, attempting to push him away, but because of the angle and close proximity, her efforts had no impact. At one point she grabbed hold of his hair and tugged furiously, only to be met by a brutal side head butt.

Back at Marlow House, Joe and Brian managed to pull their guns from their holsters in spite of the sickening pain washing over them, but not before Heather's car vanished down the street. Danielle was already on her phone, calling 911.

DARLENE GUSAROV'S spirit sat atop the ridge along Pilgrim's Point, looking out to the ocean. At one time, she might have found the scene breathtaking—now she found it utterly boring.

"I need to get out of here," Darlene groaned. She looked up to the sky and outstretched her arms. "Please! Give me a sign! There must be something I can do to redeem myself!"

She didn't hear a crack of thunder, but she did hear sirens—and they were coming in her direction. Turning from the ocean, she looked down the highway and watched as a car barreled in her direction. Behind it, some distance away, were three police cars, their sirens on.

"Something's going on," Darlene said as she watched the quickly approaching vehicles.

A moment later, she stood in the middle of the highway. Darlene watched as the first car turned the bend and headed straight in her direction. It was then she noticed the woman flattened against the driver's door, the palms of her hands pressed against the door's window, as was her face, tears streaming down her cheeks. She looked utterly terrified. The large man by her side had control of the wheel and seemed oblivious to the terror he was inflicting on the poor woman.

The vehicle was almost upon Darlene when the back tire blew, sending the car aimlessly zigzagging over the highway before heading for the bluff overlooking the ocean. Darlene had done it before, and she assumed she could do it again. Without hesitation she reached for the driver's door. It flew open and, in the next moment, she grabbed hold of the terrified woman just moments before the car sailed off the side of the cliff.

HEATHER OPENED her eyes and found herself looking into the face of Darlene Gusarov. She had never met the woman, but she had seen her picture before, and she knew Darlene had been murdered at Pilgrim's Point.

Reaching up to Darlene's face, Heather smiled. "You're Darlene Gusarov."

"You can see me?"

"You saved my life," Heather whispered.

In the next moment, the police cars arrived, sirens blaring.

HEATHER SAT in the passenger side of Danielle's car, which was now parked behind the ambulance along the side of the road at Pilgrim's Point. Joe had just finished scolding Danielle for following the patrol cars, insisting she should have stayed back at Marlow House. Danielle, in turn, had just finished scolding Heather, who refused to get in the ambulance after the paramedics had looked her over and tended to her minor wounds. Police Chief MacDonald had arrived in the midst of Joe's ranting and had intervened, telling him Danielle could stay, providing she and Heather remained in the vehicle and stayed out of their way.

Parked police cars, their sirens no longer blaring but their strobe lights still revolving, were scattered along the highway at Pilgrim's Point. Currently, the responders' attention was focused on the vehicle, which was now halfway down the hillside, teetering precariously while Baron Huxley—either dead or unconscious—slumped over its steering wheel.

"I hope my insurance company gets me a new car," Heather grumbled. "When will my bad luck ever end?"

"I'm just glad you're alive," Danielle told her. "But I really think you should go to the hospital and get checked out."

"Do you have any idea how much hospitals cost?"

"I'm sure your insurance will cover it. And if it won't, I'll help you."

"Thanks, Danielle, that's sweet. But the truth is, I hate hospitals. I'm fine. Thanks to Darlene Gusarov."

Danielle looked at Heather. "What do you mean?"

"I saw her." Heather smiled. "She pulled me out of the car. She saved my life."

"Wow. You sure it was her?"

Heather rolled her eyes. "Just who else would it be?"

Danielle, her hands on the steering wheel of the parked car, looked back to the responders by the cliff's side. "You aren't the first person she's ripped out of a car before it went off the cliff. Who would have thought Darlene Gusarov would end up being some sort of guardian angel?"

"Do you think he's dead?" Heather asked.

"I don't know. I haven't seen his spirit, so maybe he's still alive."

"Why was this guy looking for Antoine Paul?"

"He killed him," Danielle explained. "Antoine was doing some investigative reporting on Huxley when he fell in love with Huxley's wife and they started having an affair. Huxley had them both killed. His wife and Antoine."

Heather looked at Danielle with a frown. "I thought you said Antoine Paul was some sort of killer? I thought you said he strangled that woman."

Danielle shook her head. "I was wrong. Sometimes things aren't what they seem."

Heather leaned back in the car seat and gazed out the windshield just as a tow truck pulled up.

A few minutes later, the chief walked up to Danielle's car and leaned into the open window. "He's dead."

"Baron's dead? Are you sure?" Danielle asked.

"Looks like he hit his head when he went over the cliff." The chief looked past Danielle to Heather. "You are one lucky lady, Heather."

After the chief left, Heather slumped back in her seat again and said, "Yeah right, I am so darn lucky."

"You are."

Heather turned to Danielle. "Do you ever think about dying?"

Removing her hands from the steering wheel, Danielle turned to Heather. "I suppose everyone does."

"It's different for people like us."

Danielle frowned. "What do you mean?"

"We know this isn't the end. There's something more after this. Don't you ever think about…I don't know…just going now?"

"Going now? Are you talking about killing yourself?"

Heather leaned back against the passenger door and looked at Danielle. "When you say it that way, it sounds bad."

"It is bad."

Heather rolled her eyes. "Come on, Danielle, don't you ever want to just move on and see what's out there? I know your husband's dead. Don't you ever think about checking out and being with him again?"

"No. Not particularly," Danielle said dryly.

"Okay. Perhaps that was a bad example. I remember now, he was fooling around, wasn't he?"

When Danielle didn't comment, Heather said, "How about this, what if someone you really cared about—someone you were drawn to—had died, wouldn't you be tempted then?"

Danielle couldn't help it, she immediately thought of Walt. She considered Heather's suggestion a moment and then finally shook her head and said, "No. Even then, I wouldn't consider it. Life is precious, Heather. While it's comforting knowing this isn't the end, that there is something else, I've no desire to jump ship prematurely."

"Seriously? Even if the perfect man was waiting for you on the other side?"

Danielle smiled softly. "Not even then."

THIRTY-NINE

Taking a seat at the table in the interrogation room, Danielle looked over to the mirror and waved.

"Why did you do that?" Agent Thomas asked. He sat across the table from Danielle. They were alone in the room.

"Just saying hello to whoever's on the other side of the mirror." Danielle sat up straight in the chair, her hands folded together on the table before her.

With a frown, Thomas glanced from the mirror to Danielle.

"It's a two-way mirror," Danielle explained. "There's a room on the other side where they can see in."

"You've been in here before?"

Danielle leaned back in her chair, stretching her legs out under the table. "A few times."

"We found the skeletal remains in the cave you told Chief MacDonald about," Agent Thomas told her.

"Have you told Antoine Paul's sister?"

"We haven't confirmed the identity yet. But if the dental records match, someone will be getting ahold of her. I still don't understand how Huxley happened to tell you where they put the body."

"Like I told the chief, Huxley intended to kill me, so I guess he felt he had nothing to lose," Danielle lied.

"But he thought Antoine Paul was still alive?"

The story Danielle had given the chief to pass onto the FBI agents was the same one she had given Antoine's sister.

"After he saw that composite drawing in the paper, he started wondering if Paul had somehow survived and made it out of that cave. And when Paul's sister showed up in town and he saw me with her, his imagination started working overtime. He thought Antoine Paul was staying at Marlow House."

"I still don't understand, how is it he told you about how he'd murdered his wife—about how he had Paul killed?"

Danielle's fingers fidgeted nervously. "He just sort of snapped. Antoine and Melissa were having an affair, but that's not why he had them killed. He said love had nothing to do with it. It was about whatever Paul had discovered while investigating Huxley's business."

"Did he say if he killed Steve Klein?"

Danielle shook her head. "No."

"HOW DID IT GO?" Chris asked as Danielle climbed into his car in the Frederickport parking lot.

"I just lied to an FBI agent," Danielle said as she slammed the door shut.

"What choice did you have?" Chris asked as he backed out of the parking space.

"I guess I didn't have one." Danielle put her seatbelt on.

"I told Walt I was taking you to lunch," Chris told her as he pulled out into the street.

"What did Walt say to that?"

"He said I needed to take you someplace nice."

"Yeah? Where are you going to take me?"

"Pearl Cove."

"Really? For lunch?" Danielle grinned.

"You could have been killed yesterday."

Danielle leaned back in the seat and gazed out the side window. "Walt wouldn't let that happen."

"No, he wouldn't," Chris muttered under his breath.

"Heather said something strange to me yesterday."

Chris arched his brow. "When doesn't Heather say something strange?"

"She asked me if I ever considered—ending it."

Hands firmly on the steering wheel, Chris glanced over to Danielle. "Ending it? Are you talking about suicide?"

"Yes. But I guess in Heather's mind, it isn't ending it exactly, more like prematurely moving onto the next level."

Chris shook his head. "It really bothers me that her mind runs in that direction."

"After I told her no, I never had considered something like that, she then asked me, what if the perfect man was waiting for me on the other side."

Chris didn't reply. Instead, he clutched the steering wheel tighter as he drove down the road.

Still looking out the side window, Danielle said, "I told her not even then. Of course, is there really such a thing as the perfect man?"

CHRIS HAD JUST ORDERED dessert when Danielle noticed Beverly Klein enter the restaurant. She was with three young adults—two males and one female.

"There's Steve's wife," Danielle whispered.

Chris looked over to the entrance. "Who's she with?"

"I bet that's her daughter and son. The funeral's tomorrow, so I'm sure they're in town."

"And the other guy?" Chris asked.

"Well, I imagine the guy holding hands with the girl is the daughter's boyfriend."

"You're a regular Nancy Drew." Chris chuckled.

"Just as long as you don't call me Jessica." Danielle stood up.

"Jessica?" Chris frowned.

"Jessica Fletcher. Much older amateur detective." Danielle tossed her napkin onto the table.

"Where are you going?"

"I want to go say hello." She paused and then looked down at Chris. "Maybe I shouldn't. Maybe she hasn't heard about Huxley yet. He was friends with her husband."

"She just looked this way and waved. You have to go say hello now. Anyway, don't the cops think he killed her husband?"

Danielle smiled weakly at Chris, suddenly regretting jumping to her feet and attracting Beverly's attention.

A few minutes later, Beverly was introducing Danielle to her daughter, son, and daughter's boyfriend. After the introductions, Beverly pulled Danielle to the side and whispered, "Baron Huxley killed Steve."

"I guess that means you know about the accident yesterday."

Beverly nodded. "Right before we left the house to come here, Chief MacDonald stopped by. Apparently the FBI has been investigating Baron's business for some time. Chief MacDonald told me the FBI was about to approach Steve to convince him to testify against Baron."

"They have proof? That he killed Steve?"

"They know Baron killed his wife and some reporter who was investigating his business, so they believe he was also responsible for Steve's death, considering he's the one who gave Steve the tamales. He had a motive. Steve's testimony could have sent Baron away for the rest of his life."

"I'm so sorry, Beverly."

"The chief also showed me the reporter's picture; I recognized him."

"Antoine Paul?"

"That's what he said his name was."

"You say you recognized him. Had you met him before?" Danielle asked.

"Sort of. Once I ran into Melissa and she was with him. She told me he was her cousin."

"Her cousin?" Danielle muttered under her breath.

"The strange thing, I hadn't thought about that man since Melissa introduced him to me, and then the other day—that composite drawing in the newspaper of the person who had been looking into windows—it looked just like him. I thought it looked familiar, but I couldn't place him. And then the chief showed me Antoine Paul's photograph, and I remembered. Isn't it bizarre, that the peeping tom would bear such a striking resemblance to this person Baron had killed?"

"Umm…yeah…"

Beverly shook her head as if she couldn't quite grasp the coincidence. She then glanced over to her son and daughter. "This has been so hard on them. On all of us."

"SO IT'S OFFICIAL, Huxley killed Steve Klein?" Chris asked before taking his first bite of chocolate cake. The plate sat between him and Danielle.

Danielle reached over and speared a hunk of cake. "I suppose."

After popping the bite of cake in her mouth, Danielle looked over at Chris and smiled. "This is good."

"Not as good as yours. But pretty good." Chris scooped up another forkful.

"I wonder if Huxley has moved on. Don't imagine Darlene would appreciate him hanging around and muscling in on her haunt." Danielle chuckled.

"You didn't see him?"

Danielle shook her head. "Neither did Heather."

"What about Antoine and Hillary?" Chris asked. "You think they're really gone?"

Danielle set her fork down on her napkin and then picked up her glass of tea and took a sip. After setting the glass back on the table, she looked over at Chris. "I'm pretty sure they are. They both said goodbye. Hillary left first. Antoine left last night."

"What about solving all those murders?"

Danielle let out a sigh. "When Hillary was still alive, I was sort of hoping she'd help solve the murders. But with both her and Antoine gone, that's not going to be happening."

"It's probably for the best. Playing Nancy Drew can be dangerous."

Picking up her fork again, Danielle helped herself to more cake. "I did tell the chief he might want to take a closer look at Hillary's books—her descriptions of the killers. See if any of them match any persons of interests in the real crimes."

"Yeah, in all MacDonald's free time," Chris said with a snort. "None of the murders were even in his jurisdiction."

Danielle shrugged and then said, "I guess you were wrong about Antoine."

"I suppose I was. He wasn't the sinister spirit I initially imagined."

"You know, Chris, the next time I have spirits coming at me from all directions, you could at least lend a hand."

"Coming from all directions?" Chris laughed.

"There was Steve, Hillary, Antoine…and if I had hung around Pilgrim's Point long enough I might have run into Darlene, not to mention Baron."

"Hey, you had Heather with you," he teased.

In retaliation, Danielle grabbed Chris's fork, now filled with the last bite of cake, and shoved it into her mouth.

FORTY

Roxane looked out the passenger window and waved to her mother. Beverly, who stood on the front porch, waved back, waiting for Steven to look her way so she could see him one final time before they drove off. Just as Roxane's boyfriend pulled the car out into the street, Steven, who sat in the backseat of his sister's car, turned toward Beverly and smiled sadly, raising his hand in a somber salute.

Beverly stood on her porch, watching the car disappear down the street. The three were heading back to Portland. Roxane and her boyfriend would be dropping Steven off at the airport for his flight back to Texas.

Wiping tears from her face, Beverly turned toward her front door. It stood ajar. Pushing it all the way open, she stepped inside. After she closed the door, she made her way to the kitchen.

She wasn't hungry. But if she wanted to eat, there was plenty of food in the house. Her refrigerator was still stuffed with half-eaten casseroles and Bundt cakes, and there was an ice chest filled with beer and soda in the dining room.

Sitting on the counter was a framed photograph of Steve. It was one of the photographs they'd had on display at his memorial. Picking up the framed picture, she carried it to the dining room table and set it down. She walked back into the kitchen.

Grabbing a bottle of opened chardonnay off the counter, she

reached up to the overhead cabinet and took out a wineglass. After filling the glass, she took it and the bottle to the dining room table.

Staring at the photograph of her husband, she thought of his funeral. It was a good turnout; it seemed everyone in town had showed up. The last week had been a hectic whirlwind with family arriving and friends dropping by. She hadn't taken Danielle Boatman up on her offer to put up some of the visiting family at Marlow House—instead those who she hadn't managed to fit in her house got rooms at the Seahorse Motel.

Steven's sisters, their spouses and mother had stayed with her, as had her son, daughter, and daughter's boyfriend. It had been a full house. Most of them had left the day before—each fretting about Beverly being alone after they all returned home.

"Someone needs to stay with you," her mother-in-law had told her. "You shouldn't be alone." Beverly had assured her she would be fine, and considering all the people she had been surrounded by this past week, a little solitude sounded good.

Picking up the wineglass, Beverly took a sip and closed her eyes. She took another drink—this time not a sip—this time she downed half the glass. Opening her eyes, she smiled and set the wineglass on the table. Picking up Steven's photograph, she studied it a moment.

"I thought we were going to grow old together. I really did."

Setting the photograph back on the table, she carefully arranged it so that it stood up, leaning back against its little pullout flap stand. After positioning it so that Steve's smiling face looked at her, she picked up her glass again and took another drink.

"Who would have thought you'd do something so stupid like fall off the pier?" She drank the rest of her wine. Picking up the wine bottle, she refilled the glass.

"Why did you have to take up with that little skank Carla?"

Still holding the glass, she took a swig and then set it down.

"When we first moved to Frederickport, I thought it would be different. At least, I thought you'd keep your extracurricular activities out of town. But no, you couldn't do that, could you?"

Beverly wondered for a moment if she should get something to eat, but dismissed the idea.

"You honestly didn't think I knew about that ridiculous woman in the historical society? Who do you think sent her that anonymous letter threatening to tell her husband? I got her to move out of town—but it didn't stop you, did it? There was always another one."

After downing the rest of the wine in her glass, she picked up the bottle and then noticed it was empty. Letting out a curse, she stood up and walked to the kitchen, looking for more wine. There were several partially full bottles of wine on the kitchen counter. She gathered them up and took them to the dining room table with her.

Sitting back in her chair, she grabbed the closest bottle to her and removed its already loose cork. The bottle was not quite half full. Flinging the cork across the room—it hit the wall and then fell to the floor. She drank directly from the bottle, seeing no reason to bother with the glass.

Looking back at Steve's photograph, she said, "I didn't intend to kill you. Honest."

Cocking her head slightly, the bottle of wine in one hand, she studied her husband's photograph. "I was just angry. Of all people, Carla? The woman had purple and pink hair! What were you thinking?"

She took a swig from the bottle and belched. By reflex, she covered her mouth with one hand and began to giggle. "That was crude. Is that something Carla would do?"

Still staring at the photograph, she set the bottle on the table and pushed it aside.

"I loved you, Steve. I really did. But I just couldn't take it anymore. The cheating. Always the cheating."

Beverly picked up the framed photograph, holding it in both hands.

"It was surprisingly easy. I saw the tamales sitting in the refrigerator on Thursday morning after you went to work. I knew you were going to take them when you went fishing. I carefully unwrapped each one—first from the foil and then the husk."

She set the frame back on the table, positioning it so that it still stood upright. "All I needed was a can of crabmeat and a jar of taco sauce. First, I mixed the crabmeat with the sauce to hide the flavor of the fish. Then I carefully removed the meat from each tamale, replacing it with the crab mixture. And then I rewrapped them, nice and snug. It was easy."

Picking up the framed picture again, she ran one fingertip down the side of Steve's face.

"I removed your EpiPen from your tackle box and put it in your toolbox. You never even noticed."

Laying the picture flat on the table, she took another gulp

straight from the wine bottle. Setting the bottle back on the table, she looked blankly across the room.

In a whisper, she said, "I'm not really sure what I thought was going to happen. I just wanted to hurt you, like you hurt me. I didn't think it would kill you."

She sat in silence at the table for almost twenty minutes, considering her life and what she had done. Finally, she took a deep breath, exhaled, and stood up. Glancing down at Steve's photograph, she said with a shrug, "It's karma, Steve."

Smiling, Beverly turned off the light and headed for bed, yet not before taking three aspirin. She had a lot to do in the morning, beginning with cleaning out Steve's closet and getting rid of his clothes—she didn't want to have a headache when she did it.

DANIELLE FOUND herself sitting on the pier with Walt, their legs dangling over the side as they each held a fishing pole. Glancing down, she noticed she was wearing jeans and a flannel shirt, as was Walt.

"I haven't been down here in years," Walt said as he cast his line out. "Does it still look like this?" He reeled in some of the line, gently tugging on the pole as he positioned his bait.

Danielle glanced around. "Yeah, pretty much. In fact, this is where Steve fell from the pier."

Walt looked to Danielle. "So he's moved on?"

"I think so. He wasn't at the funeral. I haven't seen Hillary either."

"She said she was going to move on. I guess she was no longer nervous over the prospect of seeing her two husbands."

Danielle shrugged. "I guess not."

They sat there a moment watching their lines gently bob in the water. Danielle could hear seagulls nearby, yet there were no other people on the pier…none on the nearby beach.

Danielle looked at Walt. "Do you think he would have died if he hadn't fallen off the pier?"

Walt considered the question a moment. "I don't know. Didn't you say there was medicine in his car that could have saved him?"

"Yeah. The EpiPen he kept in his tackle box was missing, but he still had one in his car. Carla knew where it was. She could have gotten it for him; she wasn't that far, just inside the diner."

"If he hadn't stumbled and fallen off the pier and hit his head, then, yeah, he might have survived."

Gazing out to the ocean, Danielle frowned. "You know the thing I don't understand?"

"What's that?"

"If Baron Huxley really wanted Steve dead, he didn't do a very good job of plotting his murder."

"What do you mean? He might have gotten away with it if Antoine Paul's spirit hadn't shown up."

Gazing out into the distance, a frown of confusion on her face, Danielle asked, "How did he know for sure when Steve was going to eat those tamales? He could have eaten them at home and then used an EpiPen he kept there. And if that had happened, how would Baron have explained giving him fish tamales? After all, he could have decided to eat just one, not both of them. And once he had a reaction, it would have been easy to check the second tamale. If anything, that would insure Steve testifying against him and sending him to prison."

Walt shrugged. "It's possible he only put the crabmeat in just one tamale. I don't know. I honestly haven't given it much thought."

"How did Baron manage to take the EpiPen out of Steve's tackle box?"

"Maybe he came down to the pier when Steve was fishing that night and somehow got it out of the tackle box," Walt suggested.

Danielle shook her head. "No. Steve never mentioned anything about seeing anyone on the pier that night. According to Beverly, when Steve wasn't fishing, he kept his tackle box on the workbench in the garage. Did Baron break into their house?"

"Maybe he stopped by Steve's house and made some excuse to go into the garage. You said yourself it was Steve's habit to leave the tackle box on the workbench; maybe Huxley knew that."

"No…when Beverly stopped by Marlow House to return that dish, we talked a little bit about Huxley. She said he and Steve had been on the outs for a while—that he hadn't been over to their house in months. In fact, that Wednesday he gave Steve the tamales, it was the first time they had gotten together in weeks."

"See, you just said it yourself—according to Beverly, they had problems. Taking Steve those tamales was obviously a ruse. It certainly wasn't a peace offering, it was a murder plot."

With a snort Danielle said, "An unreliable murder plot. Baron Huxley had no reason to believe those tamales were going to kill Steve. The most he could hope for was that he would get really sick."

"But he did die, Danielle."

"I know…because he fell off the pier."

They sat there a moment in silence. Finally, Danielle asked, "If Baron didn't give Steve crabmeat tamales, then who did, and why?"

Standing up, Walt reeled in his line. "Steve told you those tamales were left in the refrigerator at the bank all day. Maybe one of his employees switched them with crabmeat tamales in some misguided practical joke."

Danielle cringed. "Some joke. If that's true, how could they even live with themselves? And what about the missing EpiPen? Steve told me he put some new hooks in his tackle box the night before, and the EpiPen was there. Which now that I think about it, if Baron took it, he couldn't have done it before Wednesday."

Walt shrugged and cast his line out again. "It's entirely possible Steve removed it when he was organizing the tackle box. Maybe he stuck it somewhere else without realizing it, like when Lily put the milk in the pantry last week."

Danielle reeled in her line and glanced over at Walt. "I guess there's no way we'll ever know for sure what happened."

Smiling over at Danielle, Walt said, "Life is like that sometimes. It keeps things interesting."

THE GHOST WHO STAYED HOME

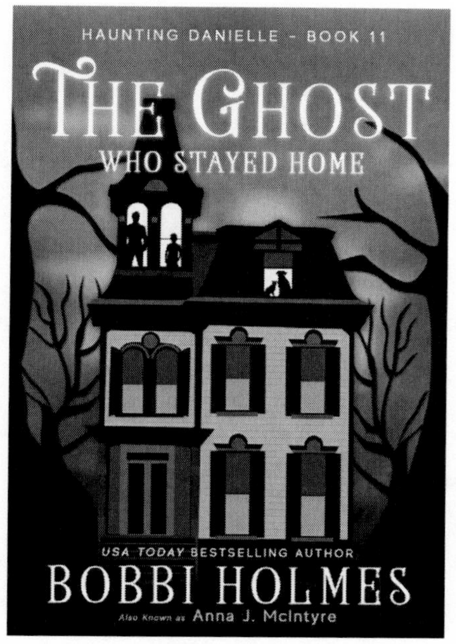

Return to Marlow House in

The Ghost Who Stayed Home

Haunting Danielle, Book 11

Left alone at Marlow House with Sadie and Max, Walt expects Danielle and Lily to return by the end of the week. When they don't, he begins to wonder what happened to them.

The ghost of Marlow House doesn't scare six-year-old Evan MacDonald. When the child sneaks into the house in the middle of the night, seeking Walt's help, the resident spirit learns something has happened to Danielle and Lily. Can a ghost confined to Marlow House and a pint-sized medium bring the people they love home?

NON-FICTION BY

BOBBI ANN JOHNSON HOLMES

Havasu Palms, A Hostile Takeover

Where the Road Ends, Recipes & Remembrances

Motherhood, a book of poetry

The Story of the Christmas Village

BOOKS BY ANNA J. MCINTYRE

Coulson's Wife

Coulson's Crucible

Coulson's Lessons

Coulson's Secret

Coulson's Reckoning

UNLOCKED HEARTS

Sundered Hearts

After Sundown

While Snowbound

Sugar Rush

Made in United States
North Haven, CT
20 March 2022